Loren Teague is originally from the Highlands of Scotland and emigrated to New Zealand some twenty years ago after travelling the world as a backpacker. Her range of occupations has been extremely varied, but eventually she found her dream job in the publishing industry as a manuscript assessor of fiction.

Loren enjoys writing romantic suspense and historical fiction. She lives in a colonial villa in Nelson, New Zealand.

For more information visit her website: www.lorenteague.co.nz

TRUE DECEPTION

In all the years that Mike McKenna has been a cop, he's never been offered a bribe. That is until Kelly Anderson rides into town on her Triumph Tiger motorbike. She is caught speeding and offers him money. Mike, suspicious about her motives, arrests her. Kelly Anderson isn't what she seems. Her Interpol file says she is a criminal: a drug courier and linked to the Triads. With a shipment of methamphetamine on its way from China, Kelly has strict orders to take control of it. Mike, convinced that Kelly is involved in shady dealings, and against his better judgement, finds himself stepping over the thin, blue line . . .

LOREN TEAGUE

TRUE DECEPTION

Complete and Unabridged

ULVERSCROFT
Leicester

First published in Great Britain in 2008 by
Robert Hale Limited
London

First Large Print Edition
published 2009
by arrangement with
Robert Hale Limited
London

British Library CIP Data

Teague, Loren.
  True deception
  1. Police- -New Zealand- -Fiction. 2. Drug traffic- -
  Fiction. 3. Romantic suspense novels.
  4. Large type books.
  I. Title
  823.9'2–dc22

  ISBN 978–1–84782–787–6

Published by
F. A. Thorpe (Publishing)
Anstey, Leicestershire

Set by Words & Graphics Ltd.
Anstey, Leicestershire
Printed and bound in Great Britain by
T. J. International Ltd., Padstow, Cornwall

This book is printed on acid-free paper

Special thanks go to Kaye Kelly and Andrew Grant for their encouragement and help with the manuscript. Also to Senior Constable Dave Colville of the New Zealand Police for his kind assistance and patience in answering all my questions. And finally, to my wonderful family and friends for being there through the tough times.

1

Mike McKenna had always wanted to be a cop. It didn't worry him that he worked long hours, unsociable shifts, and courted danger.

He'd first joined the police fresh out of school at eighteen, and graduated with honours. That had been fifteen years ago. A keen recruit, eager to catch the baddies, his first spell of duty had been in Auckland, nicknamed 'Sin City'. Sure, it had been exciting, he remembered. Front-line policing — cruising the streets at night, burglaries, domestic incidents and stolen cars. It had been good training. But when he had eventually returned to Greymouth after three years, it had just reaffirmed what he knew deep inside — that he would always have strong ties with the West Coast.

He switched off the engine in the patrol car and rolled down the window. The state highway was quiet tonight. Most people would be at home or down at the pub watching the rugby match, he thought enviously. He would have been there too but one of his colleagues had come down with the flu and so he had stepped in to take the

1

man's place. Not that he minded. Being single meant he had more time on his hands than his married colleagues, and he wasn't averse to making some extra money, especially since he had his eye on a new kayak. The last one he'd owned, he'd lent to his cousin, Shaun, and he'd accidentally put a jagged hole in it. Shaun had offered to reimburse him, but so far no money had been forthcoming. He'd no doubt Shaun would eventually pay up but in his own time.

Shifting his thoughts back to the rugby game, Mike picked up the radio handset and said, 'Comms. GMQ7.' A few seconds passed.

Mike was just about to repeat his call when the radio crackled and a voice answered. 'GMQ7. Comms.'

Mike smiled easily. 'Hey, Steve, you took your time in answering. What's that rugby score?'

'The Crusaders are winning. 21–13.'

Mike chuckled. 'Roger that. You're gonna owe me fifty bucks.'

'Huh, not if I can help it. Still got half an hour to go.'

'Oh yeah? It'll take more than half an hour to gain ten points. Out.'

Mike hung up, still smiling. At least he'd recorded the rugby match at home so he wouldn't miss any of it. He tapped his fingers against the steering wheel, then decided to take a stroll to stretch his legs. Turning up the fur collar of his navy blue regulation police jacket, he walked to the end of the lay-by, and surveyed the scenery surrounding him.

Pungas, with their long, lacy, green fronds, lined the roadside. The West Coast, a long strip of land down one side of New Zealand, was well known for its lush rainforest and long stretches of wild, hilly coastline. The bush-clad mountains — the Paparoas — loomed mysteriously, black and forbidding, like ancient sentinels guarding their valleys below. A sprinkle of snow topped the peaks, but it wouldn't last long. The warmer winds would chase it away in no time.

Only a few metres away, gigantic waves pounded the shore. Booming breakers sounding like loud drums reverberated along the beach. To Mike, it always seemed as if the surf carried a hidden message.

Perhaps the spirits of his Maori ancestors were watching over him today, he mused.

A few minutes later, he was just about to head back to the car when he heard something. Cocking his head, he listened carefully. The whine of the vehicle was coming closer, and after a few seconds, Mike decided it sounded like a motorbike travelling at high speed.

Mike scanned the highway. There was nothing in sight. But then the winding road was partially hidden by dense bush. He'd no sooner taken another step to adjust his vantage point when he saw it. A single light shone straight at him, before curving to follow the natural line of the road.

'Bloody hell,' he muttered. The motorbike must have been doing at least a ton.

Mike sprinted to the car and jumped in, switching on the siren and the blue and red strobe light, then raced out of the lay-by in hot pursuit. With his eyes focused on the road ahead, he changed into top gear and put his foot down. A quick glance at his speedometer saw it registering a 120 kilometres per hour. He firmed his grip on the steering wheel.

When he came to a corner, he lost sight of the motorbike because of the bulk of the logging truck in front of him. Ready to overtake, Mike edged out to the middle of the road but pulled back quickly at the oncoming vehicles. Damn it, he was losing valuable speed. The driver of the logging truck finally noticed the flashing light in his rear-view mirror and pulled over, letting the patrol car pass.

'About time,' said Mike, under his breath.

Hadn't the driver heard the siren?

The motorbike came into view again but only briefly — an elusive black outline, gradually growing smaller as it blended into the encroaching darkness. The rider must have known he was breaking the law, Mike thought. But there was no way a police car could compete with a motorbike. He was going to lose the man. Frustrated, he reached for the radio microphone to contact Comms, but to his surprise the motorbike slowed down just after the over bridge. He eased off the accelerator and braked. The motorbike had finally stopped at the side of the road, just before the 24-hour truck lay-by. Mike drew in sharply behind it.

Throwing the car door open, he reached the motorbike in quick strides. He noticed the rider didn't speak, didn't move, and just made an in-drawn breath, sounding like a hiss. Darkness had fallen completely and the rider, dressed in black leather, looked mean and ominous under the eerie glow of the yellow streetlight.

A black gloved hand raised the visor of the helmet a fraction and spoke. 'Is there a problem, Officer?' The voice was low and husky, with an accent.

'You're damn right there is. Didn't you realize what speed you were travelling?'

Silence. He quickly took in the rider's black expensive leathers and skin-tight boots. Whoever they were, they had style, Mike thought — and taste. His gaze roved enviously over the motorbike — a Triumph Tiger. Black, fast and efficient. He wouldn't have minded owning a bike like that himself and his fingertips brushed the sides, albeit briefly. Then, realizing he had been staring, he cursed himself for being distracted over a flashy piece of machinery. He was here to do a job and he had better get on with it.

'Where's your licence?' he demanded.

The rider, straddling the motorbike, twisted around and sprang open the saddle-bag. 'It's in here, somewhere.'

Mike stiffened. Was the suspect going to pull a gun on him? Mike wasn't armed as it wasn't routine procedure, though he carried pepper spray and a baton. Taking a step closer, curious to see what was in the saddle-bag, he tried to peer in. But before he had a chance to, the rider whipped out a small leather wallet, then snapped the saddle-bag shut. In one swoop the rider removed the helmet and swung back quickly to face him.

Mike's jaw dropped. 'What the . . . ' His voice tailed off in shocked surprise as he took in the burnished copper hair tumbling across the woman's shoulders and face.

He should have guessed the rider was a female. However, her height had fooled him and so had her slenderness. His gaze skimmed over her face, taking in the tanned complexion with a hint of hollow in the cheekbones. The streetlight made her green eyes flash menacingly like an alley cat caught in a trap.

She shoved the helmet in front of her, loosened her black gloves with her teeth and then handed him the driver's licence. 'There you are. Everything should be in order,' she said tightly. Mike backtracked towards the streetlight and looked at the passport-sized photo and the name underneath. Kelly Anderson. He did a quick calculation of her birth date. Thirty years old. The driving licence had been registered in Scotland — so that would explain the accent, he thought. So what was she doing in New Zealand? A tourist? Or an immigrant, perhaps? It would be interesting to find out. And he would, especially since she had broken the law.

Again he kept his voice level and calm. 'That was one stupid move, lady. No one in their right mind would take those corners travelling at that speed.' Admittedly, though, he'd never seen a woman ride that fast, or with such skill, but he certainly wasn't going to tell her that.

'Why are you in such a hurry?' he demanded.

She shrugged casually, though he noticed her eyes were guarded. 'I'm running late.'

'That's no justification. You could have been killed. Or worse still' — he jabbed his finger in mid-air at her — 'you could have killed someone.'

Her face flushed. 'There wasn't much chance of that. The road was deserted. Besides, I'm careful. I wouldn't take any chances, not on a strange road, anyway.'

Mike grimaced. 'That's not the point.' He paused slightly. 'Have you been drinking?'

Looking indignant, she retorted, 'Of course I haven't,' though her eyes flickered slightly. 'I'd hardly be travelling at *that* speed if I had,' she quickly added.

He snorted. 'Yeah, sure. That's what they all say.' He stood very still for a moment, trying to make up his mind whether she was telling the truth.

'Stay here,' he ordered, and abruptly walked back to the police car to fetch the breath-testing device. Commonly known as the sniffer, it resembled a small, pale blue and silver portable radio. When he returned, he pushed the buttons carefully and held it in front of her mouth. 'Say your name, please,' he instructed.

'Look here, Officer — '

He growled. 'Just say it.'

Taking a deep breath, she said, 'Kelly Anderson.' Her voice sounded muffled by the close proximity of the machine. He looked at the reading as it registered fail. Then he inserted a small plastic tube into the machine. 'Now, take a deep breath and blow.' He adjusted the tone of his voice, insinuating she didn't have a choice. 'Make sure you blow hard, please.'

'This isn't necessary,' she protested, her voice rising. She tossed her hair back from her face as if she was going to argue. It was then Mike noticed the malevolent flash of a silver snake earring dangling from her left ear.

When she made no effort to follow his command, he took a step closer. She was stalling, he realized, and his patience was running out fast.

'Didn't you hear what I said?'

'Yes, I did. But — '

'No buts,' he said firmly.

She looked at the machine in distaste. 'You look like an experienced cop. You could let me go with a warning.'

He gave a short laugh. 'I wouldn't be doing my job if I did. So move it. OK?'

Her eyes glinted, though she put the mouthpiece between her lips, taking a deep breath at the same time. Her chest rose and fell. Then she handed the machine back to him. 'There you go. Satisfied?'

'That depends.' He forced himself to concentrate on reading the machine, then stated plainly, 'You lied about drinking, but you're not over the limit.'

Kelly shrugged. 'I didn't think I would be. One glass of wine with a meal isn't a crime.'

Mike gave a grunt. She was right, he thought. But her speeding and failing to stop was. He debated whether to take her down to the station or not. The last thing he wanted was for her to end up splattered on the road from a motorbike accident. Perhaps he could talk some sense into her, and going to the station might just give her enough of a fright to make her curtail her speed.

Then, as if she guessed what he was thinking, she added, 'Give us a break, will you?' She flicked her wrist to look at her watch. 'Like I said, I'm in a hurry.'

He shook his head.

'I'll make it worthwhile,' she pleaded. 'I can pay. How much do you want? Two thousand. Three thousand dollars?' Her slim fingers skimmed across the money belt she wore around her waist.

Mike's eyebrows rose. In all the years he'd been a cop, he'd never once been offered a bribe. He decided to string her along a bit. 'What makes you think I'd even be interested?'

She gave a short laugh. 'Come on, Officer . . . everyone has their price.'

He spoke slowly. 'OK . . . fifty thousand?' He rocked back on his heels as he put his hands on his hips.

Kelly spluttered. 'Fifty thousand? You've got to be joking. What kind of cop are you?'

He took pleasure in saying, 'The honest kind,' then lunged forward and snatched the keys from the motorbike. 'You're under arrest.' He started reading her rights. 'It's a criminal offence to bribe a police officer. You're not obliged to say anything . . . but anything you do . . . '

He took her arm, intending to lead her towards the police car. 'Come on. Let's go.'

She shrugged him off. 'Hey . . . don't touch me.'

Not accustomed to repeating himself, he took her arm again and this time spoke harshly. 'You heard me. Get in the car. If you don't, I'll handcuff you.'

Their eyes met, and held. For a split moment, he was sure she was going to resist, and he'd have to tackle her, but she surprised him. With an audible disapproving sigh, she took a step forward, saying, 'OK. OK . . . you win. No need to use force.'

He kept a close eye on her as she slid on to the front seat.

'Put your seatbelt on,' he instructed.

She made no effort to move. Mike could feel his patience slipping again. His voice came out low, and warning. 'You heard me. Put the seatbelt on. Or I'll do it for you.'

Kelly's chin shot up as she scowled, and reluctantly reached over for the belt. It stuck. Seeing she was having difficulty, Mike stretched across the seat and yanked the seatbelt hard, clicking it in vigorously with a long, sharp clunk.

She leaned forward slightly, saying softly, 'Just think what you could have done with three thousand dollars.'

An image of the new kayak he'd thought about buying flashed across his mind. He answered without hesitation. 'Forget it. I'm not interested.'

He placed his hands on the steering wheel but they felt clammy. So he wiped them on his trousers. Revving the engine hard, he took off, snapping through the gears as he sped down the main highway. Vehicle lights flashed towards them as they neared the town centre.

'So what are you doing in New Zealand?' he asked, to break the silence.

'None of your damned business.'

Her reply didn't faze him. 'We'll need to know more details when we get to the station,' he retorted.

The bunker-like police station, painted white, stood out distinctly on the street. A faded New Zealand flag flew from a pole on the roof and directly below that the large crest of the New Zealand police was placed on the top half of the two-storey building.

Mike flicked his wrist to look at his watch. He hadn't expected to be back so early but now that he was, he'd process this arrest and catch up on some paperwork. Turning the police car into the car park adjacent to the building, he pulled up and switched off the engine.

'Stay right there,' he told her. Then he went round to the passenger door, but Kelly was out in a flash, surveying her surroundings.

'Come on . . . this way,' he said gruffly, taking her by the arm and leading her up the concrete steps.

She paused halfway to look at the high-wire fence surrounding the compound.

'Police stations are the same everywhere,' she murmured.

It was the last thing she said before the cell door slammed shut behind her.

2

How many times had Kelly been in a police station? It was practically her second home, but, of course, the cop who arrested her didn't know that.

The holding cell was empty. A pity, she thought. She had been hoping there might have been someone to chat with. After a few hesitant steps, she sat down and looked around the stark room, noticing the camera angled high up in the corner. She made a face at it, and sat down. An ugly brown stain on the floor had her moving away quickly to the other end of the concrete bench.

She thought of the officer who'd chased her. When she had first glanced in her rear mirror and seen the flashing blue light, she had been tempted to outrun him. But she knew he would have taken down her licence number and caught up with her eventually. Still, from past experience, if she did as she was told, she could be out of here within the hour, though it was possible they might keep her in longer.

Two hours passed. Kelly stood up. What was keeping them so long? She banged on the

14

door though she knew it would be a waste of time. Finally, the door was unlocked. The police officer who had arrested her asked her to step out.

'We need to fingerprint you,' he informed her. 'And get a photo.'

'Is this really necessary?'

'It is.'

After being showed into the interview room, she sat down on the hard wooden chair and studied the police officer in front of her.

Cropped hair, otherwise known as a number-one haircut, emphasized the strong angles of his face. But it was his grey eyes that caught her attention. Sharp and assessing, they held a glint of something else. Something indefinable. She also noticed his nose was slightly out of alignment, and wondered if it had been broken as a result of a lucky punch when he was trying to arrest someone.

'Do you need to use a phone?' he asked.

She shook her head, though inwardly debated on whether to take up his offer or not. 'No. I've got no one to call.' Though that wasn't strictly true. The problem was she didn't want him to know where she was heading.

His gaze settled on her, and hardened. 'What about a lawyer? You're entitled to call one, if you want?'

She shrugged. 'No point really. I don't know any lawyers in this part of the world.'

He slid a sheet of paper across the table towards her. 'There you are. A list of lawyers to choose from.'

Lifting up the list, she studied it carefully, then shoved it back across the table towards him.

'Save it for the next person you arrest. I don't need it.'

Mike's jaw tightened. 'That kind of behaviour isn't going to get you far.' He leaned forward slightly, his eyes narrowing. 'We're going to be here all night until I get some straight answers from you. Your co-operation would be appreciated.'

At least he was polite, she thought. Some cops she'd come across could turn into Satan himself when it came to interrogating a suspect.

He gave her a long look. 'I've got a few more questions. Firstly, what are you doing in this part of the world? You're Scottish, aren't you?'

She nodded. 'That's right. I'm on holiday,' she stated vaguely. 'Just touring around.'

He picked up his pen and started to write something on the pad in front of him. Kelly couldn't help but notice his hands — strong and firm, with tapered fingers and nails cut short. For a fleeting moment, they reminded her of another man she once knew. And yet, the man sitting in front of her was totally different both in looks and temperament.

He looked up again. 'Where did you say you were staying? In town or heading out to the backblocks?'

'I didn't.' She leaned forward. 'Why don't you just let me go? You've already booked me. What more do you want?'

He paused as if he was making up his mind about something. He fired more questions at her, but she refused to acknowledge them and merely sat there looking bored.

Finally, he said with exasperation, 'You know something? You should trade in your motorbike for a mobility scooter. That might slow you down some. Chances are high that if you keep speeding, you'll end up in one anyway.'

Kelly gasped. Did he really think she was incapable of handling a machine that size? She leaned forward even further, forgetting her earlier decision not to answer any questions or to antagonize him.

'Maybe you should just get yourself a faster police car,' she suggested wickedly, 'or even some necessary driving lessons. You could easily have caught me back there. *If* you'd had the guts to pass the logging truck.'

A red flush slowly crept up his neck. Grey eyes probed and watched her. Kelly shifted uneasily, wondering if she had pushed him too far.

He stood up abruptly, surprising her. 'OK, interview is terminated,' he said, showing her into the reception area. 'Wait here, please. You'll need to sign a release form. Then you can go.'

The duty officer, Chris Taylor, came up to Mike, his voice dropping an octave. 'She seems like a bundle of trouble.' He grinned widely. 'Makes a change from the usual arrests we have around here. She's certainly a looker.'

For once, Mike's humour deserted him. A tiny pulse beat erratically at his temple. 'She's been nothing but a pain in the ass. She's refusing to co-operate.' His gaze flickered curiously to where *she* stood at the other side of the room. How dare she accuse him of chickening out with the logging truck! He'd been tempted to tell her he wasn't about to put her life in danger, or even his for that matter, or anyone else's, to catch a biker breaking the speed limit.

Moving forward to the reception area, Mike slammed Kelly's belongings on the counter and asked her to sign a document. 'Right, there you go.' He tore off the top sheet, still feeling irritated. 'This is a court summons. If you don't turn up, there's a thousand dollar fine. Or one year in prison. As it is, chances are high you'll be given a prison sentence.'

'A prison sentence?' Her eyes flickered. 'Are you trying to frighten me, Officer?'

When he didn't reply, she added, 'So what happens if I leave the country?'

He gave a short laugh. 'You won't get far. As soon as you pass through passport control, an alert will go off. They'll arrest you immediately.'

'That's just great.' Scowling furiously, she snapped on her money belt.

Mike's gaze dropped to her waist. 'That's a lot of money you're carrying around with you.'

She opened her mouth to argue, but saw the warning light in his eyes and simply said, 'It's mine. I've earned it legally and I can do what I want with it.'

'Fine.' He wagged his finger at her. 'Just remember. Watch your speed. Or *we'll* be watching you.'

He turned abruptly and walked away, leaving her standing at the other side of the counter. The last thing she saw of him was his light blue shirt as he disappeared around the corner. Kelly, suddenly feeling cold in spite of the warm room, reached out for her leather jacket and slipped it back on. She had to get out of here — and fast.

The duty officer, Taylor, came forward and gave her a big grin. 'Need a lift back to your motorbike?'

Startled, she didn't reply straight away but when she could see he was genuinely trying to help, said carefully, 'I might. But I'd hate to put you to any trouble.'

'It's no problem. I'm heading out that way on patrol anyway.'

Unused to cops being friendly, she debated on whether to accept or not. Then shook her head. 'Actually, thanks, but no thanks.' The last thing she wanted was to be seen emerging from a police car.

He gave her a broad smile. 'Suit yourself . . . but you've got a long walk ahead of you.'

Kelly's hopes fell. Now she really was going to be late arriving at her destination. 'Is there such thing as a taxi around here?'

'Sure is.' He handed her a small card. 'There's the telephone number. It's a reliable taxi service. Wouldn't like to think you'd get lost trying to find your motorbike at night. Our town is pretty safe, but it's best not to take any chances.'

Kelly's voice softened. 'Thanks . . . I appreciate that.' This cop was certainly going out of his way to be helpful, unlike the one who had arrested her. In her estimation, there hadn't been any danger on that road. He was just some hicksville cop who had nothing better to do with his time.

Now, at last, she was free to go. After a quick call to the taxi firm, who promised the taxi would be there within ten minutes, she decided to wait outside.

When the taxi arrived, the driver threw the door open wide, and she hurried down the steps to meet him. 'Gidday . . . where are you heading, miss?' He casually shoved back his black cap on his head, while his other arm rested on the steering wheel.

Kelly slid on to the worn vinyl seat in the front. 'The twenty-four-hour truck stop. Just out of town.'

He gave a puzzled frown. 'The truck stop?'

'That's right. I've left my motorbike there,' she explained.

'Ah . . . ' He looked at her with interest and she knew exactly what he was thinking. She was part of a bike gang and had probably been arrested for some misdemeanour.

'You travelling alone?' he prompted, as he took off.

'Just me and my motorbike.'

'That so? Well, you'll like New Zealand. It's great for bikes. We've long stretches of road that you can travel on and not meet a soul for hours. But best watch out for cops, though. They'll book you in the blink of an eyelid.'

How true, she mused. The taxi driver chatted amicably but she didn't really feel like talking. It had been a long trip to reach the West Coast and she was tired. Although she had been in New Zealand for ten days, flying in from Hong Kong, her system still hadn't completely adapted to the time change.

It didn't take long to reach the service station. A few truck drivers, parked near her motorbike, gave her a curious glance as she emerged from the taxi. A wolf-whistle rang out loud and clear, piercing the night. Kelly heard their laughter and ignored it. She turned to the taxi driver, speaking to him through the half-open window.

'How much do I owe you?' she asked.

He stated his fee and she handed him some notes. He fished around in a small box for some change.

'Hey . . . don't worry about it,' she said, smiling. Money came easy in her line of work — and there was plenty more where that came from. The least she could do was improve the local economy.

'Thanks, you're very generous,' he replied, half saluting her. 'See you around, miss. I hope you enjoy your trip.'

'Thanks. I intend to.' Kelly chuckled. How about that? He'd called her 'miss'. Not lady, or hooker, or even bitch. Perhaps this town wasn't so bad after all.

The lights of the parked trucks outlined her slender shape, making her feel self-conscious as she walked across the uneven concrete yard. Her motorbike was right where she had left it and after running a quick check over the chassis, she slipped in the key. Holding the clutch in, she started the engine and revved into action before it smoothed off. Music to my ears, she thought appreciatively. Exhilaration flowed through her. Even in the dark, there was pleasure in riding her motorbike. Speed had never worried her, but still she had better be on her guard. She didn't want to be caught out a second time.

So this was Greymouth, she thought, as she drove through the town centre. Darkness prevented her from seeing the place properly but it looked similar to any other town at night-time with the bright lights and moving traffic. Verandas hung over the pavements, reminding her of those Wild West towns in the States she'd once visited. Greymouth had that sort of atmosphere — a mixture of old and new, a frontier town, originally built at the height of the gold rush way back in the 1860s.

She had to admit, since she'd been in New Zealand she had noticed the lack of crowds distinctly. But then again, what could you expect from a population of only four million?

Space. Plenty of it. No queues, friendly faces and nuclear free. New Zealand had a lot going for it in her estimation. So what else would she find here? she wondered fleetingly.

Kelly slowed down at the railway tracks running through the middle of town. Red and white poles like thick, striped candy bars stood on each side of the road. No safety gates, she realized with a start, only large warning lights that looked pretty antiquated. While travelling on the main highway, she'd seen railway tracks with neither. But what had nearly freaked her out was a road and railway bridge that cars and trains shared to cross the river.

She eased off the throttle as she reached the outskirts of town, turned right and followed the roundabout until she came to the Cobden Bridge. According to the map, if she followed the main highway for twenty kilometres directly out of town, it would take her into Moonlight Valley where her friends lived.

If she knew Shona and Brent, they'd have a hot meal and a warm welcome for her when

24

she arrived. Kelly couldn't wait to see them both. After the couple had left Hong Kong, she'd missed both of them badly. Her last words to them at the airport were, 'Maybe I'll make it down under sometime and check out that lovely, clean, green country of yours.' How was she to know her words would come true within three months of them leaving?

Kelly smiled. Sometimes, life played odd tricks like that. And she wasn't going to argue with fate about it.

Concentrating on the road ahead, she noted how it glistened with frost as she wove her way around the bends. She kept a careful eye on her speed — and for any police cars lurking in the shadows. There weren't many vehicles on the road. A cold night like this would have everyone tucked up at home beside a fire, she thought. She continued on her way, then stopped for the third time to consult the map. Shona and Brent lived in a remote place but she hadn't reckoned on it being this difficult to find them. Half an hour later, Kelly stopped again to get her bearings.

Just ahead of her she could see a gravel road turning off to the left. A small hand-painted sign nailed to a tree confirmed she'd reached the right place. Within minutes she drew into the farmyard and pulled up outside the homestead.

The house, large and majestic, had been built in colonial times, over a hundred years ago. Made of wood with the original red tin roof, Kelly took a long, slow look at the place. Bluish-grey smoke wound lazily upwards from its chimney, every so often gusting in her direction. She wrinkled her nose and sniffed at the pungent smell of sulphur. Brent had told her that the main fuel in this region was coal. When she turned around, she spotted a stack of cut logs piled high in a corner.

A dog barked nearby, but she couldn't see it. The sound of running water roaring made her wonder in what direction lay the river. It was too dark to make out. She turned back to the house, tilting her head to the side as the unmistakable sound of wind chimes caught her fancy. Sheer magic, she thought, as she gazed at the black sky with a sliver of moon hanging at a lazy angle. In spite of the background noise, she sensed rather than heard the peacefulness of the place.

Moonlight Valley.

Shona had enthralled her with tales of the West Coast. Goldminers. Raging rivers. A wilderness of native bush. And people who were renowned for their friendliness — except for cops, she amended. She closed her eyes, then opened them to make sure she wasn't dreaming.

She was here at last.

Curtains twitched, lights beamed on and the door was thrown open. Dark figures appeared from the doorway, moving on to the veranda. Boots scraped against wood and then she made out Shona and Brent hurrying down the steps towards her.

Shona was the first one to greet her, giving her a big hug. 'Good to see you . . . ' Her friend wore her black, waist-length hair in a plait rather than loose and flowing like she normally did. Her build was slim, and her skin naturally olive; a gift from her Maori mother.

Her husband, Brent, kissed Kelly on her cheek saying, 'We thought you'd be here earlier. We were beginning to wonder if you'd had an accident or something.'

'Sorry I'm late. But as you can see, I'm fine,' said Kelly, reassuring them. She gave them a broad smile while reaching for her gear strapped to the back of the motorbike. She knew she ought to explain further, sensing their curiosity. 'I got held up unexpectedly.'

'Nothing serious, I hope?' asked Shona, her expression concerned.

'Well . . . ' Kelly's voice trailed off, unsure whether she ought to give them any details or not. Perhaps later she would.

As if Shona sensed her friend's reluctance, she added with a smile, 'Don't bother explaining right now. We're just glad you've made it. It's great to see you, Kelly.'

'Thanks. It's wonderful to be here.' Kelly felt the tension ease from her shoulders. Already the incident at the police station was fading fast. Brent lifted her gear in spite of her protests that she could manage by herself. She looked at them both affectionately. Brent, with his short blond hair and fair skin, was in stark contrast to Shona's dark features.

Inside the homestead, the first thing which struck Kelly was the homely feel of the place. There was only one word to describe the living room and that was 'grand'. If it hadn't been for the television, Kelly would have thought she'd just walked back in time — at least 50 years. The high ceiling was made of dark rimu and the wallpaper, although slightly flaking off in places, looked to be in good condition. Kelly wasn't surprised to see the old-fashioned Singer treadle sewing machine tucked away in the corner.

She walked across the worn carpeted floor and shook hands with Jim McKenna, Shona's father. An elderly, stooped man, his clothes hung on him like a scarecrow, but that was deceiving. He was still wiry, with a powerful strength for his 70 years. Working on the farm had ensured that. Kelly had heard a lot about him from Shona and Brent and he obviously had heard them talk of her. He smiled at Kelly.

'Pleased to meet you, lass,' he said.

'And you,' she replied warmly, shaking his hand.

A small child toddled nearby, distracting Kelly. Immediately she scooped him up and gave him a cuddle. 'Finn, my wee darling! Hasn't he grown?' she exclaimed, holding the small body tightly. He gave a loud squawk, his grubby fingers grabbing hold of her hair as he tried to twist away. She kissed him softly on the cheek before placing him back on the floor.

Over a meal, Kelly talked of old times in Hong Kong with her friends. 'Good memories stay for ever,' she remarked wistfully.

Shona placed her hand on Kelly's arm. 'When Brent was away at the mining camp, you helped me a lot, Kelly. It wasn't easy having Finn without any family around. I won't forget it.' She gave her friend another smile. 'When I heard you were coming here, I couldn't believe it.'

Kelly laughed. 'Why not? What else could I spend my money on? I might as well use it before I fritter it away on motorbikes. Besides, I've had a hankering to see New

Zealand ever since you first told me about it.' She angled her chin. 'You know, things weren't the same after you both left Hong Kong. I figured it was time I did more travelling. So here I am.'

Shona's brows knitted together in a puzzled frown. 'But what took you so long tonight? When you phoned you said you'd be here in a couple of hours. You took five.'

A faint smile touched Kelly's mouth. 'Would you believe me, if I told you?'

Shona flicked back her plait and turned to face her. 'Try me.'

★   ★   ★

'So that's what happened,' Kelly finished, as she collected the dishes and placed them on the bench.

Shona smiled. 'I wonder if my cousin knows the cop who pulled you up. I'll ask him tomorrow when he comes for lunch.'

Kelly looked at Shona curiously, remembering Shona had once mentioned a relative who worked in law enforcement. 'What's your cousin's name?'

'Mike McKenna.' Shona shook her head. 'You wouldn't have seen him tonight though. He wasn't on duty. If I know Mike, he'd be down at the pub watching the rugby match.'

Kelly almost choked. Mike McKenna. That was the cop who had arrested her.

'How long are you staying?' Shona asked her. 'A while, I hope. You can't come all this way to New Zealand just for a couple of weeks. There's too much to see.'

With effort, Kelly focused on her friend's question. She couldn't afford to worry about Mike McKenna right now. If he showed up, she'd just have to deal with it. 'To be honest, I'm not sure. It depends on lots of things.' She smiled, injecting a note of enthusiasm into her voice. 'What about this gold panning you've told me about? I've got to try it. Who knows . . . maybe I'll find a gold nugget and I won't need to go back to Hong Kong.'

Jim McKenna, standing beside the coal range, swung around with a shovel of coal in his hand. 'There's plenty of gold in them hills yet,' he said gruffly. 'And I'm not saying where.' He grinned at Brent. 'Don't want any mining companies digging up the land around here.'

He opened the coal-range door and threw the coal in. Sparks flew out, hitting his gnarled hand, but he didn't even flinch. He slammed the door shut and slid back into his seat at the table. The kitchen was warm, not only with a physical heat but with the warmth of friends. Kelly felt it keenly.

31

Leaning his arm on the table, Brent said, 'We wouldn't dare prospect for gold around here, Jim. Not the way the local farmers feel about digging up the land.'

Jim McKenna grinned again. 'Glad you've got some sense, lad.' His gaze settled on Kelly, sitting opposite him at the table. 'Stay with us as long you want. There'll always be a bed for you here. They say the West Coast can get into your blood. Once you've had a taste of it, you won't want to live anywhere else.'

Kelly looked straight into the old man's face and at his blue eyes. Honesty and friendliness shone out at her. She swallowed, a lump unexpectedly rising in her throat.

'Thanks. It's nice of you all to make me feel so welcome.' Something told her that an offer from Jim McKenna was straight from the heart.

Later that evening, while Kelly prepared for bed, she thought about the cop who had arrested her earlier on. Certainly, he had asked her plenty of questions and, in her estimation, more than was normally required for the charges she faced. She also knew she had got his back up by refusing to answer any of them. Normally, she would have kept low-key, but sparring with him had been a challenge.

Yes, she was involved in something shady, just as he suspected. She wondered what he would say if he knew her real reason for coming to New Zealand.

3

Mike McKenna woke up with a start. Surely it couldn't be morning already, he thought with disbelief. His gaze settled on the clock beside his bed. He blinked, noting the time as just after ten.

He staggered out of the bedroom wearing a dressing gown loosely tied around his waist. After running his hand through his hair, he automatically reached into his desk drawer for a packet of cigarettes to find there was none. Then he remembered he'd stopped smoking over six months ago. Groaning, he tried to take his mind off the craving sensation that had come back in full force after a night out at the pub.

Fresh air, he thought. That's what he needed. He pushed open the French doors, and stepped outside to look at the view.

His house, perched high on the hillside, overlooked the sea and the coastline. Large rolling white surf curled and pounded the shoreline, while seagulls swooped and dived as they rode erratically on the sea breeze.

He picked up his binoculars from the window sill. Adjusting the lens, he focused on a gigantic tanker passing close to the horizon, its grey silhouette sharpened by a vivid blue sea. Another shape to the left caught his attention. It was small, moving fast. He zoomed in quickly. It was a yacht. He couldn't read the name on the hull, but he'd seen enough boats in his time to know it was a schooner. He watched it for a couple of minutes, wondering where it was from. As far as he could see, there were two men aboard, walking around the deck. After a few minutes of scouring the ocean, he placed the binoculars on the wooden table and went inside.

Now he needed a coffee, he told himself. A strong one. His mouth tasted like sawdust.

After finishing his shift the night before, he had gone out for a few drinks at the pub with some of his mates to celebrate the winning of the rugby match and ended up staying longer than he meant to.

It didn't take him long to prepare breakfast. Carrying the tray out on to the deck, he took a seat. He was just about to take a bite of his toast when his cell phone rang. For a moment he was tempted to ignore it, but his conscience got the better of him. He was, after all, on 24-hour call from the Armed Offenders' Squad, so he went inside and answered it.

A soft female voice spoke. 'Morning, Mike, it's Julie here.'

'Gidday . . . how's things?' He heard her smile.

'Oh, not bad,' she answered. 'Thought I'd give you a buzz and see what's happening. Things have been a bit slow at the newspaper. We need a few scoops to liven things up. Have you got anything?'

Mike thought of the woman he'd arrested the night before. An image of her dressed in black leather shot into his mind. He shrugged her figure away but all he could see was her green eyes laughing at him. 'Nope. Not a thing. Why don't you check in with Detective Inspector Poulsen, down at the station? He'll brief you, I'm sure.'

She gave a sigh. 'I tried to. But he's busy right now. And I've a deadline to make. Come on . . . have a heart. Remember that favour I did you last year? When you were investigating that fraud case?'

'Yeah . . . I haven't forgotten. And I know I owe you one. But I really don't have anything to give you. It's been pretty quiet lately.'

'All right, then. Forget about work for once. How about taking me out to dinner tomorrow night?'

Mike's eyebrows rose. 'Sorry, Julie, I'm working. Late shift. Duty before pleasure and all that.'

She laughed. 'That's a real shame. And I thought you liked spending time with me.'

'I do. But it's a bit difficult right now. You know how it is.'

There was a slight pause. 'Hmm . . . that's the trouble. I do. Maybe next time, eh?' Her voice sounded hopeful.

'Maybe,' he said non-committally.

'See you later, Mike . . . I've got to rush. The editor's calling me.'

Before he had time to say goodbye, the phone went dead. He liked Julie. She was fun to talk to. But that's as far as things went. He didn't want to hurt her feelings, so maybe he could take her for a drink when he had time off. And she was right, he did owe her. The fraud case she mentioned, involving local council members, had no leads until Julie turned up with some information she'd gleaned from an interview. That had given them a breakthrough. The culprits were arrested and convicted and were now doing time in prison.

Mike took a bite of his toast, then grimaced. It was cold. Someday, he'd like to be able to eat a meal right through without interruption. It seemed to be the bane of a police officer's life. Still, it was one he had chosen, and he had never regretted it.

After a shower and completing a few chores

around the place, he glanced at his watch. Midday already, he thought, with surprise. He'd been invited to the McKenna homestead for lunch. His cousin Shona and her husband Brent had returned from Hong Kong after a long-term contract working for a mining company. Shona had also mentioned something about a friend coming to stay. Mike racked his brains to remember exactly what she had said, but it eluded him. Not that it mattered. He'd find out more when he got there.

Placing the chilled bottle of Chardonnay carefully on the floor of his car, he plucked some wild flowers from the garden for Shona, and drove off down the hill.

★　★　★

The kitchen, the heart of the McKenna homestead, had retained the atmosphere of yesteryear. A long workbench, well used, ran down one side of the wall below the large kitchen window. The tiles were cracked and broken, painted with dainty Victorian flowers, and the wooden cupboards needed a thick coat of paint. But even so, the McKenna family preferred it that way.

Kelly was sitting at the kitchen table when Shona walked in saying, 'Mike's late.

Unfortunately, being punctual has never been one of his strengths.'

Kelly glanced at the clock hanging on the wall. It was one o'clock already. She continued sipping her cup of tea, hoping the warmth of the liquid would stop her stomach from clenching. Kelly heard a car draw up outside. She sat up straight, almost tempted to make a dive for her room and plead a headache but that would only delay the inevitable. Chances were high she'd end up meeting Mike McKenna again anyway.

'That sounds like him,' said Shona, her eyes bright with excitement as she rushed out on to the veranda.

Kelly heard the front door bang and the sound of footsteps and voices along the hallway. Bracing herself, she fixed a smile on her face.

Within seconds, Mike McKenna stood in front of her. His jaw dropped. 'You!'

Kelly pushed her chair back and moved forward, determined to make an effort. 'Yes. I'm afraid so.'

Before she had a chance to add anything else, he turned to Shona and said, 'What is *she* doing here?'

Shona looked indignant. 'What do you mean? Kelly's a friend of mine. *A close friend.*'

'Friend?' he exclaimed. 'Since when?'

Shona clucked her tongue. 'For a cop, you've got a poor memory. I told you last week Kelly was coming to stay. We met in Hong Kong. Remember?'

Realization crossed Mike's face. 'You're right. You did mention it.' But when he added quickly, 'Has Kelly told you about the charges she faces?' Kelly almost groaned aloud.

Shona looked at her with a puzzled expression on her face. 'What charges? What's all this about, Kelly?'

Kelly had only given her friend a mild version of what had occurred. Now how was she going to explain this to them?

Hopefully, she could smooth things over. 'It's . . . er . . . a bit complicated,' said Kelly, hoping that would suffice. It didn't. Mike obviously intended on making things as difficult for her as possible from the annoyed look on his face.

'So you didn't tell Shona . . . ' he remarked, his eyes narrowing. 'I wonder why?' He turned to Shona. 'She spent the evening in jail. She tried to bribe me.'

An awkward silence filled the kitchen, and only the creak of a floorboard could be heard as Kelly moved back a fraction. Of all the son-of-a-bitch things to say, she thought furiously. What happened to confidentiality?

Or didn't that apply in the New Zealand police?

'Bribery?' exclaimed Shona, though Kelly could see an amused glint in her friend's eyes.

Kelly pulled a face. 'Guilty, I'm afraid. Guess I've been living in Asia too long.'

Just at that moment, to Kelly's relief, Brent breezed in and clapped Mike on the back. 'Mike . . . how's it going, mate? Long time no see, eh?'

Distracted, Mike turned, his face breaking into a smile. 'Gidday . . . '

Brent's presence immediately put Mike at his ease and the two men lapsed into conversation. When Jim McKenna joined them, Shona ushered the three men out on to the veranda, each with a beer in his hand.

Kelly gave a sigh of relief and looked apologetically at her friend. 'Looks like I mucked up a bit.'

Shona only laughed. 'Oh, Kelly, what am I going to do with you? You've only just arrived and already you're stirring things up. I've never seen Mike so rattled.' She angled her head and looked at Kelly speculatively. 'So Mike actually arrested you? The way you talked about that cop, I thought he was some sort of ogre. That doesn't sound like Mike. He's one of the nicest people I know, and I've known him all my life.'

'I'm sure he is,' replied Kelly drily.

Shona gave her another smile. 'Don't think too badly of him, will you? Everyone has a different side to them at work. And who knows? Maybe he'd had a bad day. After all, it was supposed to be his day off.' Shona waved her hand dismissively. 'Let's forget about it for now, anyway. Lunch is ready. And I don't know about you, but I'm hungry.'

Kelly forced a smile, shoving her guilty feelings aside.

★　★　★

'And how's life in the police force, Mike?' asked Brent. 'Are you still hoping to make it into the drug squad?'

Mike turned to face him. 'Yeah, I am. I've put in my application to CIB. Been thinking about a change for a while.'

Kelly's ears pricked. She couldn't resist saying, 'Drug squad? I suppose that would be quite a challenge. It's pretty specialized work, isn't it?'

Mike's gaze settled on her. 'Yeah, it is. But in my estimation all police work is a challenge. We're still catching the baddies, but it's getting harder. Criminals are getting more sophisticated. Organized crime is a major worry.'

Brent agreed with him, then said, 'I'm just glad that we've got people like you in the force. Still, it must be tough. Ever think about leaving?'

Mike reached out for his beer. 'Sometimes. Everyone in the force could come up with a psychological reason for getting out. God knows, there's plenty of justification.'

'Would you?' Kelly asked curiously.

'Not yet. I'm enjoying the job too much. I've had a few years' experience now, so that's helped me cope. Maybe one day, though, I'll say, 'enough is enough'. He gave a shrug, then smiled. 'At least I don't get nightmares like I used to.'

After the meal, and helping clear the table, Kelly excused herself and wandered down to the garage to check her motorbike. She knew it would have been safe overnight, but she just wanted to give it a road check after the long haul the day before. If she was honest, it was also a good excuse to put some distance between herself and Mike McKenna. All through lunch he had asked her questions and she had skilfully avoided answering any of them directly, hoping it would put him off. But it hadn't.

She had made light of it and tried to ignore him, but it wasn't easy, and she certainly didn't want to upset her friends. As she wandered outside, the wintry sun caressed her face gently. She tossed her head back and took a deep breath. No pollution here. The valley air was fresh and sweet-smelling, carrying the fragrance of the native bush. Beech trees and manuka grew side by side as giant flax leaves unfolded their long smooth leaves. A cascade of ferns sprang out of a pile of uneven stones and she stopped to finger them, marvelling at their delicate pattern. The wind gusted, chilling her. She zipped up her leather jacket and shoved her hands into her pockets as she continued walking.

Moonlight Valley was unlike anywhere she had visited before, she decided. It would be a good place to bring up a family, with all this fresh air and space. She couldn't help but compare it to where she'd been brought up. That had been a top flat of an Edinburgh tenement. There had been no garden, only a shared green with other families, combining washing lines and a play area.

Edinburgh might not have had the grand open spaces and luscious scenery of New Zealand, but the city had taught her how to survive. As the youngest child with four brothers, she had learned to stand up for herself early in life. Her father had died of a heart attack when she was twelve, leaving her mother, Margaret, to bring them all up single-handedly. Her mother still lived in the same tenement flat. Kelly had tried persuading her to move to a nice place in the country but she had refused. Edinburgh was her home. She had lived there all her life. Kelly accepted her mother's decision, understanding her reasons. Kelly sighed. It was just a pity she hadn't been able to get home to see her mother before she came to New Zealand, but it had been necessary to leave Hong Kong for New Zealand straight away. Though if she was entirely honest with herself, another reason she hadn't gone home was because every time she did, her memories of Jeff would return with a vengeance.

Even now, she could see him so clearly. Jeff. With his blue, blue eyes which she had loved and always teased him about. God, she missed him.

After his funeral, she had decided to put everything behind her. A position working in London had come up and she had taken it without hesitation. It had been too good an opportunity to miss and, besides, she owed it to Jeff to carry on where he had left off. Only she hadn't expected to end up in Hong Kong and then New Zealand of all places.

A shadow crossed her face at the lies she had told while being welcomed into the McKenna family. For a moment, she regretted not being able to tell Shona why she had been working in Hong Kong and her real reason for coming to New Zealand. But she knew deceiving her friends was part of her plan and if that's what it took, then she had no choice. She had made her decision the day Jeff had been buried. Now, she was going to see it all through to the end.

A bird, sitting in a cabbage tree, filled the air suddenly with its haunting bell-like sound. She'd never heard a bird sing like that before. Fascinated, she wandered closer, watching it flit from branch to branch through the fan-like leaves. It was a smallish dusty-green bird, so ordinary-looking but with a wonderful, crystal-clear song. It sang for her again and then flew off, towards the shed in the farm yard.

The doors of the shed were wide open and the Triumph Tiger was parked snugly against the wall. She took a long look at its sleek black lines, splattered with mud. It needed a good cleaning. There were some rags in a box and she grabbed one and gave it a quick wipe, before bending down to examine the engine.

She didn't hear Mike McKenna come up behind her and jumped when he spoke.

'Nice motorbike, Kelly. Brand new too. That must have cost you a few wage packets.'

46

He leaned over her shoulder and put his hand on the black leather seat.

Kelly stared at his hand, wishing he would remove it. 'I'm good at saving. I don't spend my money on makeup or clothes, and I've no vices.'

'No vices? That's not the impression I got earlier.' He leaned even closer, so close she could feel his breath on her neck. It gave her an odd sort of feeling. He pointed to the body of the motorbike. 'You've missed a spot. Right there.'

She stood up, drawing herself up to her full height, but even so, Mike towered above her at least several inches. She had to angle her head upwards to look at him. 'Do you always creep up on people like that?'

Mike laughed unexpectedly, startling her. 'Nope. Only on suspects.'

'Well, I'm no suspect, so back off,' she said tartly, resenting his intrusion while she was preening her motorbike. Her fingertips brushed the steering possessively while her hips sidled up against the engine.

He stepped closer, his hand reaching out for the clutch. His fingers tightened around the black rubber.

She was tempted to move away. He was standing too close for her liking. But why should she be the first one to move? she reasoned. He was the one invading her space. She held her ground.

His gaze flicked downwards again, towards the motorbike. 'Why did you pick this model, a Triumph Tiger?' he asked curiously.

She tilted her head. Was he really interested? Or was he just making small talk? 'It's got a pretty good reputation on twisty roads,' she told him, 'and I needed something I could rely on.'

'You came through Arthur's Pass. It can't have been easy with the bad weather,' he remarked. 'A road like that takes skill and concentration, especially in those conditions.'

'No . . . it wasn't easy,' she admitted. 'There was snow and ice, plenty of it, and the road was treacherous.' She paused slightly. 'And you know what? The last thing I needed was you pulling me up.'

'I thought we'd get around to that again.' His mouth lifted slightly as if mocking her. 'But just remember, if I hadn't, I wouldn't have been doing my job.'

She didn't argue the point, preferring to leave well alone. Eager to turn the topic of conversation back to him and because she was genuinely interested, she asked, 'So what made you become a cop?'

He firmed his lips as he considered her question. 'Lots of reasons. I liked the idea of working in the community.' He shrugged. 'I grew up here. It's my home.'

'You're only a senior constable.' She tried to inject a derisive note in her voice.

But to her surprise, he didn't react to the jibe like she thought he would. His answer was quick. 'Promotion was there if I wanted it . . . but I haven't up to now.' His gaze flicked over her again. 'Some cops like being out on the streets. I suppose I'm one of them.' He didn't tell her he was a member of the Armed Offenders' Squad and had received a Police Gold Merit award for bravery.

Silence fell as he leaned back against the wall and folded his arms. He continued to look at her speculatively. 'What about you? You're a long way from home.' When she didn't answer, he added, 'Looking for adventure, maybe?' His eyes narrowed suspiciously. 'Or are you hiding from something?'

She shifted uneasily. 'I've already told you. I'm here on holiday. Been working a couple of years in Hong Kong, so figured I needed a break. New Zealand seemed like a good place to come to.'

He gave her a thoughtful look. 'You're pretty good friends with Shona. Yet you're both so very different. Seems coincidental you turning up when they've just arrived back home.'

Kelly stiffened. 'What, exactly, are you suggesting?'

'You know what I mean. But, just in case you don't, I'll spell it out for you. Shona and Brent are good people. They're also my family. And I don't want you causing them any trouble.'

Kelly felt ready to explode at his accusation. Instead she wiped her hands on her jeans, then balled them tightly at her side. 'You are just a typical cop. You've already got me judged and sentenced.' Her voice shook with disgust. 'You know nothing about me. All you can see is my motorbike and that I'm dressed in leather. Not all bikies are criminals, you know.'

He gave her a probing stare. 'You tried to bribe me. That tells me you're dishonest. So what the hell am I supposed to think?'

She couldn't prevent the tremor in her voice. 'The bribe was on impulse. I made a mistake.'

'Even so . . . ' he replied, not looking convinced.

She dropped the dirty rag in the box and said quickly, 'I'm heading back to the house.'

'Don't cause my family any grief or you'll have me to answer to,' he said softly, following her.

Kelly's mouth tightened. Before she could stop herself, the words came tumbling out.

'Harassment is a crime, isn't it?'

He growled, 'I mean it, Kelly.'

They had almost reached the homestead when to her surprise he caught her wrist and whirled her around.

'Wait . . . ' he demanded. 'I've not finished yet.'

She shrugged herself loose from his grip. 'Now what?' she said, exasperated. 'Are you going to arrest me again?'

'I might. But you'd have to break the law first.' He looked thoughtful. 'Let me buy you a drink later,' he said simply.

Kelly gasped at his audacity. One minute he was threatening her, the next he wanted to smooth things over. 'You really have a nerve, McKenna. Somehow I don't think it's a good idea. We don't have anything in common.'

'I promised Shona that I'd make amends.'

So that's why he had sought her out — because Shona had put the pressure on him. While she appreciated her friend trying to help, it would have been better to leave well alone.

'I should have known,' she replied coolly.

'We'll keep the conversation light. Even talk about motorbikes, if you want? Maybe you can even give me some driving tips.'

She heard the sarcastic, amused note in his voice and gritted her teeth. He really was the most infuriating man she'd ever met. And yet, what if he meant it? Could she really let the opportunity pass?

'I'm serious,' he added. 'Maybe I want you to convince me you're the person Shona said you were.'

Kelly was curious to know what he meant. She said carefully, 'Shona talked to you about me?'

He nodded. 'She did. She told me that while Brent was away at the mining camp, you looked after Finn when she came down with flu.'

Kelly shrugged. 'So what? I helped them out. It was no big deal. Any good friend would have done the same.'

'Wasn't it?' He gave her a searching look. 'You even took time off work.' He paused again. 'The last thing I want to do is upset Shona. If you really are on holiday, then one drink won't do any harm.'

Her eyes met his, green against grey. Something shifted. She didn't know what.

'Perhaps,' she answered.

It might be an ideal opportunity to get him off her back, she quickly realized. After all, she didn't want to upset Shona either. And arousing his suspicions even more by refusing might cause her more trouble than it was worth. Getting arrested last night had been part of her plan, but getting involved with him on any basis certainly was not.

'It's not such a big thing to ask,' he pointed out. 'One drink. Who knows, you might even enjoy my company.'

She had to laugh. 'Desperate for a woman, McKenna?'

'What makes you think that?'

'Oh . . . just my intuition. Plus the fact you don't even like me. And you don't seem like a man who'd be pressured to do anything he doesn't want to, especially by a woman.'

She had a feeling she had hit a nerve from the angry glint in his eyes.

'I don't even know you, Kelly. Though what I've seen already hasn't exactly enthralled me. But I'm still willing to give you a chance.'

She bit her lip. Then it occurred to her. Perhaps, if she did meet him, she might be able to glean some information on the drug trade.

She gave him a brief smile that she hoped indicated she was interested. 'OK, then.'

'Good.' He pursed his mouth. 'O'Reilley's pub? Eight o'clock.'

'Sounds just fine,' she forced herself to say. Then walked away as fast as she could, not believing what she had done. She had just made a date with a cop in the New Zealand police force.

She laughed at the irony of it.

4

Hong Kong

As far as Tino Chang was concerned, Hong Kong was the most illustrious city in the world. His top-floor penthouse in the Ho Lee Building at Kowloon, decorated and furnished in minimalistic white, afforded him a spectacular view of the busy harbour. He liked nothing more than standing at his wall of windows, watching the ships and boats, junks and ferries, jostle their way across the sea.

He hadn't always lived in such affluence. He'd grown up in Hak Nam, the City of Darkness, which everyone knew as the old walled city of Kowloon, in the very heart of Hong Kong. It was a place where Triads had made their stronghold, operating brothels and gambling dens and opium divans.

Someone had once told him that the old city had a reputation for being the most populous place on earth. He could well believe it. The cramped living quarters, rows and rows of washing, the cries of babies, and the pungent smells of spices and herbs, and fresh red meat hanging on black hooks, drifted upwards in the heat amongst the throng of humanity. Every day the alleys were alive with the throb of hidden machinery and the clacking of mahjong tiles, while up on the roofs, some fourteen storeys high, he used to play along-side hundreds of cooing racing pigeon housed in cages not much smaller than some of the city's homes. It was there, at aged fourteen, he had been recruited into the Triads and where a small secret ceremony had taken place. His father had been a Red Pole — one of the senior members of the Red Lion. And when Tino had eventually joined he had become a 49, a foot soldier.

But when the government had completely razed the old city nearly fifteen years ago, forcing his family and many of its inhabitants into other areas of Hong Kong, he and many of the Triads had to regroup, forge out new territories and alliances. It was then his fortune had changed.

With an astute mind, Chang had started a courier business, where he could money launder his earnings from illicit dealings. The courier business had flourished, and eventually he had become a Taipan or, in the western world, a tycoon.

And now change was in the air again, thought Chang philosophically. Not in a way he'd expected, yet it was unavoidable considering the fast pace that everything moved nowadays. The Triads were linking up with other criminal organizations and sharing intelligence on law enforcement agencies. At one time it would have been unheard of. The Triads had always been the most secret of societies, but it was a new world now.

Chang flicked his wrist to look at his gold watch. He had an appointment with his fortune-teller in half an hour. He picked up the phone and ordered his car.

Within minutes he sped down the road in the direction of Soy Street in Mong Kok.

The fortune-teller, Who Wong, an old wise man his father had known, had a good reputation. Wong also had the honour of being a grandmaster of Xiangqi, better known as Chinese chess. Chang never paid Who Wong for his forecast, but he would bring him gifts. This time he brought him a miniature ivory chess set, western style.

When he reached the old man's humble abode, he knocked on the already opened door and walked in. The old man seemed to be in a trance, his eyelids half closed. Chang placed the gift on the table next to him and Wong nodded slightly, his wrinkled mouth widening with pleasure. 'Be seated, please. It has been a while since we have talked.'

Chang took a seat on the divan and waited patiently. After a few moments, Chang prompted, 'You have news for me, wise one?'

Wong nodded, indicating for Chang to lift his hand. Chang stretched out his arm and unfurled his fist.

Wong traced his fingers over the deep creases of his palm. Then he looked up suddenly, his black eyes fathomless. 'I see many storm clouds. The journey on water will be difficult.' Wong paused briefly. 'Delay the journey. Two weeks. Otherwise you lose everything.'

Chang jolted. 'Are you sure?'

Wong nodded again. 'There is something else.' The old man looked disconcerted for a moment as if he did not like to bring bad news. 'A woman. She wears a mask. One side of the mask is white, the other red.'

'A mask?' repeated Chang, unsure as to this meaning. He gave a frown. As far as he knew, white indicated treachery, and red courage.

Wong nodded again. 'You know this woman?'

Chang thought carefully. 'I'm not sure. I know many women. Is she Chinese?'

Wong hesitated. 'I cannot say.'

Disturbed, Chang pondered on the old man's advice. Wong had never let him down before in his predictions. Perhaps he should take the warning seriously. Thanking the old man, Chang left.

Once Chang had reached his penthouse, he made a decision, but felt far from pleased. He picked up the phone. 'Get me the captain of the *King Yuan*.' He knew holding up a container ship in the middle of the ocean, destined for foreign ports, could attract attention from the authorities. But it was a risk he would have to take.

★ ★ ★

Kelly had every intention of arriving at O'Reilley's pub early. Firstly, because she needed some information, and secondly, if she was seen having a drink with a local cop, it was unlikely she'd get it. So it was just after seven o'clock when she drew up outside the pub and saw it was already busy. Even better, she thought. She'd be able to blend in with the crowd. She pushed the door open and walked inside.

It had never ceased to amaze her what information she could glean from people sitting in bars and she knew perfectly well that if she wanted to make a contact in the seedy underworld that was the place to do it. The chances were very high someone might even know the man she was looking for.

'A shandy, please,' she said to the barman, then perched herself on the high stool while she surveyed the room. Her fingers tapped gently on the wooden counter to the beat of the music from the juke-box.

A game of darts was being played nearby and a large television screen, placed high up on the other side of the room, played a rugby game. There was always a hierarchy in any bar and she looked around, gauging the politics of the people — who were the drinkers, who were doing deals.

After half an hour of getting nowhere, in spite of the casual conversations Kelly engaged in, she made for the Ladies to freshen up. Two teenage girls, most likely under age, followed her in. Kelly heard the word 'dope' in hushed whispers. Kelly's ears pricked. 'See if you can get some from Dave Williamson,' one of the girls said. 'You know him better than I do.'

The next-door toilet was flushed, drowning out any further conversation. She had missed what else they said, but she had caught the name Dave Williamson. Was he their supplier?

When she went to wash her hands, the two girls, both teenagers, were brushing their hair and applying lipstick. She wondered briefly if their parents knew where they were tonight.

For a moment, Kelly remembered her own teenage years — hadn't she also lied about her age and gone into pubs? It was all part of growing up, she reminded herself. Breaking the rules was attractive.

She glanced at her watch. It was a quarter to eight — Mike could arrive any time. She had to hurry. She went back to the bar to finish her drink, keeping her ears open for anyone named Dave Williamson. Before she finished her beer, she had found him.

Kelly took him in quickly. He was clean-cut, dressed in smart denim jeans and a silky blue shirt. He seemed harmless enough.

'Sure . . . I can do a deal with you,' he said, grinning, as he leaned against the bar.

She told him what she wanted.

'Why don't you come round to my place now and pick up the gear?' he added, giving her the address. 'I'm heading home in a few minutes.'

'Can't right now,' she explained. 'What about tomorrow?'

He nodded, and they agreed on the time.

Her first contact, she thought, pleased. At least it was something.

Within seconds of Dave leaving, Mike arrived. That was close, she thought, her heart pounding.

'Hi,' he said, sitting down beside her. 'You're early.'

She smiled. 'Fancy that. So are you.'

'To be honest, I wasn't sure you'd turn up tonight,' he admitted.

Kelly inclined her head. 'Regardless of what you think, Shona and Brent's friendship means a lot to me.'

He stared at her. 'I could almost believe you.'

Damn him, she thought. But she didn't rise to the bait.

To her surprise, Mike said, 'Fancy coming back to my place? It's a bit too crowded here.'

She was about to refuse then reminded herself that learning more about Mike McKenna could work in her favour.

'Why not?' she answered.

Kelly parked her motorbike behind Mike's vehicle in his driveway. He unlocked the front door, and switched on the light. 'Make yourself comfortable,' he suggested. 'I've got a bottle of red we can open.'

'Sounds great,' she said appreciatively.

Kelly was unprepared for the serene atmosphere the living-room projected. Pale creamy walls offset with natural wood highlighted bold prints of Maori warriors placed at regular intervals around the room. A tall, wrought-iron candlestick stood in one

61

corner with matching bright yellow candles, their wicks white and virginal, untouched by flame. She wondered fleetingly if he would light them, then dismissed the thought. Why would he waste them on her? The sofa, large and bulky, looked comfortable and she had a sudden urge to curl up on it and rest a while.

She sat down. So far, so good.

Mike carried the bottle of red under one arm, and two glasses in his hand. He placed them on the coffee table in front of her and poured her a drink.

'Thanks.' With a glass of red wine in her hand, she raised it towards him. '*Slainte*, as we say in Scotland.'

'Gaelic for good health?'

'How did you know?' She took a sip of the wine, savouring the taste. Smooth and rich bodied with a hint of spice. Nice.

'I've got Irish blood in me, from my great-grandfather,' he told her. 'He sailed all the way from Dublin. Then, when he arrived here, he married a Maori chief's daughter.' Mike set his glass down on the coffee table. '*Kia mau koe ki nga kupu o ou tupuna.*'

She arched a brow. 'Impressive. So what exactly does it mean?'

'It's an old Maori saying. Hold fast to the words of your ancestors.'

'I guess I can relate to that, being a Scot,'

she said softly. Kelly's long fingers curved around the glass 'Here's to the Celts . . . and the Maori,' she added positively. 'And as for family, they always come first. Right?'

His gaze skimmed over her. 'Seems like you and I might even agree for once.' An easy smile played at the corners of his mouth. 'How about a truce?'

She had to admit he was trying hard to make amends. But, she reminded herself sharply, not for her sake, but for Shona's. 'Possibly,' she finally replied, though she couldn't help returning the smile. 'I guess under the circumstances, I can hardly say no.'

It was then she noticed the guitar propped up against the wall, and the sheets of music stacked beside it. She reached out for the guitar.

'Yours?' she asked, surprised. Her fingers ran down the smooth sides of the instrument, feeling the polished wood. She plucked a couple of strings, their notes jarring noisily. She hadn't one iota of musical talent in her but had always admired those who did.

'Yeah, cops have hobbies too,' he said quietly. 'I'm lead singer in a rock band. When I get time, that is.'

'Rock? Now you do surprise me. You don't exactly fit the image. You're a police officer.'

He gave a short laugh. 'So?'

She shrugged, not sure how to answer. Seeing the man rather than the police officer unnerved her. It hadn't even occurred to her he might be musical.

Mike continued. 'So what you're saying is, I don't have long hair down to my waist, and I don't do drugs.'

'Something like that,' she admitted. It occurred to her that she'd arrived at his home with preconceived ideas about him, just like he'd had about her. How ludicrous could things get?

Keenly aware of a curiosity she couldn't hold back, she found herself saying, 'Do you write your own songs?'

'Yeah . . . all the time. I've been brought up on music since the day I was born. Must be the Irish in me. My father used to sing for a local band, so I guess I've inherited his talent.'

He took the guitar from her and propped it against the wall carefully.

'Tell me what you think of the country so far,' he prompted. 'I'm interested to know.'

He sounded sincere, she thought, but she was still wary. She answered carefully. 'New Zealand is different from anywhere I've been before. After living in Hong Kong, it seems like paradise.' A wave of hair fell over her face as she moved, so she shoved it back behind her ears. The silver snake in her ear jangled. 'It's one of the most beautiful countries I've ever been to. You're very lucky.'

'Yeah . . . New Zealand, land of the long white cloud . . . but we still have our problems like any other country,' he reminded her. 'The West Coast is one of the highest-growing areas for dope . . . the warm, humid climate, thick forests where plantations can be hidden. It's a lucrative business.'

Now that he was on to the subject of illicit drugs, it wouldn't do any harm to probe a little. 'And what about hard drugs?' she asked casually.

His eyes narrowed slightly. 'What do you mean? Heroin? Cocaine?'

She nodded.

'It still gets into the country but the police and Customs are doing their best to prevent it. Methamphetamine is a big worry though. Not only is it smuggled into the country, it can also be manufactured fairly easily because the ingredients are so accessible.'

'Had much problem down here on the coast?'

He shook his head, frowning. 'Not yet. There are some known drug users. But they have a tendency to keep it to themselves. They're not interested in peddling the stuff, if that's what you mean? Don't forget this is the coast. The nearest big city is at least three hours' drive from here.'

'So there's no known dealers?'

He looked puzzled. 'There could be. But why all the questions about drugs?'

'Just curious, that's all. I read something about organized crime in the newspaper the other day.' She searched her memory to remember the exact wording. 'New Zealand is thought to be a transit point for drugs to other countries, isn't it?'

He nodded. 'That's right, it is. And because of it, Customs have tightened up a lot. We work closely with them. Occasionally we find a drug shipment, so we must be doing something right.'

Tempted to ask him more, she didn't want to pursue the subject at the risk of him growing suspicious. She did, however, want to know more about Asian crime. So she pushed it a little further. 'What about the Triads? Is it true that they've forged links with gangs in this country?'

'It's highly possible. Asian Triads have been identified as a leading group in importing methamphetamine. You would have heard all about them in Hong Kong.'

'Frequently,' she admitted. 'The newspapers are full of incidents with the Triads. After all, it's a Chinese society going back to ancient times.' She hesitated slightly. 'Are you looking forward to joining the drug squad?'

He nodded. 'CIB are very selective. No doubt I'll hear in due course if my application is successful.' Mike lifted up the bottle of red. 'One for the road?'

'Just a little, thanks,' she replied. 'I'm driving, don't forget.'

He gave a wry smile. 'Glad to see the spell in jail made an impression.'

A retort was on the edge of her tongue, but when she saw he was teasing her, she relaxed. 'You're right. It did. More than you'll ever know.'

Mike poured the drinks then handed her one. Curious to know more about his family background, she noticed the photo displayed on top of the bookcase. She pointed. 'Are those your parents?'

He nodded. 'Yeah, that's my mother and father. My old man died when I was fifteen.'

'I'm sorry. I hadn't realized.'

Mike shrugged. 'I'm surprised Shona hadn't told you. He was shot.'

'Shot?' she repeated, thinking she had misheard.

'He was a cop. He'd been called to investigate a burglary at the bank. When he tried to arrest the culprits, one of them pulled out a gun. There was a fight and the gun went off.'

'That's terrible.' She stared at him. 'It must have been devastating.' Kelly found herself saying, 'I lost my dad too when I was young. There were five kids for my mother to support. Looking back, I don't know how she did it. True Scottish grit, I think.'

'That's tough.'

Kelly shrugged. 'We managed. Luckily, my mother had extended family, but somehow losing a father is hard to get over.'

Mike picked up another photo and handed it to her. 'Take a look at this. You'll recognize Shona and her twin brother, Shaun, and me when we were teenagers. The three of us were inseparable. We were always getting into mischief.'

Kelly studied the photo of the threesome lined up against the farm shed. She hadn't yet met Shaun as he'd been away but he was due back any day.

'So you did have long hair,' she accused. 'You only look about seventeen.'

He laughed. 'Eighteen,' he corrected her. 'Just before I entered police training college. I used to spend a lot of time with my cousins at their place.' He looked thoughtful. 'They were fun times. Only you don't appreciate them at that age.'

'No, I suppose you don't,' she replied softly, thinking of herself and Jeff. 'It's easy to take friends and family for granted. But when those you care about aren't there any more, you'd give anything to bring them back.'

'That's true,' he said, giving her an odd look. 'Sometimes it pays not to look back. Best to enjoy what there is to come. That's what life is all about. No regrets.'

'No regrets,' she murmured. Was he right? she wondered fleetingly. How she wished fervently she could do that. Maybe she would someday. But for now the pain was still too raw.

* * *

After Kelly had left, Mike picked up the half-full bottle of red wine and poured himself another glass. He chuckled. Its clear ruby colour reminded him of Kelly's lipstick.

Feeling a sudden urge to get some fresh air, he took his glass outside and stood on the veranda, drinking from it. The night was calm, unseasonably so, and it was chilly. His gaze skimmed over the great expanse of sea, the moon riding high in a flawless sky. It was at times like this he wished he had someone to share it with.

He thought briefly about his ex-fiancée, wondering if there was anything he could have done in hindsight to have stopped her leaving.

'You're obsessed with the job,' she'd told him a few weeks before she'd walked out on him.

Perhaps that was true . . . but it was a job he'd always done well. Only he couldn't explain to her about it. Being in the police wasn't just a job, it was a way of life. Even his mates were other police officers. The unsociable shifts probably hadn't helped things, he realized. But what he couldn't forgive were the lies she had told him. That still rankled. Still, at least he wouldn't end up divorced like some of his colleagues.

His thoughts returned to Kelly again. He frowned. He wasn't exactly sure how to describe her. Mysterious for a start. The kind of woman that could get under a man's skin — if he let her. He'd noticed her defensiveness when he'd asked about her life in Hong Kong. But still he had persisted. Everything she'd told him had seemed believable. Yet something still nagged at him.

★   ★   ★

The next day, Mike rose early. After finishing his breakfast, he stacked the dishes in the sink and, grabbing a towel from the hot-water cupboard, headed for the shower. While he scrubbed himself and shampooed his hair, he thought of the latest tune he'd been composing. Being in the shower always seemed to work well creatively as it gave him time to relax and think. Afterwards, he dashed through to his office to grab a small pad and pen and jotted down a few notes.

Playing guitar in a rock band wasn't for the money but for enjoyment. There was something very satisfying about writing lyrics and a tune to go with it. People often asked him why he didn't leave the force and go professional. His band was popular locally and they had potential, everyone said. But somehow the idea of living life without a regular income didn't appeal. He was also realistic enough to know that when you did something artistic for a living, the enjoyment faded because of the pressures involved. He didn't want to risk that. Besides, he enjoyed his job in the police too much.

As he got dressed, he turned up the volume of Don McGlashen's latest album. He rated McGlashen as perhaps the country's best songwriter and he loved playing his music loud.

The house reverberated with the sound. Lucky there were no neighbours nearby, he thought ironically. They might call the police and complain. That was one of the main reasons he'd bought the place. He liked the isolation.

After lunch he made his way to the station. In the locker room, he changed into his uniform of blue shirt and dark trousers. Snapping the leather belt on, he made sure the leather pouch hanging at his side contained handcuffs. Once he'd left them sitting on the shelf in his locker when he needed them. Really needed them. Now he double-checked every time he dressed for duty.

Kelly Anderson flashed through his mind. If he was honest with himself, she intrigued him. A girl who rode a Triumph Tiger as skilfully as she did and lived life on the edge, struck a chord in him — against his better judgement. He'd never come across anyone quite like her before. But then again, he didn't get to meet many Scottish women on the West Coast, especially one who rode a motorbike at a 180 kilometres per hour. It was obvious she skirted danger and took risks. So what else lurked underneath that cool exterior?

And what the hell was she up to?

'Where's the file on Kelly Anderson?' Mike asked Taylor, as he walked into the duty office. 'I thought I'd left it on my desk.' He rummaged through the files already sitting

72

there, but it was nowhere to be seen.

Taylor twisted his chair around. He pointed in the direction of Detective Inspector Poulsen's office. 'In there. Poulsen took it into his office earlier on.'

Mike frowned. 'What did he want it for? I haven't finished writing up the report yet.'

Taylor gave a shrug. 'Beats me. Who knows how Poulsen's mind works?' He swung back to his computer.

With quick strides, Mike reached Poulsen's office. He knocked twice on the door, without waiting for an answer, and walked in.

The detective inspector sat at his desk, his head bowed, engrossed in paperwork. He was in his early fifties, balding, with a sallow complexion and a slightly uneven moustache. His wife had started divorce proceedings recently, which explained his irritability. Poulsen could, at times, be very difficult to get on with and Mike could tell he was in a stinker of a mood.

The detective inspector looked up briefly, annoyance crossing his face. 'Yep . . . what is it?'

'Can I borrow Kelly Anderson's file?' Mike asked politely. 'Chris mentioned you picked it up from my desk.'

'What do you want it for?' Poulsen demanded. He chewed the side of his lip as he scrawled on the pad in front of him. Then he tore the page off and threw it in the bin.

'I think she's up to something,' replied Mike.

Poulsen scowled. 'Forget it. We're too busy just now to worry about a bikie who tried to bribe you.'

Mike couldn't believe he was hearing right. 'You can't be serious.'

'I am. It's not worth wasting time on.'

Mike shut the door behind him, so the other staff couldn't hear, and took a step towards the desk. He rubbed his chin thoughtfully. 'Something tells me you're not being straight with me over Kelly Anderson.'

The detective inspector took a deep sigh, then leant back in his chair. 'McKenna. I've already told you. My advice is to forget Kelly Anderson for now. She's pretty low priority in the scheme of things and I've got enough problems as it is.' He threw his pen on the desk, where it rolled to the side with a clatter. 'So if you've finished, I've got urgent things to do.'

Mike held his hands up in a placatory gesture. 'All right. But I just want to check out her background overseas.'

The detective inspector shook his head. 'Later. I'll pass the file on to you when I'm finished.'

'Finished what?' Mike pressed, not quite satisfied. 'Do you need a hand with something?' He glanced at Kelly's file sitting in full view on the desk. He needed that file. And he needed it now.

Poulsen glared. 'No, I don't need any help. But thanks for offering.'

Mike gritted his teeth, tempted to push him further but decided against it. 'Right then.' All he wanted to do was check out Kelly Anderson's background and Poulsen didn't usually stall things like this — or if he did, he usually gave some justification.

But seeing there was no shifting him, Mike headed back to his desk. The more he thought about it, the more he couldn't help thinking there was something odd about Kelly in spite of her declaration that she was only a tourist cruising around the country. Certainly any questions he'd asked her the night before should have allayed his suspicions. But they didn't. His instinct told him otherwise — and his instinct had never been wrong.

Whatever she was doing here, it wasn't tourism. He would bet on it.

5

Having a drink with Mike McKenna hadn't been so bad after all, Kelly reflected. He was sharp and intelligent and easy to talk to. Though maybe she'd better not underestimate him, she thought quickly.

When Kelly went through to the kitchen to make her breakfast, Shona gave her a warm smile. 'Help yourself to bacon. It's on the grill, keeping warm.'

'Thanks . . . but maybe later. Just a bit of toast will do.' Kelly poured herself a cup of coffee, then took a seat beside her friend.

'So what did you think of him?' asked Shona, her eyes alight with curiousity.

Kelly took a gulp of her coffee, feigning ignorance. 'Who?'

'Mike, of course.'

Kelly smiled. 'He's OK. But something tells me he's only being friendly because of you. Come on. What did you threaten him with?'

Shona laughed. 'I told him he'd have to look after Finn on his next day off. Even worse, he'd have to change his nappies.'

Kelly laughed. 'That figures. Any male

would buckle under that kind of pressure.'

'Actually, he's not so bad with kids really. He coaches the local high-school soccer team a couple of times a month. Haven't you heard the saying, 'A kid in sport stays out of court'? He's always had a lot of patience with youngsters. I keep telling him it's time he had some of his own, but he always avoids the topic.'

Kelly arched her brows, unable to keep the dryness out of her voice. 'Really. I hadn't noticed he was that way inclined.'

'You would if you got to know him better.' Shona leaned closer. 'He had a girlfriend a while back. Things were pretty serious between them. She was a typist at the hospital. But she ran out on him. And that really cut him up real bad.'

'Oh . . . ' said Kelly, trying not to appear interested, but even so, she couldn't help wanting to know more about him. 'What happened exactly?'

'They were engaged to be married, but she met someone else.'

'Maybe Mike scared her off,' Kelly said wryly. 'I'd imagine living with him would be pretty full-on.'

Shona looked at her speculatively. 'Maybe, but he's the loyal kind. Being a cop has given him a hard edge, but his heart is in the right place.'

* * *

Later that morning, while sitting on the veranda reading her novel, Kelly heard an argument between Shona and her twin brother, Shaun. Kelly hadn't met Shaun yet as he'd been away when she'd first arrived. Kelly was loath to intrude when they were obviously arguing over a family matter.

Shona's voice was full of frustration. 'If you spent more time on the farm helping Dad than with your mates in the pub, the farm might actually make some money.'

'You're a right one to talk. You've been away for a year,' came back the angry reply. 'A whole bloody year.'

'That's different,' argued Shona. 'Working overseas means we have to be away. Brent couldn't pass up such a good opportunity for his career.' Shona exhaled. 'I thought I could depend on you to see to things here.'

'Just because one or two bills are overdue — '

'One or two,' repeated Shona tightly. 'There's a whole stack of them.'

Shaun shrugged. 'I've been busy. I forgot. I would have got around to them eventually.'

'Well, *don't forget* next time.'

'Right, sis.'

Shaun's tone sounded conciliatory, so

78

Kelly decided that it would be a good time to make her appearance. When she entered the kitchen, Shona introduced her. Kelly looked at him curiously. So this was Shona's twin brother. They looked alike, she decided, though Shaun was rangy. With his long hair reaching his shoulders and tied back in a ponytail, he came across more like an artist than a farmer.

His mouth twisted wryly as he glanced at Kelly. 'Don't believe anything my twin sister says about me, will you? She tends to exaggerate my finer qualities.'

Kelly couldn't help but grin. 'I'll try not to.'

Shona passed around a plate of biscuits she'd made earlier on. 'Where's the truck, Shaun? Dad needs it.'

'I left it at a friend's place. Something's wrong with the radiator,' he replied vaguely.

'I thought the truck had just been in for repairs last week.'

'That's right. It had.'

'So what exactly went wrong?'

Shaun shrugged, sounding evasive. 'Not sure. A friend of mine, a mechanic, is fixing it. I'll pick it up later.'

Shaun didn't make a good liar, thought Kelly, noticing how he avoided his sister's gaze. If anyone could tell, she could. Deceiving people was part of her life and she was good at it. If she was honest with herself, it gave her a sense of power. She wouldn't abuse it though. She wasn't that type of person. She just needed enough deceit to accomplish her goals. That was her justification. So what exactly had Shona's brother been up to? she wondered.

★　★　★

Mike sat at his desk thinking. He leaned over and lifted some papers out of his bulging filing tray, though he hadn't the heart to tackle them. There were times he hated office work and would rather be out on patrol.

Taylor looked up from the computer. 'So you didn't get the file on the Anderson girl, eh?'

'No,' said Mike thoughtfully. 'But I will. Soon as Poulsen goes out for lunch. So if you see him leave his office, tell me.'

'You know, maybe he liked her photograph,' Taylor mused, swinging his seat around to face him.

'Yeah, sure . . . she's just his type,' said Mike with a trace of sarcasm. He drummed his fingers on his desk, still trying to fathom out why Poulsen didn't want him to pursue the issue, since he wasn't known for his leniency.

Taylor turned back to the computer screen. 'You win some, you lose some. You ought to know that, Mike.'

Mike gave a deep sigh. 'Yeah, you're right. I don't know why I'm wasting my time on her anyway.' But he did know, he thought. Kelly Anderson was different, unusual. But he couldn't get over the niggling suspicion she was hiding something. And what was more, carrying around a stack of money like she did was asking for trouble. He'd already checked her out on the national computer and she had no previous convictions in New Zealand. But that didn't mean she was innocent. Maybe he ought to try Interpol.

Mike took a swig of his coffee and nearly spat it out. It was cold. He muttered his thanks to the cleaner as she stopped to lift his cup and empty his bin. It was nearly four o'clock in the afternoon and he had two burglaries to investigate and a stack of paperwork to get through. He picked up the latest confidential report sent down from head office.

'Have you read this, Chris? Four police officers have been charged with selling drugs,' Mike asked.

'I know. But they didn't sell them for money . . . it was for information. So they could get a lead on some criminals.'

'If you ask me, they're not guilty,' Mike stated. 'It says here they've been suspended from duty pending a full inquiry. Christ, a police officer's job is hard enough without having to resort to crime to fight crime. Still, I reckon New Zealand has one of the best police forces in the world,' he added proudly. 'And our statistics prove that.'

'Yeah, but what gets me is people always seem to forget we're human beings. We still have problems just like everyone else.'

A grin tugged at Mike's mouth. 'You mean women problems. Nothing a good workout at the gym can't solve.'

Taylor laughed. 'You can say that again. Something to be said for the caveman approach. At least, that's what the psychologists tell us.' Taylor handed him a file. 'Here . . . have a read of this. It's the final report about that stake-out we did last summer. The one in Nemona Forest.'

Mike picked it up, and leaned back in his chair. 'Yeah. How could I forget?' He flicked the pages. 'That was one huge haul of weed. A lucky break, if you ask me. It's hard to believe it had gone unnoticed for five growing seasons.' He skimmed a few lines of the report, then said thoughtfully, 'How the bloody hell are we going to keep on top of things this year? We're down on staff.'

'Time we did some more community work,' suggested Taylor.

'Hmm . . . sounds like a good idea. I'll make arrangements with some of the schools and do a talk.' Mike gave a short laugh. 'It always cracks the kids up when I tell them I've tried dope. Before I joined the police force, that is.'

Taylor shook his head. 'I don't know if there are any real answers to the problem. But I do know we can't win on our own. We do need the community to help us.'

Mike agreed. 'It's not the dope growing that's worrying me right now. It's the damned P trade. It's spiralling around the country. You know what that will mean?'

'Yeah . . . violence on the rampage.' Taylor frowned. 'Look what's already happening in the cities.'

Mike grimaced. 'You said it. It's only a matter of time before it hits us down here.'

'That's the world we live in, Mike,' replied Taylor philosophically. 'We can't solve everything even if we wanted to.'

Mike's jaw firmed. 'Well, I'm damned well going to try. I don't want to see our community destroyed by drugs. We have to make a stand sometime.'

'It's bigger than us,' pointed out Chris. 'It's a world problem.'

'I'm not disputing that. But this is New Zealand. We've got good cops and we've got Customs onside. Hell, we're the envy of most other countries.'

Mike made a silent promise to himself. He'd do all he could to prevent his home and the people who lived here from being tainted with drugs. He hated them with a passion. He'd seen what they could do to a person when he'd done a stint in Auckland. He'd never forget that crazed expression on the man's face when he'd been arresting him. Inside the house, where they had been called to, he'd found two children cowering under the bed. The mother lay half naked on the bed, badly beaten. Later, during interview, the man had confessed he was a heroin addict and had needed a fix. He hadn't even remembered what he'd done. Now, from the information coming through lately, methamphetamine, or as it was often called, P, had a much worse effect, destroying whole families.

Mike tried to concentrate on his paperwork and made a concerted effort, managing to empty half his in-tray.

An hour later, a call came through. The local kindergarten had had their large sandpit cover stolen. And Mike McKenna knew exactly why.

Kelly had parked her motorbike in town and had decided to walk to Dave Williamson's address even though it was quite a distance. Walking didn't worry her — hadn't she often followed someone or avoided being followed by being on foot? Besides, she enjoyed the exercise and it was a good way to get a feel for the place.

She stopped halfway over the Cobden bridge, placed her gloved hands on the iron railings and observed the sprawling town on both sides of the river. Greymouth. Somehow on a cold winter's day, the town looked bleak and depressing. But maybe all towns looked that way when the sun wasn't shining, she thought generously.

Grey cloud scurried overhead, racing towards the sea as if competing frantically with the river below. She'd heard the river was a force to be reckoned with. It had burst its banks on more than one occasion, so finally a wall had been built to protect the town.

Kelly glanced to the left of the river neck near the edge of the port. A couple of yellow cranes loomed against the skyline. The slow rumble of a train, ready to leave, drifted up to her along with the unpleasant smell of diesel.

She turned around and leaned against the iron railings to face the mountains inland. She could see an unusual, thick white mist, very defined, slowly snaking its way through the higher reaches of the valley. Just then, a sudden sharp, cold gust of wind caught her off guard. Kelly gasped as it cut through her. 'The Barber,' she murmured. Shona had told her about the catabatic wind, which swept down from the icy mountain peaks, and its nickname.

The West Coast was full of legends, ever since the first immigrants had sailed from across the seas, lured by a life better than the one they left behind. Wasn't that what all immigrants thought when they left their homeland?

She had left her home in Scotland, hadn't she? For a moment, she wondered what it would be like to settle in one place; friends, a home, stability. Not having to worry about the next drug deal or criminal who was trying to outmanoeuvre her. The thought of permanence was enticing and yet somehow frightening.

Kelly wrapped her tartan scarf tighter around her neck before continuing on her way. Another blast of cold wind caught her and, with her head bowed low, she grasped the railings tightly for support. Unexpectedly, she was thrown back in time to when she stood on the ramparts of Edinburgh Castle looking down at her city — the one she was born and married in.

Jeff was there — but then he always had been. Scenes of them together reeled through her mind in succession. Noisy bars with folk music, walking hand in hand in Princes Street gardens in the summertime. They had been a part of each other's life for as long as she could remember. They'd even grown up in the same neighbourhood.

Jeff. Her beloved Jeff. Alive, joyful, full of good spirits and always willing to take a risk. For a brief moment, he was standing beside her, his image so real she almost reached out to touch him, but when she did it was to wipe the corners of her eyes.

She hated being catapulted unexpectedly into the past like that. Sometimes it was only a small thing that triggered the memories, but they distracted her, made her vulnerable and that was dangerous. It was better to stay in the present. Stay focused. And stay alive.

Maybe the healing would come some day. The big question was when.

Five minutes later, she found Williamson's house. Making sure no one was watching her, Kelly took the uneven steps two at a time, reaching the front door just as it opened.

Dave Williamson stood there, grinning widely, and beckoned her in. As she passed, stepping into the hallway, she immediately noticed the black snake tattoo on his right forearm.

'You got the cash?' he asked eagerly, walking ahead of her.

She nodded. She followed him down the hallway and he eventually led her into a bright, airy room at the back of the house. Boxes of seedlings were stacked next to the larger windows. Kelly knew they were cannabis plants.

'You grow these all by yourself?' she asked casually, wondering where he also planted them when the seedlings reached a certain stage of development. Though from what she had learned already, there was plenty of room in the forests at the back of town.

He nodded. 'I have help. My sister usually,' he informed her. 'She's got greener fingers than me. I just do the deals.' He flashed another smarmy grin. 'OK . . . how much do you want?'

'A couple of tinnies.' She knew exactly what to ask for: dope wrapped in tin foil.

'Are you sure that's enough?' he prompted.

'For now.'

While he handed her a small package, she added, 'Any chance of getting some ice?'

A wary look crossed his face. 'You're into P? No way, I never deal in that stuff. It's bad news, man. Take my advice. Stick to dope. It's much safer.'

'Ice isn't bad. Not if you know how to handle it. I'm keen to get some. Do you know of any dealers?'

Dave shrugged. 'One or two.'

'Can you put me in touch with them?'

'Maybe. But I'll need to check in with them first.' He made a move, ready to show her out again, but as he passed the window he looked out. 'What the — !' he exclaimed, then swore profusely. His gaze fixed on the car that had drawn up outside.

'What is it?' asked Kelly.

'A police car,' he said, with a worried frown. 'Right over there.'

Kelly peered out. 'I see it.'

Dave quickly rolled down the cane blinds, shutting out the sunlight. 'Just hope they're not coming in here.'

Kelly parted the blind slightly to look out, keeping well back to avoid being seen. 'There's only one cop,' she remarked. 'So it's hardly a raid.' She watched for a few seconds more, surveying the sole occupant of the car. Her eyes widened as she recognized who it was.

Dave took the words right out of her

mouth. 'The son-of-a-bitch. It's fucking McKenna.'

Dismay shot through her. She had to keep calm. It might only be a coincidence. After all, Greymouth was a small town. There was no chance Mike would spot her because her motorbike was parked quite a distance away and there was no way he would guess she was in this house.

'Do you know him?' she asked carefully.

'Who doesn't?' Dave answered. 'He arrested me for possession of drugs a few years ago. I got convicted, and spent time in jail.' He shook his head. 'Don't want to end up inside again.'

'Then you're taking a chance growing the stuff,' Kelly stated.

'Didn't have a choice. Needed the dosh to feed my family. I got made redundant last year from a forestry company. Big cutbacks due to the new forestry policies. You know how it goes. The government thinks more about saving trees than giving us jobs.'

'That's too bad,' remarked Kelly, sympathetically.

Dave's gaze returned to the street outside. 'Looks like he's heading into the kindergarten. Must be something up.'

'I'll wait until he goes,' said Kelly. 'I don't want him recognizing me.'

Dave let the blind drop and faced her. He frowned, uncertain. 'You've met him before.'

Kelly gave him selected details of her arrest, injecting a note of distaste in her voice for the police, and specifically for Mike McKenna. A little credibility would go in her favour, she thought quickly. 'Strangely enough, I met him accidentally in the pub after you left.'

'I'm not surprised. His band plays there sometimes.' Dave added his own stories of run-ins with the police. 'The trouble with this town is everyone knows each other.'

Feeling she was developing a rapport with the dope dealer, Kelly made her move.

'Do you know where I can find a man called Carlos Fortuna?'

Wariness came into Dave's eyes. He shook his head. 'Nope. Never heard of him.'

'If you do, can you give me a call?' She handed him a card with her name and mobile phone number.

A cunning look crossed his face. 'I might have to grease a few palms for that kind of information.'

She kept her voice level, wondering if he knew more than he let on. 'That's fine by me. As much as it takes.'

His eyes glinted. 'You must want to find him badly.' He shrugged. 'I'll ask around for you. But I can't promise anything. OK?'

Kelly nodded. In silence they watched Mike McKenna walk out of the kindergarten and drive away. Kelly followed Dave down the hallway towards the front door, then stopped as she heard a noise like a cry coming from one of the rooms.

She lifted an eyebrow inquiringly. 'That sounds like a baby.'

Dave grinned proudly. 'Yeah, you're right.' He pushed open the bedroom door. 'Have a look.'

Kelly caught a glimpse of a cot, pink covers moving and legs kicking wildly. Kelly's face softened momentarily as she saw the little girl's face framed by blonde curls.

Dave continued. 'Yeah, she's my kid. One year old next month . . . and I'll be able to buy her something nice for her birthday now.' He patted his pocket. 'Thanks to you.'

Even drug dealers have families, Kelly thought cynically. She quickly added, 'If you find Carlos for me, I'll make it worthwhile . . . very.' She slipped him some more notes. 'There's more where that came from.'

He nodded, a thoughtful look on his face. 'Sure, I'll be in touch,' he said, then closed the door firmly behind her and locked it.

Williamson dialled the number of his contact. 'I don't know what she wants . . . she wouldn't let on. But she's looking for you.'

Then he hung up and pulled out the money Kelly had given him. This had been a bonus.

★   ★   ★

The first thing Mike McKenna did when he got back to the station was place his Motorola hand-held radio on the stand to recharge. Then he made his way to his desk in the corner of the room. He swept back the curtains in order to let more light in. Streams of afternoon sunlight shone on to the wall above him, highlighting a black and white photo of a group of uniformed police officers taken in the 1960s. In the centre of the group photo stood his father. Mike stared at him for a few seconds, wondering what he would have thought if he'd known his son had grown up to be a cop. Won't let you down, Dad, he murmured silently. I'll make it into the CIB. Somehow, he had a feeling his dad would have approved.

Drawing back to the task in hand, he put his password into the computer and entered the details of the missing sandpit cover. He used two fingers only. He'd never learned to type properly, but he was fast — playing the guitar had ensured that.

Detective Inspector Poulsen breezed in. 'What's this about the kindergarten having their sandpit cover stolen?'

Mike swivelled his chair around to face the detective inspector. 'Yeah, it's a real blow. The kindergarten committee bought it a few weeks ago from all the fund-raising they did last summer. It cost over a thousand bucks. Pity they got a green-coloured one,' he added as he leaned sideways, one elbow resting on the desk. 'And you know as well as I do, we're not going to get it back. Best thing they can do is get some publicity. Maybe businesses around town will donate money to buy another one.'

Poulsen perched on the edge of the desk and crossed his arms. 'It might have been those community service workers they had there last week.'

'We don't know that for sure. Just because they're doing time in the community and not prison doesn't make them suspect number one,' Mike strongly reminded him.

Poulsen snorted. 'I bet they took one look at that cover, then came back later with their mates and hauled it over the fence in the middle of the night. The colour would have been ideal to use as camouflage over a cannabis plantation.'

'I guess that's a possibility. We could take

94

out the helicopter and scout around. See if we can locate it anywhere,' suggested Mike.

Poulsen licked his moustache. 'I wouldn't bother. There are more important things to do at the moment.' He slammed a file down on Mike's desk. 'Here, take a look at this. It's the latest intelligence on gang movements. Can you check out the rumour an outfit has moved into town?'

Mike frowned. 'Where did you hear that?'

'Some drunk we brought in last night threatened that his mates would get us. It turns out he's from the Black Snakes gang.'

'The Black Snakes?' Mike shook his head. 'Never heard of them.'

'They're new. From up north. Sounds like they're on the move, looking to set up a base here. Why, we don't know, but they've sent a few scouts down to the West Coast to check things out.'

Mike stared at him thoughtfully. 'Do you think Kelly Anderson has got something to do with this?'

Poulsen grinned suddenly. 'Now there's a thought. It seems to me like you can't get that woman off your mind, McKenna.' Poulsen turned to walk out the room, then paused under the door frame. 'About that application of yours for the CIB. Can you make the interview tomorrow?'

Surprised, Mike said, 'So soon?'

'Might as well get things moving. Now that Beattie's left, we've been under pressure.'

Mike picked up his diary, and flicked through the pages. 'What time?'

'First thing in the morning.'

'Great. I'll be there.'

When Poulsen had left, Mike thought about the forthcoming interview. There had been talk for the last couple of days about placing him on secondment to the CIB for three months. It was a trial to see how he got on, and whether they could work OK with him. Mike didn't foresee any problems at this stage apart from Poulsen, and he was the boss. Still, for the sake of the job, he was pretty sure they could iron out any differences they had.

Mike picked up the file Poulsen had given him and started to read. He'd just finished one page when the phone rang. 'McKenna.' He took note of the details quickly and then hung up.

He shouted through to Taylor as he reached for his jacket. 'There's been a car accident on State Highway 6, just out of town. I'm heading out there now.'

Within ten minutes Mike pulled the Commodore on to the verge at the accident scene. The driver of the wrecked car was already on a stretcher being transported into the ambulance. A baby screamed its head off in the background.

Mike moved towards a colleague who was standing at the side of the road, measuring the skid marks. 'Do we know what happened?' asked Mike, bending down to look at them.

The police officer nodded. 'The Holden was going too fast, skidded on the ice and ploughed into the paddock, finally stopping when they hit the tree. There's just the driver and a kid involved.'

'Are they badly hurt?'

'The driver's in a bad way. He went through the windscreen. Luckily the kid was in a car seat. It probably saved her life.'

Spectators had stopped to view the accident and Mike waved them on to prevent a traffic jam. Vultures, Mike muttered to himself. Someone tapped him on the back. It was Julie.

She gave Mike a warm smile. 'Hi. I was just passing.' She glanced at the mangled car. 'Looks nasty.' Stepping forward, she lifted her camera. 'Can I get a closer picture of the car?'

'If you want. But you'll have to wade through the ditch.'

'Doesn't matter. It's all part of the job.'

He nodded his approval. 'All right. But

make sure you don't touch anything.'

Julie scrambled down the dirt bank, through the ankle-deep water, then up the other side. Meanwhile, Mike radioed through to Comms to check the registration and found the car registered in the name of Sonya Williamson.

Half an hour later, Mike made his way to the Accident and Emergency department of the local hospital. The ambulance had arrived a few minutes beforehand. Mike stood at the counter to speak to the receptionist.

'Just waiting for details about the injured driver,' she told him. 'The nurse shouldn't be long now.' The receptionist reached up to the shelves behind her for a buff-coloured file, then leaned towards him. 'You might as well have a coffee while you're waiting,' she said cheerfully. 'I'll make you one, if you want.'

Mike glanced at the clock on the wall, debating on whether to wait any longer or return later. He might as well wait for a few more minutes. He gave a brief smile. 'No, thanks. I'm fine.'

When the receptionist returned, she continued typing, taking the details of the next person in line. Just then, Mike saw Julie walk in through the swinging doors. He went forward to speak to her.

'What are you doing here?' asked Mike

curiously. 'I thought you had your scoop for the day and would be heading back to the office.'

Julie swung her camera around and placed it on the counter. 'Yeah, I did, but when I got back my boss sent me down here. He got a tip that a teenager had been admitted for a drug overdose, so I thought I'd come along and see what I could pick up.'

Mike frowned. 'What's the angle?' He knew a straightforward drug overdose wouldn't have attracted that much attention. There had to be something more.

'Keep it quiet,' Julie whispered, leaning closer. 'This is in confidence. Someone phoned in anonymously to say a local lab is being set up, manufacturing drugs. Could be methamphetamine.'

'P?' said Mike. He pursed his lips. 'That's bad news. No idea who might have made the phone call?'

Julie shook her head. 'None. Like I said, the caller wouldn't leave his name.'

The swishing noise of curtains caught their attention. A trolley, rattling against the tiled floor, was pushed out by an orderly dressed in a white uniform. The doctor and nurse followed him. The doctor held a buff-coloured file, then handed it to the nurse.

'Looks like that's your boy over there,'

Mike indicated, as he watched the trolley roll by. A youth about seventeen years old with lank black hair lay very still, the white sheet pulled up to his chest. An older woman, red-eyed from crying, held his hand. Mike watched them walk down the corridor until they disappeared around the corner to the lift.

After enquiries at the reception, Julie got short shrift. She looked far from pleased. She turned back to Mike. 'They're not giving anything out. I might try contacting the mother later,' she said, checking her watch. 'I'll head back to the office for now. I'm nearly finished for the day anyway.' She hesitated. 'What time are you off duty?'

'In a couple of hours. Why?'

'Fancy a drink after work?'

Mike's first thought was to refuse, but then he thought he really ought to make an effort. Julie had been more than helpful in the past and it paid to keep in with the local press, especially since she was the crime reporter.

'You're on. How about meeting at Cherries, the new wine bar in town? Say seven o'clock?'

'Great.' She gave a broad smile. 'See you there.'

After Julie left, Mike's thoughts reeled as he thought about what she had told him.

Could the methamphetamine lab have anything to do with the gang rumoured to have moved into town? Meanwhile, he'd make his own enquiries. But he had to see to this MVA first. Motor vehicle accidents unfortunately were a cop's bane. A fact of life and death, as it turned out in this case.

The nurse came out to speak to him. 'The driver has died,' she said calmly, 'but the baby's OK. We'll keep her in for a few days for observation. She's pretty distressed.'

'What about the next of kin?' Mike asked, concerned. 'Do you want me to get in contact with them?'

The nurse nodded. 'That would help, thanks. We've tried ringing but there's no answer. Maybe you can go around to see them. Explain what has happened.' She handed him the driver's leather wallet and he opened it.

The name Dave Williamson and his address was listed on the driver's licence. Mike looked at it carefully, reading the man's name over and over again. Dave Williamson. Mike's forehead creased. The man's name seemed familiar somehow. Then it clicked. He had been in the same class as him at high school and then he'd busted him for drugs a few years later. If he remembered rightly, the man had been in prison, low security, but as far as Mike knew he had been living quietly since he got out. He'd run a check when he got back to the station.

It was just then he noticed a card tucked behind the thick wad of notes. He unfolded it. The name Kelly Anderson and her mobile phone number stared back at him.

What was an ex-con doing with Kelly's name in his wallet?

6

Tino Chang liked a good workout at Wushu. Traditional martial arts had been a part of his life for as long as he could remember. The movements enabled him to work off the frustrated energy that built up from too many hours sitting behind his desk.

Chang straightened his shoulders. On the wall in front of him was a full-length mirror. He glimpsed his wiry figure clothed in white cotton. His black hair, pulled into a ponytail like a Chinese warrior, smoothed against his skull with a sheen as blue as a raven's wing. Sweat slicked his face and ran in rivulets down his temples. At thirty-five years of age, Chang was in good shape both mentally and physically.

He drew his thoughts back to the teacher standing in front of the class. 'Move your fist like a shooting star . . . and your body like a writhing snake. Remember . . . the keys for winning are sharp eyes, fast hands, courage, strong stance, solid strength.'

Chang listened carefully, taking note of the teacher's words. Then he heard a noise, a discreet cough over to his left that he immediately recognized. Irritated at the interruption, he was tempted to ignore it, but eventually turned to see what it was the man wanted. Chang said in a low voice, 'This had better be urgent.'

'It is,' replied his executive secretary. 'An important message for you.'

Chang nodded. 'Very well.' He stepped away from the others to read it, then gave a satisfied smile. The container ship had resumed its course to New Zealand. Everything was going according to plan.

The martial arts class had almost finished, so instead of rejoining the group, Chan made his way to the showers. Afterwards in the massage room, the woman with black hair that reached to her waist rubbed perfumed oils over his body. Her soft slim hands glided over the dragoon tattoo on his back. The swirls and delicate blue-black lines, etched deep against the bronze of his skin, rippled under the pressure of her fingers.

Chang could feel the tension easing from his muscles. He gave a sigh. 'Feels very good.' Usually he talked to the therapist without reservation but today there were things on his mind and he lapsed into silence. For a startling moment, he wondered if she was the woman his fortune-teller had referred to. The one who wore a split-coloured mask.

Realistically, it could be one of several woman close to him, he realized. From now on, he would be on his guard.

While he lay there, Chang debated on whether to ring Kelly Anderson on her cell phone but decided against it. Let her come to him. Briefly, he considered whether it was she who posed a risk, but shoved the thought away immediately. She had extricated him from an awkward situation with the police, and on another occasion had saved him from assassination. Surely that proved her loyalty.

When he had first met Kelly Anderson, through a mutual friend, he'd been struck by her strength of intellect. What intrigued him even more was her resistance to him even when he'd showered her with gifts. He should have known that his initial approach wouldn't impress. She wasn't a woman to be bought with diamonds, or with other monetary gains. Instead, he'd wooed her with knowledge. To his pleasure, she had been fascinated with China and spoke his language fluently.

He quickly realized that the fates had brought him this woman and had put her in his path as a sign. So he'd hired her as a senior member of his staff. It had only been a matter of time before he'd entrusted her with more responsible duties. She had continued to please him, showing initiative. A woman of her calibre would be very useful indeed, especially in his overseas dealings, and so he had employed her on this most special mission of all.

★ ★ ★

'Are you sure you don't mind babysitting Finn?' asked Shona.

Kelly assured her friend she didn't. 'Take your time in town. If Brent is taking you to lunch, then make the most of it.'

'Thanks. I will.' Shona smiled gratefully. 'A break is just what I need.'

For the next few hours, Kelly had to admit she enjoyed the domestic role. At least Shona wouldn't have to face any cooking or washing when she got back. Kelly had the meal in the oven in record time. A long walk with Finn as well as playing with him made the time fly by. By the time she had taken in the washing from the line and folded it up, she heard Shona and Brent drive into the yard. Kelly peeped out the window. There was another set of car lights behind them — obviously Shaun had arrived at the same time. She opened the door to help them carry in their parcels.

'Sorry we were so long,' said Shona. 'It's not often we get the chance to get out together on our own.' She dumped her plastic bags down on the floor and picked Finn up to give him a big kiss, avoiding the chocolate smears on his mouth.

'Don't worry. I've had plenty to do,' Kelly replied, as she went forward to wipe Finn's face with a wet cloth. 'Finn was a wee darling. He even had a nap in the afternoon so I put my feet up for a while.'

Shaun came strolling in, kicking his boots off at the door. He grabbed Kelly's hand. 'Hey, beautiful. What are you doing tonight?' He whirled her around. 'Come on, get your party dress on. I'm taking you out dancing.'

Kelly laughed at this unexpected reception and pulled away. 'Dancing? Where to?'

Shaun's eyes gleamed as he looked down at her. 'A nice little place I know. Maybe you've heard of it? The Hilton Hotel.'

'The Hilton?' Kelly repeated slowly, wondering if she had heard correctly. Puzzled, she said, 'I thought that hotel was in London.'

'Ah . . . not this one. It's in Blackball. It's our local pub. Just down the road from here.'

At first Kelly was to going to refuse. The thought of a long, hot bath and an early night was tempting. Caring for a two-year-old, while fun, was exhausting. However, her conscience pricked. How could she refuse an offer to socialize?

Another trip to a pub might prove useful. It would be worth checking out. The more contacts she made, the better her network.

She smiled enthusiastically. 'Sounds great.' She glanced at the washing basket still half full. She could hardly leave it for Shona to finish after her day off.

But Shaun had other ideas. He grabbed the towel from her hands and flung it in the basket.

'Forget that. You've done enough today.' He gently shoved her towards her bedroom. 'Get changed. Put something nice on like a dress,' he said, grinning. 'That is, if you have one,' he added, and closed the door firmly behind her.

A dress? Fortunately, she had brought one with her just in case, though she usually travelled light. Rummaging through her bags, she found the little black number badly creased. She put her head around the door and asked Shona for the iron.

Shona whipped the dress out of her hands. 'I'll iron it. You put your makeup on.'

Kelly couldn't help but laugh. 'But — '

'No buts,' added Shaun, following his sister down the hallway. 'Just do as you're told. You're here to have a good time. And we're going to make sure you get one.'

Kelly gave a laugh. 'I suppose I haven't a choice.'

'Nope, you haven't.' Shaun grinned again, but the grin was wiped off his face when Shona handed him Finn.

'Here, keep your nephew amused while I iron Kelly's dress.' Finn clutched a handful of Shaun's hair and twisted it, making him yell. Kelly stifled a grin, and shut the door.

A few minutes later, Kelly, wearing her black figure-hugging dress, looked down at her boots with dismay. They spoiled the overall effect.

Shona stood in the doorway, looking at her thoughtfully. 'Wait a minute. I'll be right back.' Within seconds she returned with a pair of black and gold sandals. 'Here. Try these on. We're about the same size. So they should fit.'

Kelly did. 'They're perfect. Thanks.'

When she entered the living room, Shaun gave a long whistle. 'You ought to wear a dress more often, especially with those kind of legs.'

Kelly laughed, and slung her handbag casually over her shoulder. 'Well . . . what are you waiting for?'

'You're right. Let's hit the road.'

Shona followed them both on to the veranda. 'Don't get into any mischief,' she said, prodding Shaun in the chest. 'And remember Kelly is a guest, so make sure you look after her. That means sitting beside her, and fetching her drinks. No going off with any other women that take your fancy.'

He pulled a face at his sister. 'Spoilsport. Am I likely to get into that kind of trouble?'

'Huh, your middle name is trouble. Always has been. Ever since the day you took your first breath.'

Shaun muttered something about bossy women and looked at Kelly as he said, 'See what I have to put up with?'

Kelly whispered in Shona's ear as she passed. 'Don't worry, I'll keep an eye on him. I've got four brothers, don't forget.'

When they reached the Blackball Hilton, it was obvious from the sound coming from inside that there was a live band playing. Kelly's feet were itching to dance.

The front of the hotel was reminiscent of yesteryear with its double-storey colonial veranda and frosted window panes. The place was doing a roaring trade, Kelly judged, from the number of cars parked outside. When they entered, she and Shaun wove their way through the throng of people until they came to the bar.

The bar area had a polished brown counter curving in a half circle, enclosing two women who were working frantically to pour drinks while at the same time chatting to their customers. There was a friendly atmosphere about the place. Everyone seemed to know each other.

Kelly's gaze lifted towards the band playing in the corner of the room. She blinked twice. It was him. Mike McKenna. She drew in a sharp breath, trying to make an effort at normality.

Shaun appeared at her side with her drink. 'I see you've spotted Mike. It should be a fun night. He's pretty good on the guitar.'

A table had just become vacant and they both sat down. At that moment, Mike announced the band was taking a break and wandered over to them. Kelly glanced around the room, hoping that no one would later recognize her in conversation with a cop.

Mike pulled up a chair next to Shaun. 'This is a surprise. I didn't expect to see you both here tonight.'

'Kelly deserved a night out after looking after Finn all day,' Shaun replied easily. 'Figured it's about time we showed her some nightlife around here. We may not have the bright lights of the city, but we know how to enjoy ourselves.' He pulled at his beer, and surveyed the room. 'There's a good crowd here tonight. Word must have got around you were playing.'

Mike grinned. 'The band's been getting so many bookings lately, I've had to turn a lot down.' His gaze settled on Kelly. 'I've got tomorrow off unexpectedly, so at least that's something. Burning the candle at both ends is hard going.'

'I'm sure it is,' she replied politely.

Mike continued to stare at her. 'So what are you doing tomorrow? More sightseeing?'

'Perhaps,' she said vaguely. 'I'm not sure yet.'

'Need a guide?'

'A guide,' she repeated, unsure whether he was offering or not. 'No, I don't think so. I'm a loner. I prefer to check out the highlights of the coast on my own. But thanks anyway.'

'That's a pity. You don't know what you might miss.' He paused slightly. 'Can't I even tempt you on a picnic? I'm heading up the Moonlight track for a couple of hours in the afternoon. It will be good to get out in the bush. There's a lot of history up there that goes back to the gold rush over a hundred years ago. It might appeal to you. Sometimes I swear I can still hear the picks of the old miners chipping away at the rocks.'

'Sounds fascinating,' remarked Kelly, almost tempted. Then she reminded herself she had other more important things to do. She shrugged apologetically. 'But maybe some other time.'

He persisted. 'If walking doesn't suit you, we can fly up in a chopper. I have my helicopter's licence.'

Kelly angled her head, surprised. 'You do?'

'Yeah, use it for hunting deer mainly. Or during search and rescue. We get the occasional tramper lost in the bush. I'll even take you to places that you wouldn't normally get to see.'

'Sounds like an invitation I can't refuse. But I really do have an appointment tomorrow. And it's one I must keep.'

'OK. Just let me know when you're free. And we can arrange something.'

'Thanks. I will,' she replied, feeling surprised that she actually meant it.

Mike's break was over and the band called him back up. 'I'll be back later,' he said to Kelly. 'Just don't go away. OK?'

Kelly leaned back to enjoy the music. She wasn't quite sure what to make of Mike McKenna. Sometimes his arrogance infuriated her, but in spite of that, there was an unusual earthy and masculine aura about him. That light which entered his grey eyes whenever he asked her something probed too deeply for her liking. All the same, she wondered how he would react if he found out what she was really doing here.

Shaun interrupted her thoughts. 'Come on. Let's dance.'

'It's a ballad,' she remarked, feeling awkward.

'So?' He took her hand and dragged her up, then put his arms around her. She protested slightly, drawing back. But all he did was laugh and said, 'My girlfriend is over there. If she sees us like this, I might be able to get some response from her. Right now, she's not even talking to me.'

Kelly chuckled. 'I'm not sure I like being used like that.'

'Not used, exactly,' he explained. 'More like helping me out. That is, if you don't mind?'

'Why don't you just go over there and ask her to dance?' she suggested.

'Are you kidding? I'm going to make her suffer. Just like she's doing to me.'

She prodded him in the chest. 'You're heartless, Shaun McKenna. I thought you were the sensitive kind.'

'I am. Well, to a certain extent. But all males are heartless some time or another,' he responded lightly. 'And that includes Mike. Did you know women usually fall over themselves to get a date with him? But does he take them up? No, he doesn't. He's bloody mad.'

She found herself defending Mike, but had no idea why. 'That's understandable. He's been hurt once.' Then hastily added, 'At least, that's what Shona told me.'

Her curiosity got the better of her again. 'So why's your girlfriend not talking to you?'

Shaun gave a sigh. 'She thought I'd spent a night with someone else. But I hadn't. Only I can't seem to convince her. Not even when my mates back up my story.'

'There has to be trust between you both,' remarked Kelly.

'Exactly,' he replied with satisfaction. 'And until she learns that, things just aren't going to work between us.'

Trust was the most important aspect of a relationship, decided Kelly. She'd learned that the hard way.

When the ballad finished, Kelly returned to her seat. Moments later, as she sipped her drink, she watched Mike weave his way through the crowd towards her.

'Fancy a dance?'

She was too startled at his offer to offer any objection. 'I . . . I . . . '

He quickly explained. 'Someone's standing in for me for a while, so I want to make the most of it.'

Again she hesitated.

'What's the matter?' he asked softly. 'Scared of me?'

Her mouth went dry. 'No. You don't frighten me, *Mr Police Officer*.'

'In case you hadn't noticed, I'm not in uniform. And my name is Mike.'

'Once a cop, always a cop. It makes no difference about the uniform.'

He stood there waiting, his brows arched. 'Well?'

Reluctantly, she stood up. She couldn't quite relax in his arms, nor did she want to. His body was too close and his hand at the indent in her back too firm. Even so, she tried to pull back slightly, but he increased the pressure of his hand.

He spoke softly in her ear. 'You seem to know a lot about cops. Why the interest?'

Kelly stiffened slightly. 'Just an observation over these past few years.'

'I see.' His grey eyes pulled at her. 'So, with all this interest about cops, have you ever thought about taking up law enforcement?'

She almost choked. 'Me? Are you kidding? Sorry, but I don't do rules, nor can I stand discipline. That kind of environment wouldn't suit me at all.'

He laughed, surprising her. 'A rebel at heart, huh? That kind of attitude could get you into trouble.'

'Wrong,' she retaliated. 'It's always got me out of trouble. I'm a Scot, don't forget. Being a rebel is inherent. You only need to look at our history to see that.'

'Wait a minute,' he said slowly. 'Are you saying you've been in trouble before?'

Be careful, thought Kelly. He was angling for information. 'No. Not until the day you pulled me up at the side of the road.'

His eyes narrowed. 'I thought we'd got past that.'

'You're right. We have.'

'At least that's something we agree on,' he said wryly.

Maybe she was being too hard on him. He'd made an effort, and she was slapping it back in his face. It wasn't that she didn't like dancing; she did. It was the fact that she was dancing with him of all people.

The music stopped, yet he still held her. She gave him a quizzical look. 'Aren't you going to let me go? Or are we going to dance all night?'

'Now there's a thought.' His deep voice sent a ripple of pleasure through her. Annoyed at herself for succumbing to flattery so easily, she gave herself a mental shake, and stepped back, out of reach.

'You dance well,' he remarked.

'Thanks. You're not so bad yourself.'

Mike watched her as she moved across the room. Then he returned to the band. He picked up his guitar to tune it. Plucking a string, the sound jarred. He adjusted the tension, and plucked again. He winced. For some odd reason he found himself unable to concentrate. His fingers weren't coordinating. He yanked his gaze away from the guitar to the crowd in the room, hoping to centre himself, and get back into the spirit of the evening. Then he jolted.

Kelly had the greenest eyes he'd ever seen.

Get a grip, McKenna, he told himself sharply. He liked to know what he was up against, whether it was a new piece of music or a difficult arrest.

And damn it, this time he didn't.

★   ★   ★

Sometime later the band finished up for the night. Kelly looked around for Shaun but he was nowhere to be seen. People were drifting away, so she wandered over to where he had been sitting with his girlfriend and inquired if anyone had seen him go. No one had. When Kelly went outside, the truck had gone as well.

Damn him, she muttered. He'd left her without any transport to get home. The thought of being abandoned completely for another female did wonders for her morale. But what could she expect? She'd encouraged him to make peace with his girlfriend. And obviously he had.

The homestead wasn't far away, but she didn't feel like walking in heeled shoes and a dress along a muddy road in the early hours of the morning. Nor did she want to ring Shona when obviously she'd be in bed. She was debating on what to do when Mike came up to her.

'Stuck for a lift back? I can take you, if you want?'

Kelly hesitated. She didn't particularly want to take up his offer, but common sense told her it would be easier than trying to find her way back to the McKennas' place on her own.

'If you don't mind,' she said, stiffly. 'I think Shaun's otherwise engaged.'

'That's a polite way of putting it. I'll give him a rake up next time I see him. He shouldn't have left you on your own like this.'

'I'm quite able to look after myself,' she remarked.

'I'm sure you are,' he said drily as he led her outside. His car, a Subaru station wagon, was parked at the door. A musician's car, Kelly thought. Big enough for his guitar,

119

amplifier and speakers. But he was leaving them behind this night. She was his only passenger.

Once seated in his wagon, Mike shut Kelly's door, then made his way around to the driver's seat. Her mouth curved. She hadn't reckoned on him having manners like that.

Mike put the station wagon into reverse and backed up, swinging the steering wheel hard around to the right. When he straightened up, he put his foot down on the accelerator and took off, spraying gravel everywhere. Kelly smiled. He was acting like a cop tonight.

He spoke first. 'Enjoy your night out?'

'I did. It seemed like everyone knew each other back there.'

He smiled. 'They probably did. Small communities are like that.' He shrugged. 'You know how it goes.'

'Actually, I've forgotten. Been away from home too long, I suppose.' She hesitated. 'Do you play here often?'

'Yeah, a couple of times a month. We'll be back again in a couple of nights. Pay is lousy but it's good fun. And I get to play the songs I like.'

'Shaun is right. You're a good guitarist. Your singing isn't bad either. Reminds me of

Bruce Springsteen.' She meant it.

He threw her a grin. 'Thanks. But I'd rather you commented on my dancing. In case you hadn't realized, I'd made a special effort.'

'At least you didn't step on my toes. Shaun did. I was beginning to wish I'd worn steel-capped boots.'

He gave a chuckle. 'Those high-school dancing lessons came in handy after all. A pity my chat-up lines don't make the grade, though. Being jilted isn't exactly good for the ego.'

'Wait a minute,' she said slowly. 'Am I hearing Senior Constable Mike McKenna talking?'

He laughed again, the sound filling her with an odd sense of pleasure.

'You are.'

'Perhaps it's your approach,' suggested Kelly wickedly. Again, she was tempted to refer back to the day he arrested her. But perhaps that was being unfair. After all, they'd agreed to move on from that, and he had been kind enough to give her a lift home.

He glanced at her. 'Are you offering to give me a few tips?'

She said warily, 'I'm not the right person. Something tells me we'd end up fighting.'

'That's highly likely. I guess because we're

wired up differently. You're a female and I'm a male. All that kind of stuff.'

'Now we're talking psychology,' she mused.

'Maybe, but I'm talking about basic biology.'

'Are you criticizing women?' she asked teasingly.

'You see. That's exactly my point. I never said anything critical. I merely pointed out that we think differently.'

Because she couldn't resist it, she added lightly, 'Watch it, McKenna. I have been known to lose my temper occasionally. You might end up arresting me for assault next time.'

'Hmm . . . I wouldn't be surprised with hair that colour.'

She scoffed. 'That's a fallacy. And you know it.'

Within minutes, he'd pulled up at the homestead. He was around to her side of the car before she even put one foot on the ground.

'So?' he said, as he held the door open wide. 'What do you think? Is it a date tomorrow? A chopper flight into the mountains? Then maybe we can have dinner later on.'

'You move fast.' Her heart skittered. Maybe she could postpone that appointment she had. 'I'll think about it.'

'I guess that's better than a straight out 'no',' he remarked. 'I'll call you tomorrow then.' He slammed the car door shut and leaned against it, surveying her speculatively.

For a fleeting moment, she thought he was going to kiss her, but he didn't. Those grey eyes stared penetratingly down at her instead. She stepped out of reach, blending into the night-time darkness.

'Thanks for the lift,' she said quietly.

'My pleasure,' he murmured. But she never heard his words. She'd already gone inside.

Afterwards, Mike realized he hadn't mentioned anything to her about finding her name in Dave Williamson's wallet. Not because he didn't want to, but he wasn't on duty. It wasn't usually ethical to mix work with leisure time. But if he was honest with himself, it was more than that. He hadn't wanted to spoil the easy-going rapport that had developed between them in the car. But he couldn't hold off for ever. He needed to know what the connection was between her and Williamson.

★   ★   ★

The next day, the text message Kelly received read: *Fishing boat. Seaspray. The marina. 2 p.m.*

Kelly's eyes widened. Dave Williamson must have found the man she was looking for, and passed on her message.

The problem was she had already arranged to meet Mike. He'd even said he'd pack a picnic for them. Now she'd have to cancel the trip. Within minutes she'd left him a message on his answer phone apologizing and saying something important had come up. She'd have to make it another time. He wouldn't be pleased at the short notice, she realized. But what else could she do?

Kelly parked her Triumph outside an old hotel, which looked like a seaman's haven, and decided to walk the rest of the way to the marina. It didn't take long. Fishing boats, tied side by side, each had its own ramp. A fresh blustery wind blew straight in from the sea, making the boats rock unsteadily.

Kelly shivered. She always felt apprehensive during these meetings no matter how many times she had been through this before. A loud squawk from a black-backed seagull made her jump as it swooped down beside her to pick up some leftover scraps of fish.

A smell of fresh paint and tar mingled with the salt air. She wandered slowly down the pier until she reached the last boat. Stepping from the pier on to the wooden ramp, she found the iron-runged ladder plunging straight down on to the deck. She could see the name *Seaspray* painted on the side of the vessel.

She noticed the blue plastic crates stacked up in the corner and the orange fishing nets rolled up tidily on the bow. Yet the boat had a neglected air about it. Brown stains ran down the white-painted surfaces and the cabin windows were streaked with sea salt. Maybe the boat had just returned from a fishing trip. Or maybe it was just a disguise for something more sinister.

Kelly stepped on to the first rung, and climbed down carefully.

A man sat on a wooden crate, beside a filleting table. To one side was a large crate of fillets. On the other, several crates of whole hoki were stacked. The remains of the carcasses went into a big blue barrel set behind the table. Kelly watched him dispatch a fish, noticing the man's massive shoulders and large double chin. She weighed up the situation.

The man beckoned with the knife in his hand. The blade gleamed menacingly.

Kelly felt in her pocket for her gun. Her fingers curled around the cold hard metal. Being armed gave her a feeling of security, but she knew her wits were going to be more important.

'I'm looking for Carlos Fortuna,' she said plainly. 'Do you know him?'

The fisherman stood up, saying nothing, just staring. Eventually, he spoke. 'I might do.' It was then Kelly saw the black snake tattooed on his hand, just like the one on Dave Williamson's arm.

'Carlos is expecting me,' she told him.

The fisherman nodded. 'Just a moment.' He went inside the cabin. Within seconds Carlos came out, the fisherman behind him. She knew it was Carlos because she'd seen his photo. He was slim and dark haired, and although not tall, she suspected he knew how to handle himself in a fight. He had an air about him that immediately put her on guard.

He smiled coldly. 'Kelly Anderson?'

'That's right.' She lifted her chin. No trace of nervousness now; she was in control.

He surveyed her for a moment, then jerked his head towards the door of the cabin. 'We can talk in there. It's private.'

Kelly followed him inside, quickly recalling what she had learned about Carlos Fortuna previously. Fortuna was the youngest son of one of Colombia's top drug barons. Eager to make his own way in the illegal narcotics business his family had been running for forty years, he'd accepted a position to work with

Tino Chang and the Triads in Hong Kong on a new joint venture. Carlos wasn't averse to working with another criminal organization, she'd heard. He had plans to expand his father's business to Australasia by setting up a new network, cutting out the middle men, but first he needed to know how things operated in those regions. Kelly had never met Carlos but she had heard that he was extremely volatile to deal with.

The cabin was small and untidy with wet-weather gear strewn around on the seats. Carlos shoved it aside to make room for her.

He introduced himself. Then asked Kelly what she wanted.

She spoke quietly but firmly. 'Tino Chang sent me.'

His emotionless black eyes stared at her. 'It must be very important to send a personal messenger. *Si?*'

Kelly gave a nod. 'The Drug Enforcement Agency are on to us. They know you've entered the country.'

'I see.' Fortuna shrugged. 'I've had no problems so far. Everything's going to plan.'

'Tino is worried about the shipment,' emphasized Kelly. 'He wants me to handle things once it arrives.'

Fortuna crunched his knuckles. 'How do I know you are telling the truth?'

'Call your contacts. See if they confirm what I've said.'

Carlos whipped out his cell phone and punched in a number. He spoke only for a few moments, but all the time his gaze travelled over her. '*Si, comprendo.*' Then he rattled off a few more sentences in Spanish. Finally, he flicked shut his cell phone and said, 'One thing bothers me. How does the DEA know I'm in the country?'

Kelly shrugged. 'I don't know. But Tino Chang has his informers. He pays well for that kind of information as you well know.'

Carlos stared. 'So you're in charge now.'

Kelly gave a brief, but tight smile, sensing that underneath his manner he was furious. 'Any objections?' she asked plainly.

His eyes narrowed. 'Plenty. But then I'm not the boss here. Tino Chang is. So where does that leave me?'

'You'll still get your money, if that's what you're worried about.'

'The money isn't my priority right now.'

No, she hadn't expected it would be. She tried to sound persuasive. 'You must see the sense of this. We can't jeopardize the shipment.'

He didn't answer. 'The yacht from China should arrive in a couple of weeks. What about the couriers?' he demanded. 'Are they in place?'

'On a need-to-know basis,' she informed him. 'It's better that way. Just in case anything goes wrong.'

He frowned. 'And you think something might?'

'Not if I can help it,' she retorted. 'But there's a lot at stake here. It's not every day $130 million of crystal methamphetamine is smuggled into New Zealand.' She paused slightly. 'Just let me know when the shipment arrives. Then you can fly out to wherever you want to. Even back to Colombia.'

'I wasn't planning on leaving that quickly,' he replied sharply. 'Now that Williamson is dead, the gang he's involved in wants to do business with me.'

Stunned, Kelly stared at him. 'Dave's dead?' she repeated, unsure if she had heard right.

He nodded. '*Si*. A car accident. He was going too fast by the sound of it. A pity, that.'

Or maybe he was high on drugs, added Kelly silently. But was it an accident? Kelly wondered. Or did someone have something to gain by his death? She wasn't sure what to think. And she had a feeling that Carlos knew more than he was letting on.

★ ★ ★

Captain Lee of the container ship, *King Yuan*, stood on the bridge and punched the navigation coordinates into the computer that would take his ship just beyond New Zealand's jurisdiction of 200 miles.

His ship, built in Shanghai ten years before, was 240 metres long, and had a top speed of nineteen knots. But at the moment they were stationary, having stopped to offload their most precious cargo. The captain's gaze settled beyond the steel containers, stacked high, to the yacht being lowered by the yellow deck crane into the sea. The cradle containing the yacht was now empty and being dismantled by a group of seamen. The conditions were calm, ideal for their purpose. The captain watched thoughtfully as the yacht sailed away from the ship. Once it had reached a safe distance, he resumed the navigation coordinates, and the ship's engines gained momentum.

A knock at the cabin door had the captain looking up. It was Tino Chang's factory manager, Ho Lun Tsang, a man he had known since his younger days, when the three of them had all lived within a stone's throw in the old town of Hak Nam.

Tsang gave a cursory nod then came to stand beside him. 'How is everything?'

The captain kept his voice low. 'As

planned. We're on course for Auckland.' He paused slightly. 'And you?'

'The consignment has been packed into the yacht, the drugs wrapped well to avoid any contamination from water. We've also sealed the container.' Tsang chuckled. 'No one would guess it contained a drug lab.'

The captain admired Tino Chang's initiative. His brilliant idea of having a drug laboratory aboard the container ship had proved successful on several occasions. For one thing, the methamphetamine could be processed while at sea, with no risk of discovery. The chemicals needed to make the drug had been brought on board in large drums thought to be filled with paint. The rest of the legal cargo was made up of containers of chemicals and other resins.

By the time they arrived in Auckland, the methamphetamine secured on the yacht would already be sailing south to the West Coast.

'It's a dangerous game, my friend,' said Tsang, 'but we get well paid.'

The captain nodded. 'As long as we're careful. With an operation like this, there are many involved. Too many tongues wagging.'

Tsang laughed and patted the captain's shoulder. 'You worry too much. Remember what Chang says: 'If you have money you can make the ghosts and devils turn your grindstone.' '

The captain grunted. 'Maybe so.' He gave a sigh. 'I'm hungry. Let's get something to eat.' Both men had just reached the cabin door when a message came over the radio that had them scrambling back to their stations.

'It's New Zealand Customs here. Prepare yourself for boarding in twenty minutes.'

The captain pressed the red button on the control panel, setting off the alarm system. 'Get the lifeboats launched now. We'll use the lifeboat drill as a ruse,' yelled the captain. 'They've probably picked up that we've been stationary for some time and are investigating.'

★ ★ ★

Mike arrived at the McKenna homestead and found Shona in the kitchen. 'Something smells good.' He flicked open the oven door. 'Banana cake. My favourite. How did you know I'd turn up?'

'I didn't. And the cake isn't for you. It's for the local kindergarten raffle to raise more funds. It's such a shame their sandpit cover was stolen.' She gave a sigh. 'What kind of people would do that?'

'Ones that have no conscience,' replied

Mike without hesitation.

Shona looked thoughtful. 'Do you think they'll get it back?'

'Hard to say. But I'm working on it,' he said vaguely, knowing he couldn't give Shona any further details. The truth was he had no leads. He sat down at the table. 'Where's Kelly?'

'She's gone into town on an urgent mission.'

'Urgent? Do you know why?'

'To meet someone, I think. But she didn't say who.'

Mike already knew that from her message on his phone cancelling their picnic, but he had hoped she might have returned by now. Perhaps asking Kelly to have dinner with him tonight might be a better option.

'What is she doing later on?'

Shona gave a smile. 'I don't keep tabs on everything she does. Why don't you ask her yourself?'

'I did. But she hasn't given me an answer yet.' He gave a shrug. 'I think I'll hang around for a while. It's my day off anyway. So I've got nothing better to do.' He'd long decided the best way to keep an eye on Kelly was to stick close.

'Your day off and you're not even going kayaking?' she queried.

Mike shrugged. 'Not since Shaun put a hole in it.'

'He still hasn't paid up yet?'

Mike shook his head. 'I'm not that worried. It was time for a new one anyway.'

'You're too lax with him. Maybe you can get it through to Shaun that he needs to do more around the farm. He's always gallivanting about looking busy but not doing any work.'

'I saw him earlier on up river. He looked like he was working hard to me.'

Shona frowned. 'Are you sure? He said he was going into town.'

Mike shook his head. 'It was definitely him.' Mike hesitated. 'So when did your dad change his mind about mining for gold?'

Shona gave him a blank look. 'What are you talking about?'

'Shaun has a sluicing operation set up. At least, that's what it looked like from the air. I passed by in the helicopter earlier on this morning.'

Shona's mouth dropped open. 'He's what?'

'Didn't you know?'

'No . . . I didn't. And he had no right without consulting Dad.'

Mike thought about Shaun. So that's what he'd been up to lately. He thought his cousin had been away a lot and whenever he'd asked him what he'd been up to, his answers had been vague and secretive.

'You'd better give him a chance to explain,' added Mike.

'Explain!' exclaimed Shona, furiously. 'I'll throttle him. Dad will have a heart attack when he finds out.'

'Then it might be best not to say anything to your dad,' advised Mike. He glanced at the clock. 'So what's for lunch?'

'Tomato soup,' said Shona. 'From those tomatoes Dad froze during the summer.' She looked at him speculatively. 'Anyone would think you haven't been fed today.'

'You know what it's like being a cop. I'm always grabbing meals on the run.'

He grabbed a teaspoon and took a taste. 'Nice, but you need more pepper and salt,' he countered with a grin.

Shona hit him with the tea towel. 'I don't need you hanging over my shoulder, telling me what to do. I get enough of that from Brent. You could make yourself useful. Like bring in some more logs. The basket is nearly empty.'

'OK,' he said good-naturedly. He looked around the kitchen. 'Where's the wee rascal?'

'Finn?' Shona stopped stirring the soup, then frowned. 'He was here a minute ago.' She wiped her hands on the tea towel.

135

'Maybe I'd better check. He's far too quiet. That usually means he's up to something.'

'I'll do it,' offered Mike. 'You've got enough to do here.' With quick strides, he made his way into the hallway. After checking the living room and the boy's bedroom, Finn was nowhere to be seen. Kelly's bedroom door was open slightly though, Mike noticed. Perhaps he'd gone in there. He was right. There was Finn, sitting on the floor with a foil wrapper in his hands. He'd managed to unzip Kelly's cosmetic bag and had tipped out the contents from the look of the items strewn right across the floor.

'Found him,' called Mike. He went forward, then crouched down, so he was on eye level with the boy. 'What have you got here?' asked Mike gently. He lifted the foil wrapper out of the boy's hands, noticing he'd been sucking on the edge of the object.

'Can . . . dy,' said Finn, looking up.

'Not candy,' murmured Mike, looking closer. He wiped Finn's mouth with his handkerchief, then held the object in his hand to see what it was. He unwrapped the foil carefully and sniffed the contents.

Mike swore under his breath.

★ ★ ★

When Kelly reached the place she'd left her motorbike, she couldn't find it. She blinked twice, hoping somehow she was imagining things, but she knew she wasn't. Her heart sank.

Knowing that she was going to have to report her bike stolen to the police had her panicking but she had no chance of finding it without their help.

Within twenty minutes she had reached the police station. Mike wouldn't be there, she remembered, as he'd had the day off, so at least that was something. She breathed a sigh of relief as she pushed open the door.

In reception, she took a seat and waited her turn. There was one person in front of her. While gazing around the walls, she noticed a firearms poster pinned to the noticeboard on the opposite wall. Then her gaze settled on a stand where she reached over to pick up one of the pamphlets on domestic abuse. After she finished reading it, she gave a sigh. What was she going to do without her bike? She didn't have enough money to buy another one. And as for the insurance, that would take time to come through — and time was something she just didn't have.

A few minutes later, the person in front of her left so Kelly stood up and moved forward.

The police officer who faced her was the same one who had offered her a lift back to the truck stop the night she had been arrested. She told him what had happened. Then he filled in the paperwork in front of her and asked for her signature.

'We'll be in touch if we hear anything,' he informed her. 'I'm sorry . . . there's nothing more we can do at the moment. Stolen vehicles take time to track down. Motorbikes are notoriously difficult to trace since they can be transported to a different part of the country.'

Dispirited, Kelly left the station, wondering what else she could do. Then it occurred to her that the local Chinese contact Tino Chang had given her might be able to help track down her motorbike.

Within half an hour she had found the Chinese restaurant, The Dragon's Lair, on the main street. Kelly gave the special password, '336', a number of special relevance to the Triads, to the woman at the counter. She showed her through to the back room. Two Chinese men sat there, both typing on computers. Both gave her a blank stare.

Kelly explained what had happened.

The man in charge gave a toothless grin. 'Missy, leave this to us. We do our best. Any information we find out, we pass on to the police.'

Knowing there was nothing more she could do, Kelly wandered around the town for a while, and bought a soft teddy bear for Finn, then gave Shona a quick call to let her know why she was late. 'I'll get a taxi home. So don't worry about me.'

'No, you won't,' answered Shona firmly. 'I'll pick you up shortly.'

After Kelly had hung up, Shona went to find the ute, then remembered Shaun had taken it earlier. No doubt he'd be using it to transport mining equipment up and down the river banks. So that's why he'd been so preoccupied lately. She was just debating on what to do, when Mike came back into the kitchen, carrying Finn, a thunderous look on his face.

7

Kelly waited outside the post office building where she'd arranged to meet Shona. As she leaned against the wall, her arms folded, she watched people going about their business. It was a fascinating game to play to pass the time. To imagine what sort of lives they led and what secrets they had — and just like her, probably nothing was what it seemed on the surface. In the world she moved in, life was dangerous. You never knew from one minute to another what would happen. For a moment, she wondered what it would be like to have an ordinary life one day. Would she stagnate? Grow bored? Suddenly, her thoughts were interrupted when she saw the dark-blue car approaching at full speed. Brakes squealed loudly as it pulled up right in front of her. The driver's door was thrown open.

Kelly stepped forward, her heart sinking even further.

'Get in,' growled Mike.

Kelly looked at him sharply. He sounded in a foul mood. Immediately, she felt herself stiffen with apprehension.

'Why are you here?' she asked, as she slid on to the passenger seat. 'Where's Shona? I thought she was picking me up.'

'She intended to, but I volunteered instead.' He threw a cylindrical shape, wrapped in foil, into her lap. 'Take a look at that. Seems like we've got a big problem here. So, what have you to say, Kelly?'

Kelly fingered the small foil packet, hoping she looked innocent. 'I don't know what you're talking about. What's this?' she asked, trying to keep her tone normal.

'What do you think it is?' he asked, grim-faced. 'It was found in your bedroom, amongst your things.'

Kelly's mind worked frantically. She had to keep calm. He had nothing on her apart from the fact he had found the dope amongst her possessions. She cursed herself silently for taking it back to the homestead in the first place and not dumping it while she had the chance.

'You had no right to search my bags.'

'I didn't. Finn found it. You know what two-year-olds are like. They're into everything, given half the chance.'

Dismayed, Kelly's mouth dropped open. 'Finn? Oh — ' She started to stammer. 'I'm . . . I'm sorry. I don't know what to say.' Her voice trailed off at the seriousness of the situation.

He gave her a shrewd look as if he couldn't quite make up his mind about her. 'Are you really sorry? It's hard to know whether to believe you or not.'

'Yes . . . yes, I am,' she said quietly, wondering how on earth she was going to extricate herself from this predicament.

Still not satisfied with her answer, he put the car into gear and accelerated forward. 'Tell me where you got the dope from,' he demanded. 'Was it Shaun? If it was I'll throttle him.'

'Shaun? No, you're mistaken. This has nothing to do with him. Some guy gave it to me. I don't even know who he was.'

Mike braked suddenly. 'You're lying, Kelly.'

Kelly lurched forward and put her hand out on the dashboard to steady herself. Nerves tightened her throat. She swallowed hard, wondering what else she could say. She was desperate to prove she hadn't meant this to happen. 'It was an accident,' she stressed. 'Really, it was.'

He shot her an accusing look. 'You've put my family at risk.' Her hand rose to her breast.

A stab of guilt assailed her. 'No . . . it wasn't like that. I didn't mean to cause any trouble. I wouldn't have hurt Finn for the world.'

He sat there, waiting, just staring at her while his fingers tapped on the steering wheel. 'Well?'

'Well what?' she answered, somehow knowing her answer would make things worse, yet unable to stop it.

His voice came out so hard, it left her shaking. 'You either tell me where you got that dope from. Or I'll take you down to the station right now.'

That did it. Kelly sprung into action. She unsnapped her seatbelt. Turning fast, she reached for the door handle. But just as her hand hit the lever, he accelerated. 'No, you don't,' he growled. 'You're not running out on me.'

The pavement whizzed past. She slammed the door shut again, her breath coming in quick gasps. 'Mike . . . stop.' But her words were ignored. He increased speed.

Surely he wasn't going to arrest her? The last thing she needed was to be locked up. She'd lose the drug deal with Carlos for sure. Her stomach clenched, making it hard to breathe. She tried to plead. 'Mike, you don't understand. You've got to let me go.'

'No,' he said sharply, his gaze focusing on the road ahead. 'Put your seatbelt on.'

Knowing she had no alternative but to sit tight, Kelly did as she was told. Resentfully, she said, 'Where are you taking me?'

'My place. It will be easier to talk there.'

While she was relieved he wasn't taking her to the station, going to his house wasn't such a good idea either. 'You can't force me. You've no right.'

His jaw firmed as he shot her a quick glance. 'Can't I? I don't think you've a choice, somehow.'

Kelly sat there fuming. If he didn't release her, she'd have him arrested for abduction.

'You're kidnapping me,' she stated. 'That's against the law.'

He gave a strained laugh. 'If that's what it takes, Kelly.'

'You don't need to do this,' she told him desperately.

'That's for me to decide.'

Mike frowned as his hands tightened on the steering wheel. She was right, he thought worriedly. But that wasn't going to stop him. He wanted some answers. And he wanted them now. He might have threatened her with arrest, but he knew perfectly well that if he did take her to the station that meant his family would be drawn into the whole saga. He didn't want that. It would be better to settle with her on neutral ground. Maybe something could be salvaged, at least. Only he hadn't reckoned on the heaviness in his chest at the thought of her guilt.

Kelly watched Mike move expertly through the traffic, keeping his speed steady. Within twenty minutes, they'd reached his house. She was tempted to make her escape when she alighted from the car. But, as if he guessed what she was thinking, he shot out, 'Don't even think about it.'

Furious with herself for getting into this situation with him in the first place, Kelly decided to play it cool, not antagonize him. He might jeopardize her operation if she didn't. She could sort this out, she told herself, ignoring the momentary panic that assailed her as he led her into the house.

She heard him lock the door behind them. Then he marched her through to the living room. 'Sit down. You might as well get comfortable.'

She did as he asked. She tried to keep her heart still and cold, but the thunderous way he looked at her sent her thoughts racing for refuge.

He towered over her. 'First question. What were you doing down at the marina?'

Kelly forced herself to speak calmly as she met his gaze. 'I was taking photos. Just like any tourist would do. There's no crime against that, is there?'

He gave her a searching look. Then before she realized what had happened, he swiped her handbag that she had placed at her feet, and snapped it open.

'Don't you dare,' she protested, incredulously. 'That's private. My personal things.' She tried to wrench the bag back but failed.

When he found the camera, he threw the bag back at her, then flicked through the digital photographs one by one. He flashed a look of contempt before he said, 'Not one photo of the sea. Or even a fishing boat. Seems a bit strange since you've just been along the marina.'

Damn him. She tried to keep her breath even. 'This is harassment, Mike. I thought you were a decent cop. It seems like I was wrong.'

His lips thinned. 'You don't even know what decent means. As for harassment, you don't even know what I'm capable of. But you're going to find out very soon.'

Her chin tilted upwards defiantly, though she couldn't help the fear sliding up and down her spine. 'Are you threatening me?'

He didn't answer, just stood there. 'Take it how you like.'

Suddenly, her eyes prickled. She couldn't let him see she was weakening. He'd take advantage of her. She took a deep breath to get her emotions under control and firmed her resolve. 'I've had enough of this. I'm leaving now, and you're not going to stop me.' She grabbed her handbag, and stood up.

Only he refused to move out of the way. So she sidestepped him, ready to make a run for the door. Realizing what she was doing, his arm shot out, and grabbed her wrist. 'No, you don't,' he said. 'We haven't finished yet.'

She wrenched her arm away, but he grabbed her again. His fingers tightened on her arm and then he pushed her back down on to the couch, still holding on to her. 'Stay right there,' he warned her.

'Let me go, Mike. You're hurting me.'

'Kelly — ' The desperate way he said her name caught at her. Surprised, she jerked her head upwards, only to feel the intensity of his gaze. For a moment she lost concentration, only aware of her wildly beating heart.

'You must see how it looks,' he shot out. 'There's so many unanswered questions.'

Her voice rose an octave. 'I know. But that's the way it is.'

He exhaled, frustration crossing his face. 'Prove to me that you're not involved in anything bad.'

'Why should I?'

'Because I want you to.' Simple words. Effective. They reached her.

A knot rose in her throat. 'I can't.'

'Kelly . . . ' he pleaded.

She held his gaze, noticing the anger had dulled in his face but in its place was something more alarming. 'Don't,' she cried, her throat tightening.

'Don't what?' he asked huskily. 'Don't touch you?' His other hand tilted up her chin but she kept her eyes lowered. 'For Christ's sake, look at me!'

She did. Only to feel something pulling her towards him against her better judgement. Her gaze settled on his mouth, inching closer.

'Stop fighting me,' he murmured. 'I'm trying to help.'

Help? He was sending her crazy. She shook her head, all the time keenly aware of him and the way he looked at her. He leaned forward even more, his thigh brushing hard against hers. Her nerves sizzled at the contact. 'All right. Arrest me. That's what you're going to do anyway, isn't it?'

'I damned well ought to. But . . . ' he said, still holding her gaze. 'I need a clearer handle on the situation first. Can't you see, that's why I brought you here?'

She let out a shaky breath. 'I've already told you, I've got nothing else to say. I don't have to explain myself to you. Or anyone else for that matter.'

Stalemate. His mouth tightened. 'If that's how you want things to be.' He stared at her again for a few more agonizing moments. 'Do you know Dave Williamson?'

She jolted again. Surely he couldn't possibly know about her meeting Dave, could he? She spoke fast, hoping that he believed her. 'No . . . I've never heard of him.'

'Are you sure?'

She nodded.

'He's dead. Did you know that?'

She kept her gaze steady. 'So? What's it to do with me?'

'Your name was found in his wallet.'

She shook her head, feigning surprise. 'There must be a mistake.'

Mike's eyes narrowed. 'No mistake. He gave you the dope, didn't he? That's your connection to him.'

Kelly's first reaction was to deny his accusation outright, but then the thought of Dave dying so shortly after meeting her had her stammering, 'I . . . I suppose it could have been. It was some guy in the pub. I can't remember his name exactly.' She pretended to search her memory. 'It might have been Dave. Yes, I think it was.'

Finally, Mike let her go, his hand falling

back to his side. 'Is that the truth?'

'Yes . . . yes, it is.' She sank back into the couch, still shaking.

Mike continued to stare at her. He just couldn't make up his mind whether she was telling the truth or not. 'You'd better not be lying to me.' But when she didn't answer, Mike took her in fully. She was as white as a sheet, he realized. 'Don't move.' He made his way over to the cupboard and took out a bottle of whisky. He poured her a measure, then handed it to her. 'Here. Drink this.' Then he poured himself one. Not because he needed it. But because he wanted time to clear his thoughts. Then he sat beside her on the couch. 'Kelly, you have to help me straighten this out. Something's not right here.'

Suddenly she was tired of pretending. The shock of finding the motorbike stolen had complicated matters, as had Williamson's death. If she was honest with herself, that had really upset her. She hadn't liked him, but she had felt sorry for him. He'd been pushed into drug dealing because of his social circumstances. She'd heard that tale only too often.

With shaking hands, she lifted the glass to her lips. The liquid scorched her throat, but sharpened her mind. Her voice came out hoarse. 'OK. I made a mistake bringing the

150

drugs back to the homestead. I hadn't meant Finn to find them. That's all there is to it. Now, will you let me go?'

Mike shook his head, his jaw squaring. 'That isn't an option right now.' Then his eyes narrowed again. 'If you're in trouble, I can help you. You don't need to be afraid.'

She could handle anger, but not concern. 'I'm not. It's nothing I can't fix, given time.'

'For a moment I thought . . . ' His voice tailed off, unsure. He frowned, then moved closer again, his fingers flexing on her upper arm. 'Kelly . . . '

Perhaps, if she had been concentrating, she would have gauged his change in mood before he touched her again. There was no mistaking it now, not when his hands slid up to her shoulders, nor when he leaned forward so close. His mouth swooped down to capture hers. It all happened so naturally, she never even had time to protest. Then, before she knew it, her arms were around his neck, dragging him closer. Her own eager response shocked her. She couldn't breathe, couldn't think. Only the hot taste of his mouth registered somewhere in the recess of her mind. Disarmed, confused, she wanted to push him away, but somehow seemed unable to. When she finally managed to draw back, she gasped, 'You shouldn't have done that.'

'Maybe not.' He gave a short, uneasy laugh. 'It takes two, if you hadn't realized.'

She drew in a ragged breath, still feeling stunned. What had happened just now hadn't made any sense. From the furious look on his face, he thought so too. Appalled at her behaviour, she slid further up the sofa, trying to put some space between herself and him. She failed dismally. She was only too aware of his close proximity, and her inability to do anything about it. Every time he moved, she almost jumped, confusing herself even further.

'Are you finished interrogating me?' she finally asked, wondering if she should make a beeline for the door again while she could. Only her legs were so shaky she doubted she could even stand up, let alone run across the room.

'For now anyway.' His voice deepened. 'Maybe we ought to move on to the next stage. A bottle of wine. Dinner. Maybe the softer approach might work better.'

'What?' she exclaimed, her eyes widening. Her heart started to beat even faster. 'If you're hoping sweet-talking me will get you what you want, forget it.'

He spoke slowly. 'Of course, if you prefer to spend the night at the station.' He let the words hang. A cold, lonely cell flashed through her mind. She even heard the slam of the steel door and the key locking it.

She couldn't keep the quiver out of her voice. 'You bastard. That's some ultimatum, McKenna.'

★ ★ ★

Kelly had always taken chances. Risk was part of her nature, she'd decided long ago. But having dinner with Mike McKenna would take her into uncharted territory. Still, she couldn't ignore the fact that he kept her on edge — and for some perverse reason that appealed to her. Besides, she thought realistically, maybe having a cop on her side for once might just help things along for a while. Surely there could be no harm in spending a few hours in his company, she decided.

While Mike was inside making the meal, she stood on the deck, looking towards the ocean. Her gaze drifted over the white sanded beach. A solitary figure walked near the water's edge and for a second she identified with that person. Loneliness was something she had never been able to eradicate completely, no matter how hard she had tried.

Lifting her gaze towards the sea, she could

see several fishing boats being tossed about. Unless she was mistaken, she could also see a yacht. Could that be the *St Lucia*, she wondered? Excitement shot through her.

Mike came to stand next to her. 'I owe you an apology. I was out of line earlier on.'

She hadn't expected that. She searched his face for falseness and found none. 'That's a turn-up. You apologizing.'

'Like you once told me, we all make mistakes,' he added softly.

'There would have been a better way to handle it,' she replied.

He gave a wry grin. 'Point taken. Still . . . things seem to be a bit complicated right now.'

She heard the intonation in his voice and wondered at it. 'Am I a complication?'

'You don't really expect me to answer that.'

Her chin lifted. 'Why not?'

'Put it this way, complications tend to confuse things. But it does keep life interesting.'

'You know something? You're a surprise, McKenna. I hadn't taken you for the passionate kind.'

'Really? Think again.' He stared at her. 'We all have hidden depths. It just depends on how deep you dig. And what the provocation is.'

Kelly shifted uneasily. She wasn't so sure about which way the conversation was heading, so she turned around to face the sea again as if to shut him out. But she should have known better.

He whispered softly in her ear. 'I'm still not satisfied with your answers. But for now, I'll leave things alone.' He started to walk inside, then turned and added, 'What about some music? Something relaxing? Music is good for the soul.'

If you have one, she added silently. She whirled around to face him. 'Sure. Why not? Music soothes the savage beast.' She hoped the remark hit home. It did.

'I'll let that go,' he said drily, 'considering the circumstances.'

She laughed, saw the amused glint in his eyes, then followed him inside.

His attitude was a turn-about from earlier on when he'd been furious with her. In all honesty, she couldn't blame him. He had only been protecting his family, she realized. And if there was one thing she had learned about Mike McKenna, he thought the world of his family. But now, he seemed so different. As if he really was trying to make amends. She wasn't quite sure what to make of it.

A few moments later, he lit the candles. 'Take a seat,' he indicated. He closed the

French doors, but she could still hear the roar of the breakers curving along the shoreline. Candlelight bathed the room in gold, leaving the corners of the room in darkness.

'It's been a long time since I had dinner like this,' she admitted, moving towards the table. She saw it had been set for two.

He held her chair out while she sat down. Those old-fashioned manners of his popped up when she least expected them. It gave her a nice feeling. 'Thanks.'

He served the main course, putting the casserole dish in the middle of the table. 'Help yourself.'

'I hadn't realized you were such a good cook.'

'Just one of my many talents,' he said drily. 'Normally, I don't usually go to much effort. I guess living alone has that effect.'

'I'm impressed,' she couldn't resist saying, and meant it.

Later, over coffee, and sitting side by side beside the log fire, she told him about her travels and the people she had met. Most of it was true. But she was selective. He would never understand what made her choose a life built on secrecy and lies — and with dealings that were against the law.

As if her confidences had spurred him on, Mike told her about his family and how he

156

had grown up in Moonlight Valley. He told her tales of the early pioneers and of his Nga Tahu ancestors. He explained about Maori spirituality, and the West Coast legends. The police stories were amusing and there were plenty of them, although she didn't know whether to believe them or not. From what she had seen of the coast already, she was inclined to.

She didn't know whether to ask him about his ex-fiancée in case she spoiled the mood of the evening, but she was curious. The question slipped out before she realized it. 'Are you glad you didn't get married?'

He shrugged. 'That's a hard question to answer. Things didn't work out between us. But I got over it.'

Which is more than most of us do, thought Kelly, when you lose someone.

He poured her another glass of wine and asked, 'What about you? Got a boyfriend tucked away somewhere?'

She laughed. 'No, I haven't. There's nobody special. I'm always travelling. So there's no time to get serious with anyone. Nor do I want to.'

'At least you're honest about that.'

No, she thought. She wasn't being honest. She was just being practical. And it was safer to be that way.

Feeling as if she had said too much already, Kelly laid her empty coffee cup on the table, then glanced at her watch. 'It's getting late.' She angled her chin. 'Are you going to let me go now?'

'That depends. The night's still young.' He reached for a CD and slipped it into the stereo. Bruce Springsteen belted out 'Dancing In The Dark'.

'Rock music at midnight,' she murmured. Whatever next?

He came over and pulled her to her feet, but she protested loudly that she was too tired and had eaten too much.

'Come on,' he said softly, giving her an encouraging grin.

At first she felt awkward. It seemed odd just the two of them dancing together, but she finally slipped off her shoes, kicking them under the chair.

Then she got the beat. After that, it was easy. At the end of the song, another one began, a slower one this time.

'Something tells me you should do this more often,' he remarked, holding her in his arms.

'I used to. But I guess I've forgotten how.' She tried to ignore the pleasure she felt as the warmth of his body infused with hers.

'It's never too late to learn again.

Sometimes when I've had a hard day on the beat, I come home, pour myself a beer and put on some music. Then life suddenly seems worthwhile again.'

'Sounds like you're easy to please.'

'Maybe. But I enjoy the simple things in life. It's easy to lose sight of that being a cop. Here on the West Coast, you can forget the cities and the crime. I know I wouldn't want to live anywhere else.'

When the song finished, he said, 'I'll take you home.'

Mike picked up her jacket which was draped over the arm of the couch. As he held it in his hands, his fingers probed over a familiar shape. He was so taken aback, he didn't say anything. At least, not immediately. Then he slipped his hand into the inside pocket, confirming his suspicions. 'Kelly . . . what are you doing carrying a gun?'

His question hit her with full force. Fear of what he had found, but mostly of herself, made her speak more abruptly than she meant to. 'For protection.'

'From what?' he demanded.

'I'm a woman,' she emphasized. 'On my own. Need I say more?'

He frowned. 'Have you got a licence for this?'

She could lie, but she knew he would check

up on her. 'No. I haven't.'

'You're committing an offence,' he pointed out. 'The minute you'd purchased this, you should have applied for one.'

Kelly met his gaze unwaveringly, her green eyes turning tawny as the candles in their dying throes flickered and hissed, spitting hot wax on to the floor. She swallowed hard. 'Just take me home, will you?'

Once seated in the car, Kelly leaned back into the seat, her mind turning over the events of the day. Mike knew she'd had dealings with Dave Williamson and, on top of that, in the heat of the evening she had forgotten about the gun. How could she have been so lax? So stupid?

Why had she let herself be drawn into spending the evening with him? There were so many contradictions, she thought. It was hard to make sense of them. Or, admittedly, even of herself at times.

They drove all the way back to the homestead in silence. He didn't even attempt to put on some music, so the silence almost drove her crazy.

'Are you going to put in a report about this?' she asked, stealing a glance at him, somehow hoping that he wouldn't, but knowing he'd probably have no choice.

To her surprise, he said, 'Not if you come

into the station tomorrow and declare the illegal firearm. We might be able to sort something out.' His shoulders lifted slightly as he concentrated on driving.

She bit her lip, not keen to make any promises. 'I'll think about it.'

When they pulled up outside the homestead, Kelly turned towards him. She would feel churlish if she didn't show some appreciation for the wining and dining. She slipped her hand into his briefly, squeezing his fingers. 'Thanks, Mike. It was a great evening.' No matter what the outcome, she had enjoyed herself, she decided, even if it had begun and ended on a bad note. At the very least, she wanted him to know that.

He gave a grimace. 'Don't kill anyone, Kelly. I'd hate to see you up on a murder charge.'

'Don't worry . . . I'll give you plenty of notice, Mr Police Officer, who plays by the book.' She didn't see the glimmer of a smile that crossed his face, nor the worried look that followed it.

Once inside, she thought over the night's events. Tonight she had found she liked Mike McKenna a great deal. Sure, he had demanded answers. But she couldn't blame him for that. Though now she had made a mistake of letting things go further between them. She had been adamant there would be no room for anyone in her personal life. And her conscience reminded her she owed it to Jeff to keep on going. What about the promise she'd made to him before he had died? She would see things through to the bitter end regardless of anyone else.

Numbly, she threw her clothes on to the floor and slid into bed, feeling cold in spite of the warmed room. But even as she tried to sleep she kept seeing him, even though she didn't want to. Not Jeff this time. But Mike McKenna. Her mind whirled with scenes of them together.

But it was only one night and the sooner she accepted that, the quicker she could get on with what she had to do. There was no future for her here. She had to remember that. As soon as she had the methamphetamine shipment, she'd be out of here fast.

Only what was she going to do about Mike until then?

8

Tino Chang answered the phone on the third ring. He frowned. The captain was late with his report. If it hadn't been anyone other than his friend, Captain Lee, he would have reprimanded him.

'The yacht is on its way,' the captain informed him. 'Had a slight problem though. Customs paid us an unexpected visit.' He told Chang about the lifeboat drill. 'It fooled them.'

Chang's mind worked quickly. The least said over the phone the better, he thought. The line was encrypted, but he didn't want to take any chances.

'Proceed with your next stop at Auckland. Unload the cargo. Then return to Shanghai.' Chang terminated the call, and slipped the mobile phone into his pocket. He raised his glass to the men sitting around the boardroom table.

'Join me in a toast, gentlemen. The goods are on their way.'

The five men, all Triads, smiled, each speaking to him in turn.

'Congratulations,' said one.

'A genius plan,' said another.

The others echoed their feelings on this, Chang's newest venture. Only his sister, Miriam, didn't look pleased. Chang frowned slightly. He knew what was worrying her. He had told her about the fortuneteller's forecast about the woman who wore a mask.

'Someone may betray us,' she pointed out. 'Wong has never been wrong before.'

It worried Chang too, but there was simply nothing he could do about it.

'Now to business, gentlemen,' said Chang. 'Who would like to invest in my floating lab? I have plans for several more, all over the Pacific. It is a scheme that will make us very rich.'

★ ★ ★

Mike hadn't heard from Kelly in over a week in spite of his phone calls. What the hell was she playing at?

'Leave her alone,' Shona told him. 'She seems upset about something . . . and I have a feeling it's to do with you.'

'You don't understand. I think Kelly's hiding something. She might even be in some sort of trouble.'

Shona scoffed. 'You're wrong. Kelly seems fine. If anything was wrong, I'm sure she'd tell me.'

164

'Not necessarily. Maybe she doesn't want you to know. Have you thought about that?'

'For goodness' sake. There's no way she's involved in anything sinister like you're trying to make out. So stop being so ridiculous.'

'Yeah, so what exactly did she do in Hong Kong? Can you tell me that?'

Shona stammered, 'Well . . . she . . . she . . . worked for some sort of courier firm. I dropped in to see her one day at her office. It's all genuine.' Shona took a deep breath. 'Look, if it makes you feel better, I'll ask her if there's anything wrong when she gets in.'

'No,' he said sharply. 'Don't do that. Not yet. I'll call round later. Talk to her myself.'

When Mike arrived at work, Chris Taylor was the first to congratulate him. 'About time you made it into the CIB.'

Mike grinned. 'News gets around fast. I only heard myself first thing this morning. Poulsen rang me at home.'

'Guess you'll be moving office then?'

Mike laughed. 'Yeah, down the other end of the corridor, right next door to Poulsen. I just can't wait.'

'Need a hand to move your stuff?' offered Taylor. 'I've got a few minutes spare.'

By the time Mike was ensconced in his new office, he'd decided that having his own space wasn't so bad. He spent the next hour being briefed by Poulsen, going over routine duties. Afterwards, Mike found Taylor.

'Did you run that check on Williamson?' asked Mike.

'Yep, here it is.' Taylor handed him a report. 'According to this, after his previous conviction for possession of cannabis, he's been living quiet. There was some talk about him being recruited into a gang while he was in jail. But certainly no evidence of it.'

'A gang?' Mike's eyes narrowed. 'Do we know who they are?'

'Yep. The Black Snakes.'

An image of Kelly's silver snake earring dangling from her ear shot into his mind. He recalled the intelligence report recently circulated on every known gang in the country. 'Haven't they got Asian connections?'

Taylor nodded. 'So it seems.'

Mike returned to his office and found Kelly Anderson's file was sitting on his desk.

'About time,' murmured Mike. He flicked it open. Poulsen had obviously already run a check through Interpol. Mike skimmed through the basic personal details quickly, noting with surprise Kelly had a master's in criminal psychology, and could even speak fluent Chinese. But when he turned to the next page, his jaw dropped.

She had been arrested for possession of dope and selling drugs in Edinburgh five years before. Since then she was known to have connections with high-profile criminals in Britain and Asia as an interpreter. She was thought to be employed by the Triads. She had even done time in prison.

'Bloody hell,' he muttered. He couldn't believe it. But the facts were there, right in front of him. Suddenly, he thought of the night when he had held her in his arms. He remembered their disagreement about the gun and her defensiveness when he had asked her about it.

Was it really possible she was guilty of all these things? He had suspected something, but never anything as bad as this. Worriedly, he rubbed his hand over his face. A sudden urge to find her, and ask for her side of the story, came over him. He quashed it, and instead went into Poulsen's office and threw the folder on to his desk in front of him. 'So what's all this about?'

The detective inspector looked up. 'Makes interesting reading, doesn't it? A message came through from the Hong Kong Narcotics Bureau to keep an eye on her. They've had an intelligence report that the Triads intend to smuggle a shipment of methamphetamine into New Zealand. They reckon she's involved somehow.'

Stunned, Mike said carefully, 'In what way?'

'We're not sure yet. But they suspect she's a liaison person for this Hong Kong drug cartel.'

'Are you going to bring her in for questioning?'

'Not yet. But she's under non-obtrusive surveillance. She has been since she arrived here.'

'Surveillance?' said Mike, in amazement. 'Why the hell didn't you tell me?'

'I didn't have clearance from the powers above. But I do now. Besides, you're in CIB now. One of the team.' Poulsen gave a thin smile as he leaned forward. 'So tell me, Mike. What is she doing staying at the McKenna homestead?'

Calmly, Mike answered the question, explaining her connection to his cousin. As far as he was concerned, his family had nothing to hide. 'That's all there is to it.'

Poulsen still looked suspicious. 'Are you sure there's no more to it than that? Didn't the farm have money problems? It could be an ideal chance to make some extra money.'

'Shona and Brent have got nothing to do with this,' said Mike adamantly, 'and besides the money problems aren't as bad now since my uncle has sold some of the land. My family aren't involved in anything criminal. And neither am I.'

'Come off it, McKenna. Everyone knows you're a straight cop. You wouldn't be in the CIB if you weren't. But you're not responsible for your family.' Poulsen frowned. 'And what about Shaun? What's he up to nowadays?'

Mike chose his words carefully. 'He's working on the farm. Why?'

'He's been up for possession of cannabis in the past.'

'That was when we were teenagers, for Christ's sake. It was just harmless experimentation. If you're suggesting he might have something to do with any drug dealings, you're way off mark. I know Shaun well. He's against anything like that.'

'Maybe. But he's got a criminal record. He's a Greenie. Pro-active and all that. Could be a recipe for trouble in my estimation.'

'Yeah, a police record for anti-logging protests. He loves trees. And in case you've forgotten, he was charged with obstruction. That hardly makes him guilty of drug dealing.'

'Even so . . . ' Poulsen let the words hang.

The phone rang, disrupting their conversation. Mike perched himself on the edge of the

169

desk to wait until his boss had finished with the call. He was tempted to tell Poulsen that Kelly had had dinner at his place, but the situation looked bad enough. Then it occurred to him that Poulsen might already know, especially if he'd been kept up to date on her movements by the surveillance team. He hadn't done anything wrong, he reminded himself, so he'd wait until Poulsen mentioned it.

The detective inspector hung up. 'That's the hospital. Boxes of painkillers and medical supplies sent from a pharmaceutical company have gone missing.'

Mike frowned. 'When?'

'First thing this morning.'

'How were they transported?'

'MacBeth couriers.'

'Perhaps there's some truth in what Julie told me at the hospital. If a drug lab has been set up, the gang could have stolen the equipment. For a start, they'd need pseudoepinephrine to manufacture the methamphetamine. And that's found in painkillers. They'd also need equipment like scales, rubber gloves, that type of thing.'

Poulsen agreed. 'A pity you can't get that teenager to talk. We might have been able to get a name.' Poulsen chewed his lip. 'If this gang is setting up here, we don't know who or where they are. There's been no reports from the public of any unusual activities. Or of any trouble except for that one guy we threw in the detox cell overnight.'

Mike looked thoughtful. 'Something is bound to turn up eventually. Though I'm surprised Kelly even put in a report about her stolen motorbike. If you think about it, attracting attention to herself doesn't make sense.'

Poulsen shrugged. 'Quit analyzing her, McKenna. Criminals don't need a reason to commit a crime.'

Mike could see his point. 'So who are the officers on surveillance?'

'No idea. They're keeping very quiet. Still, they'll ask for back-up if they need it. That's when we'll get involved.'

Mike had to admit that whoever the surveillance team were, they had done an excellent job of keeping under cover. He groaned inwardly as he thought about the evening with Kelly. He only hoped like hell they didn't have any long-range cameras, or had planted any microphones in his house.

He made a quick decision. 'I don't want my family mixed up in all of this. I'll need to warn them. Make sure they ask Kelly to leave straight away.'

Poulsen leaned forward. 'You do that, and

she'll suspect something's up. We could lose her. And that means the surveillance team won't be pleased.'

Mike couldn't believe he was hearing right. 'For Christ's sake, the safety of my family comes before any drug bust.'

'You could give it a few more days,' Poulsen suggested. 'At least, until we track down her motorbike.'

Mike wasn't so sure but he had no intention of telling the detective inspector that.

Later, on his way to the McKenna homestead, Mike thought about what he was going to say to Kelly. He was breaking every rule in the book by warning a suspect, but that was exactly what he was going to do. Staying with his family put them in danger. And if telling her was what it took to get her out of there, he was willing to risk it.

★　★　★

Mike found Kelly down by the river, reading a book. He paused on the slope above her and allowed himself a few moments to appreciate her. She had a natural athletic grace in the way she stretched her limbs over the grey rocks.

'Enjoying the sun?' Mike asked quietly.

'Mike!' she exclaimed, looking up. 'What are you doing here?'

He hesitated. 'We have to talk.'

'That sounds serious.' Kelly spoke carefully. 'So what's up?'

'You tell me.'

Kelly raised her brows.

He spoke quickly. 'Don't plead innocence. I know you've done time in prison. And you're involved in some drug-trafficking deal. That's why you're here, isn't it?' When she didn't answer, he continued. 'That's an impressive criminal history you've got too.'

Her voice came out defensive. 'You've been checking up on me.'

'Not me. My boss.'

Kelly stared at him. 'So why are you telling me this?'

He shrugged. 'Lots of reasons. I'm intrigued to know how you managed to get this far for a start. You've fooled a lot of people. And that takes a lot of skill.'

'What I do for a living is nothing to do with me staying here with Shona and Brent,' she said adamantly.

'You can't justify your way of life like that. So don't even try.'

'I'm not justifying anything,' she shot out angrily.

Exasperated, Mike replied, 'If you really

care for Shona and Brent, you won't put them in danger like this. Surely you see that?'

Kelly's eyes widened at the implications. 'I hadn't meant to cause them any trouble. But you're right.'

His voice took on an urgent note. 'You've got to get out of here. Find somewhere else to stay.'

She stood up. 'I'll pack right now.'

'And what about us, Kelly?' The words came out strong, questioning. 'Didn't the other night mean anything to you?'

She shrugged, knowing what she had to do and hating herself for it. 'There's no point in starting something. It was only a momentary attraction. That's all. It was fun while it lasted, but — ' She steeled herself. 'Don't expect anything more than that.'

'Fine. If that's how you see it,' he said coldly.

It wasn't, she thought. Not really. But what else could she say to him?

Side by side, they walked back to the house in silence.

'Where will you go?' he eventually asked.

'I don't know. I'll find somewhere.' She took a deep breath. 'Please . . . don't tell Shona and Brent about my past. I couldn't bear it.'

He gave a short laugh. 'You surprise me. I

didn't think you'd care what people thought.'

'Shona and Brent aren't just people. They're friends,' she emphasized.

'OK. I won't tell Shona and Brent. But you have to leave now.'

She nodded her agreement. 'I'll get my gear. Can you give me a lift into town?'

'Sure. I'm heading that way anyway.'

It didn't take long for Kelly to pack her belongings. The house, luckily, was deserted. Everyone was in town. She left a note on the kitchen bench explaining something urgent had come up and she'd had to leave in a hurry and that she'd be in touch soon. Kelly knew Shona would understand. It wouldn't stop them picking up their friendship again whenever she returned. If she ever returned, she corrected herself. She'd miss Moonlight Valley and the McKennas and as for Mike, her decision was made quickly and with certainty — she couldn't give him any hope. It wouldn't be fair. She just wished that she didn't feel so miserable about it.

Before leaving, she placed the teddy bear she'd bought Finn on his bed, and smiled. She knew he would love the present.

She didn't see Mike watching her from the doorway.

A few minutes later, Kelly sat in the car, aware of the silence lengthening. 'You've taken a risk warning me.'

'Yeah, I have,' he admitted.

'Thanks,' she murmured.

Half an hour later, once they entered the town, Mike turned to her. 'Where do you want to be dropped off?'

Kelly braced herself, knowing he wasn't going to like what she was about to say. 'At the police station.'

He braked suddenly, and pulled on to the side of the road. 'You what? Are you crazy?'

She gave a short laugh. 'Hmm . . . maybe I am. But I'm not going anywhere until I check out if my bike has been found yet.'

'You're worried about your damned motorbike at a time like this? I thought you might have been on the first train out of town.'

Her eyes flashed again. 'Stop telling me what to do. I can take care of myself.'

Mike's fingers tightened around the steering wheel. 'All right. Let's compromise. I've got somewhere you can stay. It's a house truck, near the beach. It would do until you make other arrangements.'

'A house truck?' she repeated, taken aback.

'It's fairly basic, but comfortable,' he added, turning to face her.

'You don't have to do this.'

'Yeah, I know.'

Mike hadn't known exactly what had

prompted him to help her. But something told him he couldn't just let her walk away like that with nowhere to go.

He looked in his rear-view mirror. No car was following them. Strange, he thought. Where the hell were the undercover surveillance team? Then it occurred to him. Maybe they had planted an electronic recording device on her. He swore silently. If that was true, they'd probably heard everything he'd said.

A few minutes later, Mike pulled up outside an old house truck. Kelly recognized the truck part of the home on wheels as a Bedford. The house on the back was a construction of wood and tin. It sat sideways on to the beach front.

'A home on wheels,' remarked Kelly. 'Impressive.'

'It's usually rented out during summer,' explained Mike, 'but it's vacant just now. So you might as well have the use of it.'

He unlocked the door and Kelly stepped inside. The interior had been lined in natural pine, giving it a log cabin feel. 'It's really nice,' said Kelly.

Mike gave a smile. 'Glad you like it. I did the renovations myself. Took it for a trip down south a while ago to test it out, then parked it up. I never got around to using it again.'

'Why not?'

Mike didn't answer straight away. He exhaled slowly. 'Because I'd built it for my honeymoon. It was supposed to be a surprise for my fiancée, but since that all fell through, I decided to rent it out.'

'I'm sorry,' she said softly.

Mike shrugged. 'Just one of those things, I guess.' He continued. 'It's winter, so it's pretty quiet around here. You'll have the place to yourself.'

'Being on my own doesn't worry me.'

'Somehow I didn't think it would.'

Her brows arched. 'What's that supposed to mean?'

'You just don't let anyone in, do you?'

'Mike . . . I . . . '

He shook his head dismissively. 'Forget it. We don't have time to argue.'

Kelly felt awkward. She knew she had hurt him by her cold attitude earlier on and yet here he was trying to help her. He'd even confided in her why he'd built the house truck. She suspected anything to do with his ex-fiancée still grated.

He quickly pointed to the log burner as if to change the topic. 'By the way, that works. There's some logs outside. Dry kindling in the basket if you get cold. It can get a bit chilly being right next to the sea.'

Kelly turned to the cupboard and pulled open the door. 'There's pans and dishes, and even a small cooking stove,' she remarked, peering inside. 'It's well equipped. So at least I can make a meal.'

By the time she brought her gear in and threw her sleeping bag on to the bed and unrolled it, the place looked more like hers. Mike waited for her outside, initially checking that the house truck was connected to the electricity box. He flicked on a switch, stating, 'You've got power.' He pointed. 'The toilet block and showers are at the other end of the camping park, so you've got a bit of a walk.'

'Doesn't worry me,' she replied. She turned to face the sea. At night, she would hear the sound of surf beating the shore. She swung back to face Mike, not completely understanding why he was helping her.

'Thanks again,' she said, suddenly feeling uncertain of herself. 'For a cop, you're not so bad, after all.'

'Is that supposed to be a compliment?' His eyes glinted in amusement.

'Take it any way you want.' She smiled.

'I'll be on my way then,' he said. He started to move away, then turned to take one last look at her. She looked so vulnerable in the fading light of the day. God, he wanted to hold her in his arms like he had the other night. But he couldn't do that. He had to walk out of here, right now, before he said or did anything else he might regret.

★ ★ ★

Mike sat in the squad car and took out his notebook. Earlier on he'd spoken to the chief pharmacist of the local hospital about the theft of the medical equipment and painkillers. Security was pretty tight at the hospital and they hadn't had any other problems of theft within the building to date. MacBeth Couriers had been delivering their supplies for years and were found to be reliable. Unfortunately, the pharmacist hadn't been able to give Mike any more information than what had been reported previously. He provided Mike with a detailed list of what had gone missing.

Mike surveyed the list. He had been right. Everything on it could be used to manufacture drugs.

After leaving the hospital, he returned to the station to put in a report to the National Drug Intelligence Bureau.

His next stop was MacBeth Couriers, situated off the main road into town. He was shown into a small office while the manager

180

fetched the driver. It was a woman. She introduced herself as Melissa Scott.

He gave her a reassuring smile. 'I'm Detective Constable McKenna. I just need to take a few details from you about the stolen supplies,' Mike informed her politely. 'Can you tell me exactly what happened?'

The driver's forehead creased slightly in thought. 'I do several runs a day with the deliveries, and on my first run, just after nine in the morning, I loaded the boxes into the van. My first stop was the railway station to make a delivery.' She took a breath. 'I had to wait for the clerk to sign for the packages, then I returned to the van.'

Mike interrupted. 'How long were you in the railway office?'

She pursed her lips. 'About five or six minutes, I think. Then I headed off to the hospital to make their delivery. Only when I got there, and opened the back, I discovered their delivery was gone. They must have been stolen while I was parked outside the train station.'

'You sure it was loaded into the van in the first place?'

She nodded. 'Definitely. There were six brown boxes. My manager checked them off the delivery sheet before I set out on my run. I even stood right next to him while he counted the boxes.'

'Did you leave the door unlocked at the railway station?'

'No,' she said sharply. 'I didn't. I always lock them. Security is paramount. The manager is always drilling that into us.'

Mike wasn't sure whether to believe her or not regarding the locked van doors. He had a feeling that to speed up the deliveries, the door might have been left open. Locking and unlocking the van every time she stopped on a busy run would incur more time than it was worth.

'Is there anyone else who would have a key to the van?' he asked.

'There's a spare key in the administration office, just in case the driver loses his keys. Though there isn't much chance of that because we keep them on a chain hitched to our belt.'

'What happens to the keys when you're finished with them?'

'I hand them in to the office, and sign the register to say they've been returned. It's pretty efficient really.'

Mike completed his notes, then read them out loud for verification. The driver agreed that the statement she'd given was correct. He handed her a pen. 'If you could just sign there, on the dotted line.'

After a quick scrawl, Melissa handed the pen back to him.

'Do you think you'll catch them?'

Mike gave her the standard reply: 'We'll do our best.' He gave her a brief smile, then stood up. 'Thanks. We'll be in touch if we need any more information.'

Before he left, he obtained a list of the staff at MacBeth's. It could come in useful later.

When Mike returned to the car, he went over what the courier driver had told him. He'd have thought a red courier van would have been noticed parked outside the railway station.

Perhaps, though, he ought to give Julie a call at the newspaper. Often the paper ran details about various crimes and asked the public for any witnesses. It often paid off. With that in mind, he returned to the station to file his report.

★ ★ ★

Kelly rolled over and hugged her pillow. She'd woken at about four in the morning and although she had tried to go back to sleep, it had been impossible. Her mind had been thinking over what the next day might bring.

Kelly sat up. Today she had to appear in

court. Her stomach churned at the thought of standing up in the dock, facing Mike. He'd be there for sure. He had been the arresting officer, so he would read out the charges. That was the usual procedure.

Kelly turned up at the district courthouse early. She wanted to get a feel for the way things were done in the New Zealand courts. Forewarned, she thought. She took the opportunity to listen to a case that was being heard, though it was hard to concentrate. Her heart started to beat faster knowing that she would be the next one standing in the dock. The current prosecution was against a teenager with outstanding fines. He admitted a plea of guilty, and was ordered to make an arrangement for payment. She hoped that her own case would be just as straightforward.

'Kelly Anderson,' someone called. Kelly stepped on to the stand, and faced the judge and the people sitting in the courtroom. She didn't dare look at Mike, though she was keenly aware of his gaze.

'Have you seen the duty solicitor, Miss Anderson?' asked the judge.

Kelly tilted up her chin, her gaze meeting the judge's. 'Yes, Your Honour, but I want to speak for myself.'

'You are entitled to apply for legal aid and a solicitor may be appointed for you,' he reminded her.

Kelly shook her head, affirming her earlier decision. 'I appreciate that. But no thanks.'

'Very well,' answered the judge. 'Let us proceed.'

The sergeant in attendance read out the charge and then Mike was asked to read out his statement. The judge asked Kelly, 'How do you plead?'

Kelly swallowed hard. 'Guilty.'

The judge stared at her. 'Are you sure of that?'

'Yes,' she said, keeping her voice level.

The judge rustled the papers in front of him. 'Have you anything to say in response to the charges?'

'Only that I'm sorry. And that I did apologize to the officer who arrested me.' She glanced briefly at Mike.

The judge nodded. 'You are a mature woman, Miss Anderson. I do not need to lecture you about the consequences of breaking the law. But I need to remind you strongly that you are a visitor to our country, and as such you have to respect our laws. Bribery is a serious offence. The penalties may include imprisonment for up to fourteen years.'

Kelly gave an audible gasp. Fourteen years? She kept her gaze focused on the judge, hoping he'd be lenient. Seconds ticked by as she watched him study the paperwork in front of him. She could feel those sitting in the courtroom staring at her. When her gaze glided over the throng of faces, she was startled to see Carlos — and the two Chinese men she'd met in the Golden Lair restaurant. She hadn't reckoned on them being here. How had they found out about her court appearance?

The sergeant in attendance handed the judge a document, and then whispered something to him as he leaned forward across the wooden bench. Surprise crossed the judge's face as his gaze lifted, then locked on to hers.

The judge cleared his throat. 'Miss Anderson. Since it is your first offence, you'll be fined $3,000. But let that be a warning to you.'

'Yes, Your Honour.' Kelly closed her eyes in relief.

★　★　★

'I know you're flat out. And you're not a uniformed cop any more. But you'd be the ideal person to take the journalist out on patrol,' said Poulsen smiling at his subordinate. 'The *Greymouth Evening Star* is doing a story on the police. A day in the life of a police officer. I think we should oblige. It will be good for public relations.'

Mike groaned. 'But why me?'

'The editor requested you especially. And since you help out with the youth soccer teams, you're a familiar face in the community.'

Mike gave an exasperated sigh. 'Right at the moment, there are more pressing things to see to. What about this investigation on the stolen medical supplies?' Mike's gaze swung to Taylor, hoping he would back him up. 'Isn't that right, Chris?'

But all his friend did was grin widely. 'Looks like you're out of luck, Mike. No one else is available anyway.'

Mike gave in, though he wasn't pleased. 'What time do I pick the reporter up?'

'Now,' answered Poulsen. 'It's Julie Thomas.'

Mike gave him a look of disbelief. Julie Thomas? He should have guessed. 'Why do I get the impression this is a set-up?'

Poulsen grinned. 'No set-up. Honest. I thought you liked her anyway. She's always keen to speak to you when she rings up.'

'Don't I know,' muttered Mike, under his breath. 'I've still a few urgent things to do. So she'll have to wait.'

The detective inspector waved his hand dismissively. 'Chris will handle them.'

'Great,' said Mike sarcastically, and reached for his jacket.

By the time Mike arrived at the building that housed the *Greymouth Evening Star*, Julie was already waiting outside. She opened the car door and slid into the seat beside him. 'I was hoping it might be you,' she said, looking at him in anticipation.

Mike grunted. 'Let's make this quick.'

'What's the matter? Had a bad day?'

'Not exactly, but I'm pretty busy just now.'

'I'm aware of that. But I'm following orders, just like you are.'

Mike could see the sense in that. He made a concerted effort to relax and be friendly. 'Sorry. Just feeling a bit pressured right now. New job and all that.'

Julie gave him a bright smile. 'I'd already heard. It's quite an accomplishment making the grade to CIB.' She leaned back in the seat. 'Anyway, where are we heading first?'

'We'll go for a drive along the highway,' he informed her. 'See what's happening there.' But no sooner had he put the Commodore into gear when Comms HQ came over the radio. A shoplifting incident had occurred at one of the shops in town. Mike confirmed his attendance and headed for the location.

The interview at the shop lasted about half an hour. The culprits, both teenagers, had run out of the clothes shop after they'd been caught red-handed. Two uniformed police were already in attendance, but Mike took a copy of all the details saying, 'We're cruising around for a while, so we'll keep a look-out for them.' After that, he had another call to make. A woman had been receiving abusive phone calls. It was mid-afternoon before they'd finished. 'Might as well head back to the station,' he suggested.

'Come on, I'll buy you a coffee first,' offered Julie. 'It's the least I can do. Besides, the newspaper is paying for it, so we might as well go somewhere nice.'

Mike agreed.

While sitting in the corner of the trendy café Julie had chosen, she explained how the feature in the newspaper would be set out. 'It was actually my idea and the editor loved it. I thought we ought to do something positive for a change. Especially since the police have had some bad press over the last few years.'

'How do you mean?' asked Mike cagily.

'You know. The trial of the assistant police commissioner and two of his colleagues, on those sexual misconduct charges.'

'The assistant police commissioner was

found not guilty by a court of law,' he reminded her.

'True. But his two colleagues weren't. There is some suggestion of police abusing their power where women are concerned.'

Mike could feel himself becoming defensive. 'I can't really comment on that particular case. Don't forget it happened some years ago. No organization is perfect. But at least we have a reputation of being one of the least corrupt police forces in the world.'

'I'll be sure to mention that point too,' she replied with a smile.

Mike flicked his wrist to look at his watch. 'We really ought to get back.'

Julie concentrated on her notebook. 'Wait a minute. Can we go through a few more questions? Please. It won't take long. The detective inspector wanted us to do a closer profile of what you do. He reckons it might help with the recruitment issue.'

Mike nodded, seeing the sense of that. 'Right. Fire away.'

Julie switched on her small note recorder. 'What sort of person would the police look at recruiting?'

Mike thought for a moment. 'Probably someone who is physically fit for a start. They'd have to have integrity, exercise good judgement, and be committed to the community they serve. Actually we have a motto: 'Safer Communities Together'.' Mike hesitated. 'You could mention that any members of the police officer's family have to understand the nature of the job. It can be stressful at times.'

Julie gave a quick smile. 'Great! I figured I'd get a better picture of the job from you rather than talking to your personnel department.'

'Personnel can give you the specifics,' suggested Mike. 'So it would still be worth talking to them as well. For example, there are various assessment tests to undergo. It's a fairly rigorous selection.'

'I suppose it has to be. My brother once applied but he was turned down. He didn't meet the height specifications.'

'He should reapply. A minimum height is no longer a prerequisite,' pointed out Mike.

'Oh . . . why's that?'

'Due to the shortage of recruits. They've had to compromise on that one.'

Julie listened carefully. 'There's been some talk about recruitment from the UK and the US, hasn't there?'

'It's happening already. Some of the recruits are already patrolling the streets. We hope to have an ex-Los Angeles sheriff working with us sometime soon. The personnel department are keen to have a wide representation of nationalities in the police. It reflects what our country is made up of.'

'What about the undercover programme?'

Mike said carefully, 'That I can't comment on. It's highly confidential. Otherwise it could compromise investigations.' His eyes narrowed suspiciously. 'I thought this feature was angled at recruitment anyway.'

'Hmm . . . seems to me the police always get touchy whenever I want to talk about undercover cops. Do you know any I could interview?'

Sure he knew a couple. But he wasn't about to tell her that.

'That topic is off limits,' he said firmly. 'Next question?'

Julie laughed. 'From that answer, I reckon you know more than you're letting on.'

★ ★ ★

Mike woke with a start. The phone was ringing. He reached over to answer it, and grunted, 'McKenna.'

It was Chris Taylor. 'We've found Kelly Anderson's motorbike. We had a tip-off from someone who rang in. He didn't give his name, but he had an Asian accent. Maybe

Chinese. I'm not sure. Anyway, he said he saw a motorbike dumped at the side of the road, a couple of hours out of town.'

Mike sat up, rubbed his eyes, and glanced at the time. It was nearly six in the morning. He was due at work soon. He tried to clear his thoughts. 'Good. Give me the location and I'll arrange to have it picked up.'

A few hours later, Mike rode into the camping park on the back of the Triumph, but Kelly was nowhere to be found. Earlier on, he'd rung her but she hadn't answered her mobile phone, though he'd left a message. He peered through the window of the house truck. Her gear was still there, so she couldn't have left. Debating on what to do next, he considered there were two options. He could either park the motorbike and leave the keys for her at the camping park office, or he could take it back to the station, and she could pick it up later. He chose the latter. It would be better to keep it safe, he reasoned, especially since she had to sign the paperwork for its release. Luckily, it hadn't been damaged apart from several slight scratches, so at least that was something.

By the time he finished his shift and arrived home, it was nearing midnight. It had started raining earlier, and now there was a steady downpour. After closing the curtains, he made his way upstairs and had a hot shower. He'd be glad to get to bed, he thought, feeling weary. With a towel tied around his middle, he had just entered the bedroom when the front doorbell rang. He swore. It had to be something urgent for anyone to be calling at this late hour. Reaching for his jeans, he hitched them up and slipped on a black pullover.

When he opened the front door, Mike blinked, wondering if he was dreaming. Somehow hoping he wasn't.

Kelly stood there. 'Hello, Mike.' She spoke softly. 'I got your message.'

'You did?' He tried to get his thoughts into some semblance of order. Of course, she wasn't here to see him. She'd be after the motorbike. He nodded. 'Your bike's safe. No damage, just superficial scratches.'

'Thanks.' She stood there, dripping wet, shifting from one foot to another. 'When can I pick it up?'

'Tomorrow at the station. First thing.' He took her in quickly, noticing she was shivering. 'You're soaked through. You'd better come in.'

'It's not a good idea,' she protested. 'I could be under surveillance.'

'You know?' he asked, taken aback.

She gave a smile. 'I put two and two

together. If Poulsen knows about me, then others will too.'

Mike swung the door open wider, saying, 'To hell with the surveillance,' and stepped back to let her in.

She put her finger to her lips as if motioning him to be quiet. Then she mouthed, 'Your house could be bugged.'

Mike shook his head. 'No. I've already checked. It's clean.'

Once inside, Kelly removed her sodden leather jacket. 'I couldn't find a taxi so I walked. It was further than I thought. Then it started to pour.'

'You should have rung. I would have picked you up.'

She shrugged. 'It doesn't matter. Honestly.'

He couldn't take his gaze off her face. In her eyes, something flickered, and sent his heart unexpectedly thudding against his ribs. 'You must be frozen,' he added. 'I'll make you a hot drink,' he offered quickly, closing the door behind her.

She gave a brief, grateful smile. 'Thanks. I could do with one.' She shivered again.

He led her into the living room, then retrieved his dressing gown from the bedroom and handed it to her. 'Here, you'd best put this on. I'll put your clothes in the dryer.'

She angled her chin, looking unsure. 'I

don't want to put you to any trouble.'

He gave a wry grin. 'You're not.'

A few minutes later, while she sat next to the log fire, she cupped her hands around a mug of cocoa and talked about her court appearance earlier that day. 'I suppose you enjoyed watching me get a lecture from the judge?'

He grimaced. 'I'm not that kind of cop.'

Kelly looked sheepish. 'I'm sorry . . . I didn't mean that. I'm kind of edgy right now. Fronting up in court isn't exactly a pleasant experience.'

He gave a chuckle. 'It's not meant to be. It's meant to be a deterrent.'

'I was lucky the judge only fined me. I almost thought from the way he was talking he was going to deport me as well.'

Mike agreed. 'Admittedly, he was pretty lenient. Something bothers me though. That envelope handed over to him looked important. Any idea what might have been in it?'

She shook her head. 'Not a clue. It may not even have been to do with me. If it was, wouldn't it have been read out aloud?'

Mike stared at her, still puzzled. 'Possibly, unless it was confidential. For his eyes only.'

Kelly shrugged. 'It was probably nothing. Maybe it was from his wife . . . ' She let her words trail off.

Mike took the empty mug out of her hands and laid it on the coffee table. Kelly shifted. Mike caught her movement, her gaze lowering as if she had something on her mind. He sensed her internal fight, but what she was fighting against, he didn't know, didn't understand — but he'd try to if she let him.

Unable to hold back any longer, he asked, 'Do you want to talk some more?'

Her head lifted. 'What about?'

'Anything you want.' He shrugged. Then decided the direct approach was best. 'Crime.'

'That's a fairly large topic. Anything in particular?'

'Yeah. You.' He hesitated. 'I guess there's some things I'd like to know. Why did you turn to that kind of life? I'm curious.'

'That's not something I can answer easily,' she said warily. 'I don't think we should go there.'

'Why not? I'm a good listener. We've got all night.'

She looked confused. 'But aren't you on duty tomorrow?'

He shrugged again. 'So? It wouldn't be the first time I've worked a shift with no sleep.'

An odd resigned tone entered her voice. 'I don't know what to say. Except that turning to crime was something I was forced to do. OK, I'll admit it. The kind of life I lead is exciting. The pay isn't bad. And I get to meet people from all walks of life.' Her gaze levelled with his. 'Including cops like yourself.'

'Kelly . . . ' growled Mike.

She gave a small, teasing laugh. 'I can't really tell you, Mike. I wouldn't even know how to begin. How can I explain what drives me?'

He considered her words. 'Maybe someday you'll trust me enough to tell me.'

She smiled, though her eyes shadowed. 'Trust? That's a big ask.' She shook her hair back from her face. 'Let's not talk about *that*. The minute I walked through your front door, I wanted to leave it all behind.'

He could almost understand her reasoning. 'You really think that is possible?'

Her eyes met his. 'Why not?'

Mike watched her. Somehow the only thing that seemed important right now was the two of them being here alone, together like this. He could see the dressing gown was far too big for her slender body. Her hair had dried, now tousled from running her hands through it. She looked as if she belonged here, with him, he thought suddenly. Something pulled in his gut.

He found himself saying, 'Kelly . . . you don't have to go through with this drug deal. You could turn yourself in to the police. Something might be salvaged. I'd even put a good word in for you.'

'You'd do that for me?'

He nodded.

'Mike . . . don't even ask me to. I'd end up disappointing you.'

He threw his palms in the air. 'OK. But I guess you can't blame me for trying.'

She gave a smile. 'I suppose I can't.'

She leaned forward, her green eyes shifting in shades, reminding him of the greenstone he'd once searched for along a wild, deserted beach.

'You're a good cop, Mike. But I'm past redemption,' she added. 'What you would call a dark angel.'

'Dark angel?' he repeated. He pulled her towards him. 'Yeah, like hell you are.' When his mouth took hers, he fought to gentle his kiss, but couldn't. Her lips opened for him, releasing a sultry sound of pleasure that spurred him on. His mouth raced over her face, then slid downwards until he reached the hollow in her throat. Momentary reason slammed into his mind. He was an officer of the law making out with a criminal. Not even an ordinary criminal but a woman involved in drug running. The thought left him stunned, yet somehow he just couldn't help himself.

Kelly tried to pull back. 'Mike . . . we shouldn't.'

A note of resignation entered his voice. 'Yeah, I know.'

Any further protests were swallowed as his mouth found hers again.

Kelly sank into the kiss. The roughness of his unshaven jaw scraped against her skin, and his hand, firm and hard, curved against her waist. He dragged her downwards on to the floor and she went willingly.

Her dressing gown had loosened and his fingers found the curve of one breast and the warm soft skin of her belly. His hand ranged lower. Realizing things were going further than she had envisaged, she pulled back slightly, breathless. 'Mike . . . I — '

He cut in sharply. 'Having second thoughts?'

'No. It's not that . . . '

His face broke into an easy-going smile, easing her fears. 'Then why don't we just take things as they come?'

He was right, she thought, and she appreciated his consideration. 'Maybe I shouldn't have come here tonight.'

A muscle pulled in his jaw. 'I've no intention of letting you go.'

'Mike,' she whispered vehemently. 'There is

only here and now. No matter what happens tomorrow or even the day after. Will you remember that?'

He stared at her. A low sound grated from his throat while he propped himself up on one elbow. He said slowly, 'All right. Though I can't promise I won't want to see you again.'

Kelly's eyes softened. 'You know something? For a cop, you say the right things.'

'Christ. Forget that I'm a cop for once. I'm a red-blooded male with a gorgeous woman in my arms.'

He traced his finger down her cheek. Tenderness, he thought suddenly. That's what she needed. But when he saw the tears glittering in her eyes, he paused. He'd crossed one line. Now she had to cross another. He said quickly to reassure her, 'If you think I'm into one-night stands, you've got me wrong.' Mike lifted up her hand, kissed her palm gently. 'Seems to me we need time to get to know each other properly.'

'I don't know how long I'll be here.'

'Then we'll make the most of the time we've got.'

'And then what?' she asked, curious.

'I don't know. I can't see into the future.'

'None of us can,' she answered. 'Perhaps that's just as well.' And why shouldn't she take what happiness she could? she justified. Kelly pushed aside doubt and caution, keenly aware that something was happening between them, and she was unable to stop it. For the barest moment, Kelly saw something in his eyes that was reflected in her heart. It would be so easy to fall in love with him, she thought suddenly. Perhaps she already had, and hadn't even realized it.

So when he pulled her up and led her upstairs, she went willingly. Her mind whirled with the wanting of him, conscious of a need she'd so far been able to suppress. Yet the moment he'd touched her, any promises she'd made to herself vanished.

He'd left the lamp on, the light softening the bedroom in a golden glow. The covers on the bed were already rumpled, noted Kelly. Her legs refused to hold her, and she sank on to the edge of the bed. It had been so long since she'd felt like this. His melting tenderness combined with the hunger from his eyes as he slipped the dressing gown from around her shoulders made her feel as if she was the only woman he'd ever touched. Even so, she still trembled. He must have sensed her apprehension because he said softly, 'You look beautiful.'

She shook her head, her hair falling over her face, and couldn't reply. Somehow words stuck in her throat. She tried to swallow, to say something in return, but her thoughts seemed to fade away into nothingness as she took him in.

She fell backwards against the sheets, and watched him step out of his jeans. Lean and hard bodied, he moved closer. His strong arms encircled her. Perhaps she could find solace with him for a while, she thought. Though she reminded herself sharply that in spite of what he'd said earlier, he was still a cop. Some cops wore their badge for ever. She had a feeling Mike would be one of them.

As they lay together, it was easy to forget her troubles. Her own sensuality responded in ways she had no control over, only conscious of the hardness of his chest and the warmth of his hands as they smoothed over her body.

★ ★ ★

Daylight filtered through the windows, casting soft patterns on the walls. Mike lifted his head from the pillow to see Kelly lying next to him. The events of the night flashed through his mind. He smiled.

Moving quietly, he slipped out of bed and slipped on his dressing gown. With a backward glance, he saw Kelly still snuggled under the covers, her face peaceful and content. He resisted the temptation to wake her, kissing her gently on the forehead instead. She didn't even stir.

Last night it had been hard to be so close and not ask questions. When she had cried, he had wondered if it was because she was ashamed of her past. They had shared the most incredible lovemaking. Yet he felt the distance between them was as great as ever. It seemed ironic that she was under surveillance, and here she was with him. He wondered what the surveillance team would make of that. Still, he didn't give a damn if they knew. He had nothing to hide. But Kelly did, he reminded himself.

She hadn't broken the law again, so they couldn't arrest her. But he had a feeling it could only be a matter of time before she was taken in for questioning. As far as how it would affect him, well, he'd handle that when the time came.

Intending to make coffee, he put on the kettle. The milk, freshly delivered, would still be in the postbox outside, so he walked down the path barefooted. At least the fresh air would help clear his mind.

The fierce winds and torrential rain the night before had left their legacy. Broken branches and curled-up leaves trailed across the concrete drive and collected in the corners of the retaining brick wall. The ferns, heavy with water, drooped sullenly. Mike's gaze swung towards the lawn, noticing a large pool of water had formed. It would take the morning sun to dry it up.

When he returned to the house, it didn't take long to make breakfast and he took the tray into the bedroom.

Kelly had already woken. She sat up. 'Mmm . . . a hot drink. Just what I need.' She sat up, yawning. 'What time do you have to be at work today?'

'Soon,' he answered. He placed the tray on the bedside table and handed her a mug of coffee. She took a sip, then said, 'You've only had three hours' sleep . . . will you survive the day?'

His mouth slid into a grin. 'After last night, I reckon I could survive anything.'

She hit him with her fist but all he did was laugh at her. Then held her down, kissing her until she was breathless. When she finally emerged from the tangle of sheets, she pushed her hair back, and ran her finger up and down her ear lobe. 'Oh . . . I've lost my snake earring.'

'It will turn up. If it doesn't, I'll buy you another one made of greenstone. Something to remind you of the West Coast.'

'I might just hold you to that promise.' She slipped her hand into his, looking at him intently. 'I've got the feeling that things will never be quite the same again.'

'Nothing ever is,' he remarked. 'Every action has a consequence. Even ours.' He looked at her thoughtfully. He had to ask her — it had been on his mind since he woke up. 'Kelly, tell me about Tino Chang.'

Kelly's smile faltered. 'What do you want to know?'

'Whatever you can tell me.'

She shrugged. 'He's my boss. He owns the courier firm in Hong Kong.'

'Are you working with him on this drug deal?'

She gasped. 'Mike . . . I thought we'd agreed . . . '

He cut in sharply. 'That was last night. Things have changed between us. Just answer me, damn it.'

Kelly sucked in a breath. 'I just can't.'

He stood up, his grey eyes hardening. 'Can't or won't?'

9

Tino Chang was mentioned in Kelly's file, Mike remembered. A suspected Triad member using his courier firm in Hong Kong for money laundering. Recently, he'd gone into shipping, mainly transporting chemicals in the Pacific.

He also had a reputation for being ruthless with no compunction about killing. Only the authorities could never prove anything against him. And to confuse matters, he made hefty donations to charities to keep up his appearance of being a law-abiding citizen. Mike frowned. The thought of Kelly being connected to Tino Chang and any Triad organization made him feel sick.

Kelly had refused to answer any more questions, so he'd had no choice but to let things go for now.

Mike arrived at work just before lunchtime. Poulsen called him through to his office.

'What's up?' asked Mike.

'I hear that Kelly's staying in a house truck that you own.'

'That's right. She decided to leave the homestead, so I offered her the use of it.

Besides, at least you know where she is,' justified Mike.

Poulsen disagreed. 'It could cause difficulties. You're aiding a criminal.'

'Renting out a house truck isn't illegal. And she hasn't exactly broken the law yet apart from the bribery and speeding charge. She's already appeared in court and been fined. Anything else hasn't been proven yet.'

'For Christ's sake. Sounds like you're defending her.'

Mike shrugged. 'Just stating facts.'

'All the same, you'd better be careful. Your actions could be misinterpreted.'

'I'll cross that bridge if it happens.'

Poulsen made a note in front of him. 'Have you read up on Tino Chang?'

Mike nodded. 'He's a Cho Hai. A Grass Sandal. Or in simple terms, the Triad's frontman. Only he's too clever to get caught by the authorities. Several members of the Hong Kong government count him as a personal friend. That gives him added protection.'

'He's also Kelly Anderson's lover,' added Poulsen drily.

Mike's stomach clenched tight. 'He's what?' He stared at the detective inspector in disbelief. 'That's not in her file.'

'Maybe not, but Joe Rogers of the Scottish

Crime and Drug Enforcement Agency informed me. And he would know. He's got an agent working close to Chang and Kelly in Hong Kong, reporting their movements.'

Mike tried to steady himself. Could it really be true? He didn't know what to think.

Poulsen frowned. 'Is everything OK?'

'Yeah, just fine,' shot out Mike. He picked up Kelly's file and opened it, reading through a few more pages and hoping that would buy him some time to think. Eventually, he looked up. 'As long as I've been a cop there's been talk about the Triads trying to infiltrate New Zealand.'

'Not just the Triads. A Colombian drug cartel are also showing interest. The Scots faxed through some details they thought we should know. It's rumoured that the Fortuna cartel in South America have hooked up with Tino Chang.'

'The Triads and the Colombian cartels in business together. That doesn't bode well. So why are the Scots interested in all of this?'

'Fortuna's cartel has been smuggling cocaine into Scotland for several years and the police have been unable to stop it. Now with Fortuna's father ailing, and favouring Carlos's older brother to take over their business, it's suspected that Carlos is looking at other options. On top of that, China has opened up trading-wise.'

Mike understood straight away what the detective inspector meant about China. With an increasing amount of goods being exported from China by sea and air, there'd be more opportunity to smuggle out drugs to other countries, including New Zealand. Illegal drug manufacturing was rife. Only the week before liquid methamphetamine had been found in perfume bottles being imported into New Zealand. Drug-trafficking syndicates were continually evolving more sophisticated methods to evade detection.

'And Kelly? Where does she fit into this?' asked Mike.

'She's a translator for the Triads, and an employee for the courier firm Chang owns. I'd say if she's close to Tino Chang, she'll be carrying out his orders.' Poulsen hesitated. 'You'd best keep it quiet for now but the SCDEA and our Customs are planning a stakeout eventually. Intel reports that the shipment of methamphetamme has left Hong Kong. It's due here, in Greymouth. Thought to be coming in by sea.'

Mike's heart slammed up against his chest. 'A stakeout? Do you know when?'

Poulsen shook his head. 'No . . . not yet. But we'll know soon enough.'

It didn't take Kelly long to reach the marina. She'd received an urgent message from Carlos. He needed to see her.

When she stepped off the last rung of the ladder, nothing stirred on the boat. She made her way along the deck carefully, then stopped outside the door to the main cabin and knocked. No answer. She waited for a few more seconds. Still no answer. Without hesitation, she slipped inside.

Her gaze swept the cabin quickly. A large map had been spread out across the table. Moving forward, she examined it closely. A red cross marked a spot somewhere off the west coast of Greymouth. Could that be where they were meeting the yacht from Hong Kong? she wondered. But when? Nothing else had been written on the map. Surveying the cabin, she made her way to a bench. Papers were stacked untidily so she flicked through them at random, hoping to see something that might give her a clue. There was nothing of interest and no handwritten notes to indicate any rendezvous. 'Damn' she muttered. Surely there had to be something.

Again surveying the cabin, she spied the wet-weather coats hung on the back of the door and although she did a thorough search of the pockets, she found nothing of interest there either.

Frustrated, she checked her watch. It was a quarter to three. Carlos would be here any minute as she'd arranged to meet him at three o'clock. She'd better wait outside or he might suspect that she was snooping around.

It was just as well. Within seconds, Carlos appeared and jumped on to the deck. 'You're early,' he stated.

'My watch must be fast.' Thankfully she had set it fast earlier on just in case she needed that as an excuse.

He opened the cabin door and she followed him inside again. When he saw the map on the table, he quickly folded it up, tucking it into a drawer. 'We've got a problem.' His lips drew back in an unpleasant smile. 'The police have been snooping around.'

'The police?' Kelly repeated, frowning. Her heart started racing. 'When?'

'This morning. Two officers walked up and down the marina, watching the fishing boats. They were asking questions. Making notes.'

She had to reassure Carlos. 'It could just be a routine check,' she added, trying to keep calm. But Carlos didn't seem convinced.

He took out a cigarette. 'I hope you're right.' He lit it, inhaling deeply, then added,

'The last thing we need are the cops sniffing around. If they get suspicious they could alert the coastguard.'

'There's nothing to worry about,' she repeated firmly.

He nodded. 'We'll see.'

When Kelly left the boat, Carlos watched her until she was out of sight. Then he turned to the blonde-haired woman who had emerged through an internal door leading into the bowels of the vessel. She came to stand next to him.

'She was searching the cabin,' the woman said. 'I saw her. She didn't see me though. I was next door, on Paddy's boat, having a cup of tea with him.' The woman sniffed. 'If it hadn't been for her, Dave might have still been alive. She must have given him something. The autopsy report said he was high on drugs when he crashed the car. Dave never took P. He always stayed away from the stuff.'

The Colombian's eyes glinted. 'You could be right. Kelly Anderson is bad news. But we'll get to the truth eventually.' His arm slipped around the woman's waist, pulling her closer to him. He whispered in her ear softly, 'Veronica, stop worrying. Your brother Dave would have wanted me to look after you.'

Two days later Carlos stood on the bow of the fishing boat as it heaved in the ocean. Night was falling, the sun sinking quickly in the west, leaving long red-streaked clouds in the sky. The navigation lights were switched on. Suddenly the radio burst into life. One of the men shouted to him and Carlos hurried inside.

Within half an hour the yacht was in view. It hove to and the skipper steered them on a course to intercept it. Black rubber tyres squeaked as the two boats sidled up against each other and mooring lines were exchanged.

On the yacht were two men, both Chinese, but they spoke English. Carlos greeted them, then stood by and supervised while the pair began ferrying large plastic wrapped cartons from below deck and passed them across to the two deck hands on the trawler. They in turn stowed them in the hold. It took less than a quarter of an hour for the transfer of the drugs to be completed.

It was dawn when Carlos and the fishing boat finally made it back to port. Pale clouds scurried along on the early morning wind. The boat lifted its bow then plunged violently as sea spray soaked the deck then ran downwards, draining out the scuppers.

Carlos felt queasy. He wasn't used to boats, having lived all his life in the city. Still, he was willing to put up with virtually anything if this deal paid off. Developing contacts with other organizations would strengthen his father's business in narcotics. Competition was fierce and rival cartels were always trying to get the upper hand. While primarily he was working with the Triad boss, Tino Chang, he was keen to talk business with the New Zealand gang, the Black Snakes, if the opportunity arose.

He stared out of the murky, salt-stained cabin windows. Up to now, the plan had been for six couriers travelling from New Zealand to several European cities carrying the methamphetamine. If they all got through, Tino Chang would make millions.

In a few days' time, Carlos would head to the city. He'd been looking forward to spending some time in Auckland, using the extra cash he'd planned on making from the methamphetamine. But that had gone by the wayside since Kelly had turned up. It annoyed him that she intended taking over the next stage of the deal. He took the switchblade knife from his pocket. The eight-inch blade snapped into place. With a vicious throw, his aim was spot on — the razor-edged blade thudded into the wooden bulkhead right in the centre of the red buoy hanging on the front of the cabin.

He took out a small bottle of whisky and swigged from it. Then he wiped his mouth with his sleeve. Carlos held on to the rails and looked towards land. The sea spray had formed a thin mist on the shore, clinging around the native forest of nikau palms and ferns like an undulating shroud; sometimes showing the tops of the mountains, sometimes not. The sprawling town of Greymouth nestled in the valley, slept quietly, the streetlights emitting a mysterious haze of amber on the deserted streets. Curtains were still pulled and smoke tailed from chimneys like dark veins against the early morning sky.

Carlos saw the car parked at the end of the pier. As the fishing boat neared the wharf, the car started its engine and drove slowly along the pier to meet him.

★   ★   ★

She was jeopardizing the operation, thought Kelly worriedly. Up to now she'd always thought she could handle the psychological pressure of leading a double life, but lately she'd been slipping. She was losing her focus.

Hadn't she been taught that allowing personal feelings to get in the way mucked things up big time? How many times had she

216

been told that? If any of the drug dealers heard about her fraternizing with a cop it would completely ruin things. Even worse, if Tino Chang heard about it, he wouldn't hesitate to dispose of her, and anyone else close to her, and that included Mike.

Firming her resolve, but despising herself for it, she knew she had to put an end to the affair with Mike, at least temporarily, until all this was over. It wasn't going to be easy though. Over the last couple of weeks, every time she saw him she'd tried pushing aside her growing feelings for him, but it was proving impossible.

Restless, she decided to go for a long motorbike ride, to see some of the tourist sights Mike had told her about. She felt in the mood for it, and maybe it might ease some of the tension she felt. On her way back she had arranged to meet Shona, having received a phone call from her earlier on asking to meet up. It would be good to see her friend again.

She'd only travelled a few kilometres along the highway when there was a hold-up because of an accident. A bus had gone off the road and into a ditch. A tow truck was already there, trying to winch it out. Kelly waited patiently in the queue of cars, wondering if she should phone Shona to let her know she'd be delayed. She decided against it. It would only be fifteen minutes at the most.

When Kelly walked into the café, Shona beckoned her over to the table. 'About time. I thought you weren't going to turn up.'

Kelly quickly explained what had happened.

Shona gave her a warm smile. 'Well, at least you're here now.' Shona called the waitress over. 'Two coffees, please. Both black.'

Kelly surveyed the café. There was a mixture of tourists and locals, some sitting and others standing. She always took in the way people moved, more so than their appearances. It paid to be careful, to ensure that no one had followed her. Appearances could easily be changed; a wig or a scarf, the type of clothes, but it was the way people held themselves, even a slight hesitation, that gave them away. Kelly, satisfied that she saw nothing to worry about, relaxed and focused on her friend.

After the waitress delivered her coffee, Kelly told Shona where she was staying.

'I already knew,' replied Shona. 'Mike told me. But I still think you should come back to stay with us sometime. We all miss you.'

Kelly felt warmed at her friend's offer. 'Thanks. I hope to, but I can't just yet.'

Shona gave her a searching look. 'It all

sounds a bit odd. But I knew you must have had a good reason for leaving.'

Kelly took a sip of her coffee and wondered how to answer her friend's question without giving too much away. 'It's not something I can talk about. At least, not just yet.'

'Hmm . . . well, whatever it is, Mike's been asking a lot of questions about you. He even asked if I had any photographs of you in Hong Kong. So I showed him the one I took of you at Finn's birthday party.' Shona looked thoughtful. 'He seems very worried about you. He thinks you're in trouble. Is he right?'

Kelly smiled, hoping to ease her friend's concerns. 'No. I'm fine. Honest I am.'

'That's exactly what I told him. But he didn't seem to believe me.' Shona hesitated. 'Seems like Mike has more than just a professional interest in you. The way he talks about you . . . ' Shona shook her head, a serious glint in her eyes. 'You won't let him down, will you? It's just that after the last time he got involved with someone, he took it hard when things fell apart. I don't want to see him go through that again.'

★   ★   ★

She'd better get it over and done with, Kelly decided. Much later that day, she called in to see Mike. She tried to appear normal but it was forced. She wasn't looking forward to telling him she was leaving for a while. He'd assume the worst. And the worst thing was, he was right.

Mike had just come out of the shower. Wrapped around his waist was a towel. Water still glistened on his chest; tiny beads of water. Towel-drying his hair, he stood and faced her. 'Something on your mind?'

She jolted. He was starting to read her too well. 'Sort of. I'm not sure how to tell you this. But I'm going away for a few days.'

'This is sudden news.' His voice sounded strained. 'So when are you coming back?'

How could she put a time limit on a drug deal? Kelly swallowed hard as the familiar feelings of guilt took their toll.

'I'm not sure. Maybe next week,' she managed to say. It was the nearest thing to the truth she could manage.

'Kelly, don't go — '

'I have to.' Her voice softened. 'Wait for me, Mike. That's all I ask.'

He covered the space between them, his hands curving around her shoulders. 'What you're doing is dangerous. It can only end in prison. Can't you see that?'

'Nothing will happen to me,' she reassured him.

She reached out a hand to touch his cheek, wanting him to know she still felt the same way about him. He caught her hand, bringing it to his lips. His tenderness and concern had reached her like no one had ever done before. He was breaking down her barriers, one by one.

If only she could unburden herself to him, before she left. But if she did, she'd be giving up everything she had worked hard for these past few years. Most of all, Jeff would have died in vain. That she would never allow to happen.

Mike exhaled slowly. 'I still can't understand you. Does the money mean that much? I had hoped that maybe things had changed. You and I . . . ' His voice trailed off.

She had to let him down gently. 'The money is only part of it. There are other reasons.'

His jaw hardened. 'Like what?'

'I can't tell you. At least, not yet. Please . . . please . . . be patient.'

He didn't believe her, she realized, her heart sinking fast. She could see it in his eyes.

His voice came out low, urgent. 'It's always later, never now. It's just not good enough.' He threw her an angry look. 'So . . . this is really goodbye then.'

'I never said that.'

'No?' His jaw tightened. 'But you implied it.'

'I didn't,' she retorted, feeling that things were spiralling out of control. 'I asked you to wait for me. Is that really so hard to do?'

He didn't answer. Instead, he stared at her intensely. There was nothing else she could do or even say that could ease their parting. Feeling sick at heart, she said, 'I've got to go now, Mike. Please . . . please . . . don't make it difficult for me.'

She slipped past him, and without another word made her way to the door.

He called out, 'Kelly!'

No, don't turn around. Keep on walking.

Her legs were heavy, yet her feet made no noise on the soft woollen carpet as she descended the stairs. A few more seconds and she would reach the front door.

She half expected and hoped he would follow her, but he didn't. It was pride, she supposed. He wasn't the type of man to beg her to stay, and she wasn't the type of woman to plead more than once.

The latch gave a click. She stepped outside, closed the door. Darkness enveloped her. *Empty. That's how I feel, she thought. So empty. So lost.*

Her hands covered her face. *What had she done?*

Get a grip, she told herself miserably. Forcing her thoughts into order, she fumbled with the key for her motorbike, almost dropping it in her haste to slip it into the ignition. As she straddled the seat and gripped the throttle, the power of the motorbike flowed into her, recharging her spirit like a hidden force.

* * *

Mike stood at the window, looking below. Kelly had gone; only the drone of a motorbike could be heard in the distance. She was just going to slip out of his life and there was nothing he could do to stop her.

What had happened between them was special; he was convinced of that, if nothing else. But perhaps he had been the only one to feel that way. He'd never known such a complex woman. And just when he felt as if he was getting to know her, she said or did something totally unexpected. Like now, when she said she was leaving.

He hadn't tackled her about being intimately involved with Tino Chang. The reason was, he'd have had to declare where he had got the information from. He couldn't do that. It might compromise the undercover operative planted near Chang.

He picked up the phone, ready to dial Poulsen.

Maybe it was time to admit his depth of involvement with Kelly before any further reports from the surveillance team reached his boss. Although somehow he was loath to bare his soul to him of all people. Mixing his personal life with that of a suspect would attract a lot of criticism and maybe even suspension. Cops were above reproach. They had standards to maintain in law and duty. They were there to protect the public. But they forgot one thing, he thought ironically. They were also human and they fell in love.

He slammed the phone down.

★ ★ ★

The following day, Mike couldn't delay it any longer. He caught the detective inspector after their morning briefing. 'Got a minute? I need to talk about Kelly Anderson,' said Mike.

Detective Inspector Poulsen looked interested and waved a hand towards his office. 'Fine. Take a seat.'

Mike pulled the chair forward, sitting opposite him. 'I might as well be straight up and down about this. Kelly and I are involved.'

Poulsen looked at him blankly. 'You mean Kelly Anderson?'

Mike nodded.

Poulsen whistled. 'How the hell did that happen?'

Some things he wasn't about to explain. Mike shrugged. 'It just did.' He took a deep breath, knowing what he was about to say would make things worse. 'Kelly's left. Last night. I don't know where she's gone. But she knows she's under suspicion.'

'You told her.'

'No. She already guessed. She even knew about the surveillance team.'

Poulsen looked shocked. 'She did?'

Mike nodded. He felt a jab of guilt. What had happened to that oath he had taken when he'd joined the police force?

'I'll need to inform the SCDEA,' said Poulsen, picking up the phone. 'I don't know how I'm going to explain this.'

'Let me talk to them,' offered Mike. 'I'll take full responsibility.'

Poulsen gave him a disgusted look. 'You're damn right you will. I don't suppose in the heat of the moment you stopped to think how this would affect your colleagues?'

Mike exhaled. 'I thought of every angle there was. But like I said, that's how things worked out.'

'Did you get any information from her? I could put it to the SCDEA, make out that's why you got involved,' suggested Poulsen.

Mike nearly choked. 'No, I damn well didn't.' And even if he had, he wouldn't have betrayed her, he added silently.

'You bloody fool. You just got a promotion into CIB,' said Poulsen, giving him a frosty look. 'You'll probably be suspended over this.'

Mike flinched. He was in deep trouble but he wasn't going to shirk from the repercussions. He'd face it head on. 'I realize that.'

'But . . . ' Poulsen emphasized. 'I'll suss the situation out from the surveillance team. You've got a good work record so far. You won't be the first cop to lose his head over a woman.' Then he added drily, 'Even if she's on the wrong side.'

'Our relationship had nothing to do with law enforcement or even crime. We're just two people who enjoyed each other's company.'

Poulsen scoffed. 'In that case, maybe I'd better refer you for psychological counselling. Seems to me you've got issues with your sex life, Mike.'

Mike stood up, furious. 'You do that, and I'll shove your psych referral right where it belongs.'

Poulsen gave a strained laugh. 'We'll see.'

He hesitated. 'For Christ's sake, sit down, will you? We need to discuss this further.'

'There's nothing else to say.'

Poulsen grimaced. 'Oh, but there is. Firstly, I don't want this to get around the office. It's between you and me. Do you hear?'

'I hear.' Mike didn't like it. He wanted everything out in the open. But Poulsen was his boss.

Poulsen continued. 'Secondly, if Kelly gets in touch with you, you're to inform me immediately.'

Like hell, thought Mike. 'That depends.'

'It's your call, Mike. Misconduct is a serious matter. Don't make things worse for yourself.'

Mike nodded. He returned to his desk and tried to reason out Poulsen's reaction. He couldn't blame his boss for trying to extricate him from the situation. But it was the way he operated, at times, that annoyed Mike. Picking up a file, he tried to concentrate on the paperwork, but couldn't. He was just too worried. Not so much for himself but for Kelly. He shouldn't have let her go.

Taylor came in with the newspaper in his hand. He gave Mike a sideways look. 'Everything OK?' He pointed to Poulsen's office. 'Or is *he* pissing you off?'

'More like the other way around.' Mike

gave a sigh, followed by a brief smile. 'Yeah, everything's just fine.'

No matter what the outcome was, until he was suspended, he still had a job to do.

Taylor handed him the newspaper. 'Here, take a look at this write-up. Julie's written a good article about the missing drugs and medical equipment. Hopefully, we'll hear something from the public in the next few days.'

Mike read the article. 'Hmm . . . not bad. You have to give it to her, she can put out a good story.'

The following day, the first phone call came in. A man who'd been walking his dog near the railway station remembered the courier van being parked outside. Even better, he'd seen a couple, a man and a woman, lifting the boxes out of the van and depositing them in a green Holden utility. He was even able to give a description.

'Thanks, that's a great help,' said Mike, taking down the details. Then he turned to Taylor and grinned. 'Looks like we've had our first lucky break.'

★ ★ ★

Kelly sat on the step of the house truck deep in thought. The same questions tormented her mind. Would Mike ever understand what had driven her to commit the crimes she had, even though circumstances had forced her to?

Mike had showed her that life was out there for the taking, if she took the chance. An unexpected ache flowed through her as she thought of their argument about her leaving. You've been through worse, she told herself.

But this was different.

She closed her eyes and let the cool sea breeze wash over her face as if cleansing her. Unfortunately, the feeling didn't last long. Her eyes opened, recalling the phone call from Carlos earlier on. The shipment of methamphetamine had arrived.

'Where have you stored it?' she'd asked calmly.

'Somewhere safe.'

'Can we meet?'

'*Sí*, at the Brunner Mine, just out of town,' he'd said. 'We can talk about the next stage in the operation. Who's distributing.'

'I've told you, Carlos, you're not a part of the next stage. So there's no point. Just tell me exactly where the goods are and I'll take over from there.'

'No,' he said sharply. 'We need to discuss it first.'

Realizing she wasn't going to get anywhere

arguing with him over the phone, she finally relented. 'OK. In two hours.'

He'd agreed.

How was she going to play this? she wondered. Carlos had the upper hand. She didn't want to phone Tino Chang, at least, not yet, and tell him about Carlos. It would look as if she hadn't been able to handle him. Damn Carlos, she thought.

Perhaps a walk along the beach might calm her nerves.

A golden labrador came bounding up to her, then ran towards its owner. A man with blond hair surveyed her from a distance. Kelly recognized him immediately. It was Mike's colleague, Chris Taylor.

And Kelly knew, if he saw her, he'd tell Mike.

She hurried back to the house truck and slammed the door behind her.

★　★　★

Mike studied the description, given by the courier driver, of the two suspects thought to have stolen the medical supplies. The woman had blonde hair and was slim. The man was thickset and dark-haired. Mike flicked through the images on the computer screen until he came to Dave Williamson and reread the man's family history. He remembered Williamson had a sister with blonde hair, and had met her briefly when he'd called round to inform Williamson's wife of his accident.

The sister's name was Veronica Williamson and she lived in Cobden, not far from where her brother had lived. Within minutes Mike was knocking at her door. No one answered. He noticed the junk mail overflowing from the letterbox and was just about to head to the neighbours to make further enquiries when a man came out of the house next door and leaned over the fence. He said, 'They've gone. Been away for a couple of weeks now.'

'Any idea where they might have gone to?'

'Nah ... but some foreigner was staying with them.'

'Foreigner?' queried Mike.

'Spanish, I think. Not very friendly. Kept to himself, if you know what I mean.'

The neighbour seemed to be in a talkative mood, so Mike pressed on. 'Notice anything strange going on?'

'Strange? They seemed to come and go, all times of the night. That's all I can tell you.'

Mike thanked the neighbour. 'If you remember anything else, give me a call.' He slipped the man his card.

Later, when Mike returned to the station, he filed his report to Poulsen. 'The foreigner could be Carlos Fortuna. He doesn't fit the description of the suspect we're looking for, but the woman, Veronica Williamson, does. There could be some link here.'

'I'll pass the information on to the SCDEA. It could be useful,' said Poulsen. 'Meanwhile, we've got other things on the agenda. I had a call from HQ earlier on. We're going to trial the new tasers and we'll need someone to attend the course in Wellington.'

'Are you suggesting I go?'

'Yep.'

'But isn't it Chris's turn? It's only been a few weeks since I last went on a training course.'

'Officers in the drug squad will need to know how to operate the taser. Many of the offenders are violent. Taking them down by taser is probably the best way.'

'I agree. But — '

Poulsen waved his hand in the air. 'You don't have a choice in this, Mike. Your flight is booked. It's a two-day course.'

Mike gritted his teeth. Why did he get the feeling that the detective inspector was trying to get him out the way?

10

It was late afternoon when Kelly climbed on to her Triumph. The mountains in the distance stood black and mysterious against an ice-blue sky. She couldn't help but admire their beauty. They were young mountains compared to the ones in her native country Scotland but even so there was a certain mystique about them. With the deep ravines and tea-coloured creeks, it was a different world from any she had ever experienced.

Mike had told her he still wanted to show her the real New Zealand bush away from the tourist areas and what better way to do that than by flying in by helicopter to places that were inaccessible by foot? He'd spent a lot of time in the mountains, not only through scouting for cannabis plantations but for his own recreation and knew his way around well. Dare she even hope that she could take him up on the offer? Just the two of them, spending time together away, would be a dream come true, she thought.

The West Coast, New Zealand's last frontier, had something indefinable about it, not just because of the beautiful native scenery but something deeper, almost spiritual, and Kelly was gradually falling under its spell.

A cold, sharp wind blew. She zipped up her leather jacket and tied her tartan scarf tightly around her neck. She was glad she had put on an extra layer underneath as it would be chilly up the valley. After patting the small automatic gun in her pocket, she consulted the map and set off. The Brunner Mine was situated about eleven kilometres from Greymouth and, since the road was tar sealed, it was relatively smooth going.

By the time she arrived, dark shadows were closing in and the light was fading fast, leaving the sky in the distance suffused with pink. The first stars were out, glinting silver, and the atmosphere was pure, almost virginal. Only the ragged tail of a high-flying jet marred the great expanse. Kelly breathed in deeply, absorbing the crisp evening air.

The derelict mine was on the other side of the Grey River, but there was no way she was going to chance driving over the old rickety suspension bridge to reach it. She parked at the side of the road and made her way down the rough track towards the river, intending to cross the bridge on foot.

Kelly hopped over the railway tracks. Old rusty coal wagons stood ready at the side as if waiting for an engine to come puffing along and tow them away. Her heeled boots made a clattering noise as she walked across the wooden planks of the old bridge. The Grey River swirled below, the current unpredictable and dangerous. The sound of the bridge ropes straining against the wind, making a humming sound, put her nerves on edge.

Once on land again, she followed a small path past the beehive ovens, then sat down on the crumbling stone wall to wait. A morepork hooted mournfully in the bush above her.

Kelly remembered reading about the Brunner Mine in a book she'd found at the McKenna homestead. Sixty-eight miners had died in an explosion over a hundred years ago. Being brought up in Scotland, tales of spirits and ghosts easily played on Kelly's mind. Perhaps that's why Carlos had chosen this place, to unnerve her.

Kelly steeled herself. She'd been in worse places than this but if something did go wrong, Carlos could dispose of her in one of the mine shafts and she'd never be found again. Her spirit would walk forever with those miners who had died here so long ago. She shivered at the unpleasant thought.

Nervousness ate at her for a few minutes while she waited, impatient to get the meeting over and done with. She heard a sound in the bushes and turned to see a man emerge from the shadows. It was Carlos. He wasn't alone either. Two accomplices walked beside him. She hadn't seen them before, but she saw the black snakes tattooed on their bare forearms.

Carlos didn't speak straight away; just looked her up and down. Something emanated from him which instantly put her on her guard. She could handle it, she told herself, taking several breaths to calm herself.

'Carlos . . . ' she greeted him.

He nodded. 'Anyone with you?'

'No . . . should there be?'

'That depends. You've been seen visiting a local cop,' he accused.

Kelly stiffened. 'What are you talking about?'

'Mike McKenna.'

She could deny it again, but it was clear Carlos knew about her and Mike. She'd need to bluff her way out of this. 'So, what's the problem? Mike's a contact of mine. He's on the take.' She could see from the way his eyes narrowed that he didn't quite believe her.

'Is he now? That's not what I heard.'

Her chin lifted. 'And what did you hear?'

'That he can't be turned.'

Kelly gave a smile. 'There are other methods, other than money.'

Carlos leered, though she saw the admiration in his eyes. '*Sí*, I should have known, eh? I bet Tino Chang will be interested in knowing about your cop lover.'

The last thing she wanted was Chang finding out that particular piece of information. She said smoothly, 'No point in getting Tino riled up over nothing. Mike McKenna doesn't mean anything to me. But he is useful.'

'It's too risky.'

'The benefits of getting inside information outweigh the risk. Mike doesn't know anything.' She paused slightly. 'Where's the shipment?'

'It's safe.'

Kelly knew he was stalling again. Damn him. She tried not to show her frustration. She gave a small laugh. 'So safe, you're not going to tell me where you've hidden it.'

'*Sí*.' He grinned again. 'But I can tell you how we brought it in. Even if Customs had searched us at sea, they would never have found it. The shipment was in the water. In a special capsule we towed along on a wire. If we had to ditch it in a hurry, we'd mark the spot. Then we'd go back to retrieve it when it was safe. It had a remotely operated buoyancy aid.'

'Very clever,' remarked Kelly, impressed.

'Who thought that up? You or Tino Chang?'

'Chang.'

'He never told me,' she said, sounding disappointed. 'So the shipment is now on land?'

'It is. But, since you've informed me I'm not part of this deal, I've been forced to change my plans.' He stepped forward, a sneer on his face.

Before Kelly could draw the gun in her pocket, a hand clamped over her mouth from behind. She struggled, unable to free herself. She razed her heeled boots down the man's shins, and to her satisfaction heard a yell of pain, but his grip still held her tight.

Carlos came so close she could feel his stale breath on her cheeks. He pulled out a flick knife and the blade snapped into place with a metallic snick. 'Quit struggling or I'll slit your throat.'

Her mind paralysed with fear as she felt the point of a knife pressing against the base of her neck. She did exactly as she was told, all the time staring at the knife. Carlos wouldn't hesitate to kill her.

'You're an informer,' stated Carlos.

She shook her head. 'No, no, you're wrong.'

'Then convince me. Why did you want Mike McKenna in your pocket?'

Kelly's mind raced. 'I needed some information about Dave Williamson.'

Carlos frowned. 'What sort of information? Williamson is dead. He crashed his car.'

'I know. But I think he might have been murdered. I wanted to find out why.'

Carlos grunted. 'What made you think that?'

'Just a feeling I had.'

Carlos laughed out loud as if he'd just heard a very funny joke. 'You want to know the truth, *sí*? Williamson was becoming a nuisance. So I laced his drink with P. By the time he got into the car, he was flying so high, he'd have been in heaven before he even hit that tree.'

Kelly gasped. 'You killed him?' She hadn't reckoned on dealing with a psychopath. She had underestimated Carlos. 'You could have wrecked the drug deal. Killing someone like that in a small community has repercussions. His sister worked with him on the drug deals. She'll suspect something.'

'I doubt it. She's in love with me. So you see, there is no risk. Williamson was interfering in a business deal I had proposed with the Black Snakes. He left me no choice.'

Kelly frowned. 'What kind of business deal?'

'None of your business.'

'You can't move those drugs without me,' she said. 'I'm the only one who knows who the couriers are, and how to contact them.'

'Then you'd better start talking.' His voice was heavy with threat.

'Why? So you can use them yourself?' she accused. 'You just want to find out the distribution channels so you can use them for your own cartel.'

'*Sí*, what's wrong with that? It's narco business. We gave Tino Chang inside information on the American market.'

Kelly shook her head. 'Not this time. The couriers belong to Chang. They're specially selected. Highly trained.'

'So? They might want to work for me. I'll pay well.'

She said drily, 'Chang wouldn't allow it. Let me go, Carlos, and we can forget about this disagreement.'

'No way.' He gave a laugh. 'Scream all you want. No one can hear you.'

'If I don't meet Mike McKenna tonight, he'll inform the police about the whole operation. You'll never make it out the country. Not even by boat.'

Carlos's face turned thunderous. 'You said he didn't know anything. You double-crossing bitch.'

She had pleasure in saying, 'I lied.'

He lifted his hand to strike her.

'Wait!' she shot out. 'There's something else. Mike's in on the deal. Don't you realize what that means?'

Carlos gave her an uncertain look, then lowered his arm to his side. She could tell he was debating on whether she was telling the truth or not. She pushed harder. 'Mike's working with the Criminal Investigation Bureau. They've set up a special task force to combat narcotics. That means we can be one step ahead all the time with his help. Tino Chang has plans for more shipments. And you're eventually going to bring in cocaine, aren't you?' She smiled, hoping he'd take the bait. 'So . . . are we still in business?'

★ ★ ★

Two hours later, Kelly stormed into the incident room at the police station. 'Where's Joe Rogers? I need to see him. Right now.'

Chris Taylor looked at her uncertainly. 'Just a moment.' He quickly disappeared and returned in record time. 'This way, please.'

Joe Rogers, her controller in the Scottish Crime and Drug Enforcement Agency, sat at a desk studying some papers. As soon as she entered, he stood up. 'Kelly — '

'Where the bloody hell were you?' she

241

demanded. 'That psychopath was going to slit my throat.'

Joe Rogers looked grim-faced. 'Kelly, I'm sorry — '

'That's not good enough.'

'All right, I'm *very* sorry. We had men hiding in the bushes very near to you, ready to pounce as soon as I gave the word. But we held out, hoping Carlos would tell you where the shipment was.'

Kelly exhaled. 'Well, he didn't.' She looked around the room. 'I need a bloody drink, but I'll settle for a damn coffee.'

Rogers got up and headed for the tearoom while Kelly fell into a chair. The strain of her encounter with Carlos had left her feeling tired and vulnerable.

Joe Rogers returned and placed a coffee mug filled with a strong black brew in front of Kelly. 'There you go. It's fresh.'

'Thanks,' she muttered. At the smell of the coffee, bile rose in her throat, making her feel nauseous. She pushed her coffee mug away. Then stood up, feeling the need to walk around to steady her nerves. She closed her eyes for a moment, put her hands to her cheeks, but she could still see the knife glinting in front of her, and feel the cold steel of the blade as it pressed against the hollow of her throat.

Rogers touched her on the shoulder and said calmly, 'You're shaken up. I can imagine how you must feel.'

She whirled around. 'Can you?' Her voice cracked a little. 'I don't think so. You're not a woman for a start.'

'You're right,' he said, looking apologetic again. 'Why don't you just sit down and relax? Let's talk this through.'

She took his advice. 'That makes sense, I guess,' she said, and tried to steady her breathing.

Joe took out a small pewter hip flask from his jacket and poured a drop of amber liquid into her coffee. 'That will put the colour back into your cheeks.' He gave a grin.

She managed a weak smile, lifting the mug to her lips. 'I've never been a whisky drinker.'

'I know. But it's all I've got right now. I don't know these Kiwi cops well enough to ask if they've got anything else.'

'They're just cops like us,' she reminded him, thinking of Mike. Wondering where he might be.

Joe's face took on a serious expression. 'A pity Carlos didn't give us the location of the methamphetamine. Now I'm not sure what to do.'

Her voice rose. 'Is that all you care about? Finding the drugs?'

He looked uncertain. 'I thought that was what you wanted too.'

'It is, but . . . ' Her voice trailed off. But what? she asked herself. Had she had enough? Had she lost her nerve? Sure she was in shock, but she could get over that. So what was it?

'But what?' he pressed, his brow furrowed in concern. She took a good look at him. She trusted Joe Rogers one hundred per cent.

'I don't know,' she said lamely. That wasn't strictly true, she thought.

'Look, Kelly, in spite of what's happened, you're going to have to go back undercover.'

'Are you kidding?' she gasped. 'Carlos is already suspicious about me. It's pure luck he didn't discover my cell phone held a listening device.'

'He's suspicious. But not sure,' argued Rogers. 'That means you still have a chance. They still think you're a part of the operation. And now they think McKenna is in too. That could work in our favour.'

Her shoulders rose then fell. 'I'm not so sure. Things are getting too messy. I don't want Mike brought into this.'

'You know as well as I, there are no set plans in this game. We move according to circumstances. It's the only way to go.' He hesitated. 'Mike is a police officer. Now that he's in CIB, it would be only fair to give him a chance.'

Kelly shook her head, not convinced. Yet she reminded herself that being an under-cover operative meant improvisation. She'd lied to Carlos about Mike, but only because her life was in danger. Extreme measures were called for, but she'd never willingly have got Mike involved. Only now it had backfired on her, with Rogers wanting to use him to increase their foothold within the criminal fraternity.

'You were close,' reminded Rogers. 'Very close.'

'But I screwed up. Damn it . . . I should have known Carlos would try to double-cross me. I shouldn't have agreed to meet him there. But he told me he was hiding the methamphetamme at the mine. I should never have believed him.'

'The drugs aren't at the mine. We've been watching him closely.'

'So what has he done with them?'

Rogers shrugged. 'Beats me. He's clever though. When that fishing boat came in, we were convinced the P was on it. But after a routine Customs check, and search, it wasn't. His confession about the underwater capsule explains why. That method has been used before, of course, in the UK. But I must admit I didn't expect them to use it this time. We did search around the boat once it was tied up but nothing was found. I'd say he probably sent another craft out later on to retrieve the capsule. The deserted coastline stretches for kilometres. They could have landed the gear further down the coast. All they'd need is a pick-up truck to meet them.'

Kelly lifted her head, knowing what she was about to say wasn't going to go down well. 'Joe, I can't go on with this. Get me out now.'

Rogers stared at her. 'What? You can't mean it. You seriously want to throw it all away after everything we've done? The sacrifices *you've* made?'

Kelly's cheeks flushed. She knew exactly the sacrifices Rogers was referring to. 'You don't have to bring that up.' She hoped Mike would never find out the lengths she'd gone to so as to gain Tino Chang's trust. He'd hate her for it. There were times she even hated herself. But things had changed for her, she realized. Mike had changed her. But how could she tell that to her colleagues?

Roger's face was sympathetic. 'At least take a while to think about it. You're still shaken up. Not thinking straight. Why not take a few days off?'

She nodded, realizing he meant well. 'If I

do, it will be harder to re-establish contact with Carlos. And we might lose the shipment.' She hesitated. 'I'm so confused. I don't want to let the team down.'

'You won't be. There's only so far we can push you,' stated Rogers. 'I don't want to lose you altogether. There'll be other assignments. The war on drugs will continue long after we've hung up our badges.'

'You know something? That's just what I like about you. You have such a positive nature for a cop,' she said drily, and was rewarded with a wide grin. 'I guess after five years of working together you can't blame me for wanting to pull out for a while.'

He gave a short laugh. 'If I could entice you to stay on with money, I would. But I know I'd be wasting my time.'

Kelly's smile faltered when Detective Inspector Poulsen entered the office. Although she hadn't been introduced formally, she had been informed of the detective inspector's role, giving back-up where needed.

'Sir,' she acknowledged, shaking hands with him.

'Things didn't go according to plan,' he said.

'We tried our best,' she answered. 'I'm sure Joe would have filled you in. It's all on tape if you want to hear it.'

Poulsen nodded, then turned to Rogers. 'So what's the next step?'

Kelly butted in. 'We haven't decided yet.' She hesitated. 'Can I see Mike? I need to explain a few things to him.'

Poulsen shook his head. 'I realize that. But it's not priority. Let's keep McKenna out of it for now. He might be in CIB but this undercover operation is highly confidential.' He hesitated. 'That is, unless you've decided to bring him in on this operation.'

'No,' said Kelly sharply. 'I just wanted to talk with him.'

Poulsen sat down opposite her. 'Are you sure that's a good idea? Mike's in trouble anyway.'

Kelly stared at him, not liking his insinuation. 'Trouble? What exactly do you mean?'

The detective inspector grimaced. 'Mike knew you were a suspect, involved in shady dealings. He read your Interpol file thoroughly. Yet he helped you and, even worse, lied about your movements. He really should be suspended. There'll have to be an inquiry into his actions.'

Kelly was silent for a moment as she digested his words. 'That's ridiculous. Mike's an honest cop. He only acted in the best interests of everyone. He never once crossed that thin blue line.'

'That's open to debate. Seems to me he stepped over it, then back again when it suited him.' Poulsen grimaced. 'Nevertheless, it's not looking good for him. His career in the force might be in jeopardy. I'll have to put in a report about his involvement with you.' Poulsen looked directly at Rogers. 'He came down here earlier on and confessed everything.'

Kelly gasped. 'He what?' How much had Mike actually told Poulsen? She just couldn't believe he would do that. Betrayal shot through her.

'Mike McKenna's the least of our worries right now,' remarked Rogers. 'I'd like Kelly to go back undercover, but she's reluctant.'

'I see,' said the detective inspector, his gaze settling on her. 'You do realize the last thing we want is to lose these criminals. Organized crime is a real threat.' He paused slightly. 'Of course, I could be willing to overlook McKenna's actions if you were to go back undercover.' His voice was full of meaning.

Kelly's mouth tightened. 'Are you black-mailing me?'

The detective inspector didn't answer. He swapped glances with Rogers instead.

Kelly stood up, furious. She was just about to tell the inspector to go to hell when

Rogers, realizing what was about to happen, intervened. 'Putting pressure on Kelly isn't a good idea, even if your offer is meant as an incentive.'

'At least I know who's on my side,' muttered Kelly, throwing a grateful look at Rogers. 'Thanks for backing me up, Joe.'

Rogers gave an embarrassed grin. 'You're part of my team, Kelly, but I suggest we listen to what the detective inspector says. We are working in conjunction with the New Zealand police force, don't forget.'

Even so, Kelly knew Poulsen had her just where he wanted her. To use another cop's career as leverage to make her do what *they* wanted didn't go down very well. Yet no way could she leave Mike in this position.

Kelly had met cops like Poulsen before. They were willing to make deals to get what they wanted. Deals that weren't ethical but, nevertheless, worked in their world — and they usually got away with them. He didn't intimidate her but she was fearful for Mike. It would be all her fault if he got into trouble. She cared too much about him to let him take the flak for helping her.

She tried to keep her voice even, knowing it was time to play a few rules of her own. 'Joe, I know I didn't tell you about Mike, but I kind of guessed you'd know from the surveillance what was going on between us.'

'We knew you were seeing him,' Rogers admitted. 'But it was open to speculation as to why. It didn't help that you turned off your recording device every time he was within arm's length.'

'Some things I just wasn't about to let you record. You'll have to take my word for it about Mike.'

Rogers looked thoughtful. 'Is there any possibility that he could be a bent cop? After all, some of the things he's done are suspect, just like the detective inspector mentioned.'

'No way,' she said sharply. 'He's a damned good cop. He doesn't follow police procedure blindly. He prefers to use his common sense when making decisions. If we had more cops like him, we'd have a lot less problems within the force.' She leaned forward as if to emphasize her next words. 'His loyalty has never been in question.'

Rogers spoke quickly. 'Regardless of that, I still think if there's a chance to find the drug shipment, you have to go back undercover. I've got a feeling you're close, Kelly . . . really close. A lot of people are depending on you. The New Zealand police are asking for our help. I really don't see how you can refuse.'

'But if I'm not up to it, you could send someone else in, couldn't you?' she pleaded, feeling cornered. But even as she said the words, she knew it would be impossible.

'You know as well as I do that would take time. We have to move now before the shipment goes underground. If that happens, Carlos will distribute the P throughout New Zealand. The whole drugs trade in this country will spiral. That's what the detective inspector is worried about.'

Kelly's hopes sank. What was she going to do?

Needing time to think, Kelly walked across to the window, and parted the curtains to look out on to the dimly lit street below. A supermarket opposite was closing up for the night, the shop assistants collecting the basket trolleys scattered in the car park. For a few seconds Kelly wondered what it would be like to be an ordinary person in an ordinary job. When you finished for the day, so did the job. Envy struck her. And yet part of her knew that an ordinary life wouldn't have held her for very long, unless ... maybe ... Mike wanted her to stay.

It hit her. Could this be happening? Had she really fallen for him? To love someone meant opening up and trusting them, didn't it? She hadn't got to that stage but only because her circumstances had prevented her. And yet there was something special between them. She cared about him deeply. And he had helped her at his own cost, knowing her past, thinking that she was a criminal involved in drug-running. Oh God . . . what would happen when he found out that she was an undercover agent?

How much proof did she need that he felt something for her? Her gaze drifted below to the pavement. In the dim street light, the man approaching the station looked like Mike. Now she was starting to imagine him appearing, just when she needed him. She strained her eyes. The man was dressed in denim jeans and a tight black pullover, and he even moved just like him, she thought. Her heart started to beat faster.

* * *

Mike received a phone call late afternoon. The taser course had been postponed due to one of the lecturers falling ill and would run the following week. Not that he'd minded. Right at the moment there were other things on his mind. Kelly being one of them. He hadn't wanted to be out of the region in case there were any new developments.

Since one of his colleague's wife had gone into labour, Mike had offered to fill in on his night shift.

'I'll be along as soon as I can,' he'd told Detective Constable Steve May, the proud father-to-be. Since the night shift wasn't due to start for a couple of hours, he went into the station early anyway, figuring he could catch up on some paperwork beforehand. It might take his mind off the current predicament.

As soon as Mike entered the station, he could see something was up. The place buzzed with people.

'What's happening?' he asked Chris.

'Not sure yet. We've been invaded by the Scottish Crime and Drug Enforcement Agency. They've all been ensconced in Poulsen's office for the last hour.'

A knot twisted in Mike's stomach. Police officers from Scotland meant only one thing. 'Is this to do with Kelly Anderson?'

'I think so. She's in the interview room right now. Poulsen's looking positively sick. I don't know why. There's another cop talking to him, Joe Rogers. He seems to be in charge of the SCDEA team. Seems an approachable guy, but isn't saying anything about what's going on. From what I can glean, they've had an operation going and something's gone wrong.'

Mike grimaced. 'Any idea what?'

Taylor shook his head. 'No . . . not yet. But I expect we'll be briefed soon. You'd better stick around for a while.'

'What about Kelly? Is she under arrest?'

Taylor gave him an odd look, but Mike wasn't about to explain why he wanted to know. 'Doesn't look like it. She turned up voluntarily to see Rogers. Oddly enough, he didn't seem that surprised when I told him she wanted to speak with him.'

Mike's heart thumped. 'You mean she gave herself up?'

'No, it didn't seem like that.' A confused look crossed Taylor's face. 'She marched in, demanded to see Rogers. And when he came out of the office, he whipped her into the interrogation room as if he knew her. She's still in there.'

Mike wondered if he ought to go in to see what was happening. After all, he was part of CIB, but Poulsen had left strict orders they weren't to be disturbed. So he would wait; suss things out when Kelly came out.

Somehow he had a feeling things were going to get interesting.

★ ★ ★

Detective Inspector Poulsen looked expectantly at Kelly, his eyes hardening. 'Well?'

She turned to face him. 'If I go back undercover, I have some conditions.'

'Conditions?' he repeated. 'Like what?'

'I want your agreement that Mike McKenna is vindicated of any wrongdoing.' Her mouth set in a determined line.

'I'm not sure I can do that,' answered Poulsen. 'That's not procedure.'

'We don't have procedures when we're working undercover,' said Kelly hotly. 'You do it, or I walk off the job.'

Poulsen hesitated; swapped glances with Rogers. 'I don't know.'

Rogers moved forward and sat on the edge of the table. His Glaswegian accent thickened noticeably. 'We can go higher than you, Poulsen. So what's it to be?'

The insinuation that power could be taken right out of Poulsen's hands quickly had the desired effect that Kelly had been hoping for.

'All right,' Poulsen said finally, with something approaching a resigned sigh. Though she could see the detective inspector wasn't pleased, he picked up his pen and did a quick scrawl, then handed her the sheet of paper. 'There you go. An official statement saying that I'm satisfied Mike acted in good faith.'

She skimmed the contents briefly. 'Good, that'll do for a start,' she conceded. Unable to resist needling Poulsen, she added, 'So what if I change my mind and walk out of here?

Renege on the bargain?'

'If you go back on your word, I'll see to it Mike never gets promotion around here. I know how keen he is to stay in the drugs squad. His secondment to CIB is still only temporary, don't forget.' Poulsen had a smug edge to his voice.

Kelly fumed. She might have the letter, but he could still block Mike's career in the force. Still, she wasn't going to let Poulsen have his own way completely. Quickly she weighed up the consequences. If she told Mike she was an undercover cop and explained what she was doing for him, he'd refuse to let her. That arrogant streak of independence would bode ill for him. He'd insist on facing the accusations himself. There'd be an inquiry. Maybe he'd come out OK. But what would happen if he didn't?

Kelly hoped her next plan would work. 'Actually, I might as well confess. Mike knew I was a cop all along,' she stated, her gaze never faltering.

Poulsen gave a snort. 'Like hell he did. Nice try, Kelly.'

Her voice was deceptively cool. 'Why don't you call him in and ask him?'

The detective inspector shifted uneasily. 'Mike's not here. He's away on a taser course.'

257

'Really?' said Kelly coolly. 'That's odd because I just saw him walking into the building.'

Poulsen looked startled. 'You did?' He rose to his feet. 'I'll just check that out.'

Once Poulsen had left the room, Rogers's worried gaze settled on her. 'I hope you know what you're doing.'

Kelly didn't answer, at least, not straight away. Gambling had always been part of her nature. She only hoped she could play Poulsen at his own devious game. 'It's the only thing I can do. I won't have Mike take the blame for anything.'

A few minutes later, Mike entered the room with Poulsen behind him. Mike's eyes met hers, but he said nothing as he took a seat.

Poulsen spoke first. 'The taser course has been cancelled, so Mike's filling in tonight for a colleague.' Poulsen turned to Mike. 'You'll be wondering what all this is about?'

'Yeah, you could say that.'

'We've got a few questions. It won't take long,' added Poulsen.

'Take as long as you like,' answered Mike calmly.

Poulsen cleared his throat. 'Did you know Kelly is working undercover for the SCDEA?'

Mike's gaze settled on her and she could

see the betrayal in his eyes but she felt helpless to do anything about it. Kelly found herself curling her nails into her palms. She wanted to scream at him to say yes. Her whole plan depended on his answer. If Mike said yes, then the accusations the detective inspector had come up with wouldn't be any good in an inquiry. Helping an undercover cop was no crime. But if Mike said no, that meant he had helped a person he thought was involved in drug dealing. That was a serious matter. And worse still, Poulsen would always have leverage over her, preventing her from pulling out of the assignment at any time she wanted.

Mike's mouth tightened. 'And if I did?'

'Just answer the question, Mike,' pressured Detective Inspector Poulsen. 'Did you know she was an undercover agent?'

Mike shifted his gaze to his boss. Finally, he spoke. 'Yeah, sure I did. Kelly told me right from the beginning. But she told me I couldn't trust any of my colleagues. So I promised I wouldn't say anything. Not even to you, sir.' Mike hesitated. 'I wasn't completely honest with you when I confessed my involvement with her.'

Detective Inspector Poulsen looked from one person to another. He stood up, his mouth tightening. 'You're both lying.'

Rogers intervened. 'For Christ's sake, this isn't getting us anywhere. And we're wasting time.'

'Oh ... but it is, Joe,' answered Kelly smoothly, eager to get the better of the DI. 'It's time a few things were discussed. So what have you to say, Detective Inspector?' persisted Kelly.

Poulsen's jaw set tight. 'All right, you made your point. But like I said, I'm willing to overlook all this if Kelly goes back under-cover.'

Kelly stared straight at Mike, begging him for understanding. She tried to explain. 'We've lost a drug shipment. That's what all this is about.' Another plan quickly formed in her mind. Her gaze swung back to the detective inspector. 'Wait. There's something else.'

'Another demand?' replied Poulsen, sarcastically.

'You could say that. I want to stay in New Zealand. To do that, I'll need a passport and a new identity. Can you get them for me?'

'That's Immigration's department,' the detective inspector replied. 'We do have a witness protection scheme, but it still has to go through the Department of Internal Affairs.' He threw his hands up in the air. 'I can't make promises that aren't mine to give.'

Rogers looked thoughtful. 'I'll see to it, Kelly. We've been working with the Department of Internal Affairs for some time now. This is a joint operation. I'm sure if I made a request, they'll agree.'

'Thanks,' replied Kelly, feeling satisfied at the turn of events. 'If I'm going to claim that new identity afterwards, you'd better just make sure all the paperwork is in order. Plus, you'd better get surveillance to keep a close eye on me from now on. Things could be moving quickly.'

'Kelly . . . surveillance is out,' announced Rogers flatly.

Kelly blinked. 'What? But why?'

Rogers answered quickly. 'Think about it. Carlos will be watching you closely. We can't afford to take the chance. Not if he's got the slightest suspicion about you.'

Poulsen agreed.

'Well, I don't,' added Mike sharply. 'You're asking Kelly to put her life on the line here. It's far too dangerous. They're vicious thugs you're dealing with.'

Kelly had lived with danger for a long time. But Mike was right. Not having surveillance did put her at a very high risk. Still, she could see Joe's point too. She made a quick decision.

'OK. Let's compromise. No surveillance.

But I'll keep in close contact. I won't even meet with Carlos unless I've verified the meeting with you first. That way you can put a tail on me if need be.'

Mike shook his head. 'No. That's not good enough. Kelly should have surveillance from the moment she walks out of here. If you don't, then I'll do it myself.'

'Mike,' uttered Kelly, surprised. 'You don't have to do this. I'll be careful. I promise.'

'I know you will. But something bad could happen.' He snapped his fingers. 'Just like that. And you'd have no one there as back-up.' He swung around to look at Rogers and Poulsen, who were about to protest strongly at his interference. He glared at them. 'Don't even think about trying to stop me.'

* * *

An hour later, Poulsen said, 'We've had another intelligence report come in. The connection between Carlos and the Black Snakes is strengthening. The gang has offered to pay Carlos more money for the drugs than he's getting from Tino Chang. But the deal is he hands over the shipment completely.'

'Are you sure this Intel report is genuine?' asked Rogers.

Poulsen nodded. 'We've got an informant

262

on the inside. We're paying him well. He's been accurate in the past.'

'As long as you're sure,' stated Kelly. 'And it's not a set-up. What do you think, Joe?'

Joe rubbed his chin. 'It makes sense. Carlos is totally unpredictable. We know that already. I suspect it's not the money that's his priority, but forging partnerships with the Black Snakes.'

'But that's not all,' said Poulsen, skimming the report. He looked up. 'A bidding war has started with the other gangs around the country in competition with the Black Snakes. It seems everyone knows about the shipment, but no one knows where it is.'

'That's just great,' said Kelly, frowning. 'Who knows what Carlos will do next?' She hesitated. 'I'll need to ring Tino Chang. He needs to know the situation. Besides, he'll be expecting to hear from me.'

'All right,' agreed Rogers. 'Let's see what his next move is. You could try getting him over to New Zealand. That way, with luck, we can round them all up in one go.'

Kelly shook her head uneasily. 'I can't see Chang coming here. He wouldn't take the chance. He'd send his men to do any dirty work.'

'You don't know that for definite,' pointed out Rogers. He switched on the tape to record Kelly's phone conversation. 'Do what you can anyway.'

Kelly dialled the special telephone number in Hong Kong. She was put through to Tino Chang straight away.

'Carlos is out of control,' Kelly told Chang. 'And now he's hidden the P. So he's got everyone exactly where he wants them.'

Chang was furious. 'I'm putting a contract on Carlos. I'm not letting him get away with this.'

'You can't,' said Kelly. 'If you do that, we might never find the methamphetamine. Or if it falls into the Black Snakes' clutches, they'll take over, and the drugs will be distributed here. You'll have lost everything.'

'So what do you suggest?' he asked carefully.

'You could come to New Zealand. Talk to Carlos face to face. Make him see that double-crossing you isn't going to work. You could point out that his father and the Fortuna cartel won't be pleased at him stirring things up. Everyone knows his father keeps his word, whether it's legal business or narco dealings. If he screws up this deal for you, no one will do business with him again. It would reflect on the Fortuna cartel as a whole.'

'That makes sense.' Chang drew a breath.

'But no, it's not possible for me to come over. The authorities will know if I enter the country. There must be another way.'

There was a long silence. For a moment, Kelly thought the connection had been cut. 'Tino, are you still there?'

'Yes,' he said slowly. 'Just thinking.'

Kelly mouthed to Rogers, 'What now?' Rogers signalled to wind up the conversation. Kelly nodded.

'OK, Tino . . . leave it with me a while longer. I'll see what I can do. I'll try talking to Carlos again. Once I have the shipment, Carlos will have lost his power. So that's what I'll aim for. As for the couriers, they're all in place and will wait.'

Chang growled. 'You've got one week. If he hasn't handed over the shipment to you by then, I'll send men over. If I kill Carlos, it will mean an all-out war with the Fortuna cartel. But they've left me no choice.'

★ ★ ★

'I'll alert the Hong Kong police,' said Rogers. 'They can keep tabs on Tino Chang.'

'He could leave unofficially,' remarked Kelly. 'He has the contacts.'

'That's possible. We'll just have to wait and see.'

Kelly took a walk down the corridor, stopping at the water fountain. She had just reached for a paper cup when Mike approached her.

He whispered, 'Poulsen's made it clear to me to stay out the way. I'm not to contact you. He's even allocated me other duties.'

'But I need to talk with you now,' she urged. 'Please — '

He shook his head. 'Later. Just make sure you stay at the station all night. Don't go back to the house truck. At least not yet.' He paused slightly, checking no one was within earshot. 'Call in at my place as soon as you leave here. I'll be home by then. We can talk about surveillance.' With a quick squeeze of her shoulder, he was gone.

While she appreciated Mike's offer, it could only complicate things. Carlos already knew about Mike and while he was willing to accept that a cop on the take could be of use, she didn't want Mike placed in any danger. In Kelly's estimation, it was safer for Mike to keep a low profile. She was used to undercover operation; Mike wasn't.

In reality, undercover work couldn't be taught in a classroom. It was an art more than a science, and very few people were good at it. Kelly had been able to adapt according to circumstance. It had saved her life more than once.

It didn't take long for her to reach Mike's house. Kelly had been especially observant, making sure none of Carlo's men were following her. But as she approached, she saw a white car with *Greymouth Evening Star* written on the side pull up into his driveway. Kelly slowed down, but didn't completely stop. She watched as a woman climbed out of the car. So this was Mike's journalist friend, Kelly realized. The one he'd told her about.

Kelly didn't dare call in now in case the reporter got curious about her. There was nothing else Kelly could do but head back to the camping park for a shower and breakfast, and ring Mike from there. After that she could plan her next move.

* * *

Mike opened the door on the second knock. Instead of Kelly, whom he'd been expecting, Julie stood there on the step, looking bright and cheerful, dressed in green linen trousers and a white blouse. Her make-up was immaculate as per usual.

She smile broadly. 'Hi.'

Mike hesitated. 'Hi. What brings you here so early?'

'I start work at seven, so thought I'd call in.

267

Heard something's up. You know how news travels fast in a small town like this.'

Mike almost groaned. 'Oh . . . like what?'

'Don't plead ignorance, Mike. My sister works at the airport. She said several official-looking men, all with Scots accents, arrived yesterday. Two police cars were there to pick them up, including your boss, Detective Inspector Poulsen.'

'I can't tell you anything,' said Mike firmly. 'It's classified. My advice to you is to head back to the paper and wait for an official press release.'

Her eyes glittered. 'I knew it. There is something going on.' She edged forward as if she was trying to sneak a look into the room behind him. 'Aren't you going to invite me in for coffee?'

'Nope. I'm expecting someone.'

'Really? Who?'

Mike could feel his patience slipping, but he tried to keep his voice friendly. 'Julie, I'm a bit busy right now. Just off night shift.' He yawned appropriately. 'And it's been a helluva night. So if you don't mind.'

Her features sharpened. 'I won't take that personally, seeing I'm wearing my journalist's badge.'

Mike laughed uneasily. 'Look, there's nothing going on.' Seeing her look of disbelief, he added casually, 'I have a friend calling around soon.' He flicked his wrist to look at his watch. 'Any time now.'

'Oh . . . ' she replied. 'You mean the woman in black leather . . . on a motorbike.'

Mike said nothing. Damn, he thought. How the bloody hell had she found that out?

Julie continued smoothly. 'Actually, she was here, a moment ago. But when she saw me, she took off. Mind you, it's not the first time I've seen her around. Kelly Anderson is her name, isn't it? She's from Scotland.'

Mike said nothing.

Julie pursed her lips. 'I was in court the day she was summonsed on bribery charges. That's interesting how you happened to be the officer who charged her. Also, the fact that our editor didn't want to publish the details in our court pages. He wouldn't even tell me why. Now don't you think that's a bit odd.' She paused slightly. 'It's almost as though he'd been told not to.'

Mike started to feel uneasy. 'I can't answer any questions, Julie. Sorry, but I've got to go.' He tried to close the door, but Julie jammed her foot in the gap, stopping it from closing.

'Mike, I'm not about to give up that easily. You do realize that I can get that information anyway. The Freedom of Information Act gives me the legal right.'

'Not in this case, I suspect.'

'Why's that?'

'Because confidentiality is needed to protect those involved. And besides, I'm asking you not to.' His voice lowered. 'As a friend.'

Julie chewed her lip, undecided. 'That's a big ask, Mike.'

'Yeah, it is.'

Mike stared at her, realizing there was an edge to her he hadn't seen before. Maybe she was getting the hard word from her boss. She'd mentioned something about the newspaper's new tactics in getting a headline. Sales had been flagging and they'd had to do something. Redundancies had even been mentioned. Perhaps even her job was on the line.

'You could buy my silence?' she suggested. She arched a brow. 'What about dinner, champagne . . . and in return I'll delay my investigations. But only for a few days, of course.'

Mike groaned inwardly. 'Jesus . . . you drive a hard bargain.'

Julie smiled. 'Blame those male journalists. They taught me a lot of tricks. I want to be the first to cover this story. So what do you say?'

★   ★   ★

Kelly had just climbed off her Triumph, when her phone rang. She recognized the voice immediately as DI Poulsen.

'There's been a change of plan,' he said. 'Surveillance has been reinstated. Rogers asked me to give you a call to let you know.'

Surprised, she asked him why.

'Mike put the pressure on. So Rogers relented. He didn't want Mike getting in the way, causing trouble.'

'But I haven't heard from Mike,' she stated, worried. 'Is everything OK?'

'Fine as far as I know. I expect he'll be in touch soon.'

'And what about Joe? Maybe I'd better check in with him about this. He was so adamant about not having any surveillance.'

'Rogers is tied up right now, talking with the Hong Kong police. I'll get him to ring you as soon as he's free.'

Since there didn't seem to be anything else she could do, Kelly decided it would be beneficial to have some time out. She would call in later to see Mike to straighten things out between them. He'd want to ask her questions, and this time, she'd be ready to answer them.

Until then, she decided to go for a spin on the motorbike. She needed to get away for a while to think things through. Prepare herself for what was to come. Maybe she could even call in and see Brent and Shona. It would be good to see them, and being on the bike she doubted any of Carlos's men would keep up, even if they were following her. She phoned through her plans to Poulsen, leaving a message for Rogers, and got the go-ahead.

When she arrived at the homestead, Shona made her welcome, insisting Kelly stay for dinner. It felt good to just relax, forget about everything. Kelly rang Mike again but he hadn't picked up his phone. She couldn't understand it. Tempted to leave a message on his answer phone, she realized it would be foolish to do so. Someone other than Mike might get hold of it.

'It's so late. Are you sure you won't stay the night?' asked Shona, concerned. 'The bed is already made up, if you want it?'

Kelly smiled. 'Thanks. But I've got some things to do first thing tomorrow.'

It was after one in the morning when she cruised into the camping park. She glanced at the ocean and the full moon above. Rays of silver reflecting in the water threw a ghostly aura over the sea. For a few seconds, she stared at it, fascinated. There was something about the moon which captivated her even as a child.

When she entered the house truck, the first

thing she did was to reach out for the light switch. Sensing something was amiss, she paused. Moonlight filtered through the stained glass window, casting eerie shadows on the wall. A creak of the floor alerted her and she spun around to see a figure step out from behind the door. She gasped. The door was slowly being pushed.

Without hesitation, she whipped out her gun and aimed it, focusing carefully on the black figure. 'Hold it right there,' she said, her body tensing.

The figure moved, stepping forward into a stream of moonlight. His outline was unmistakable.

'What are you doing here?' she said, her mouth dropping open.

11

'I've been waiting for you,' said Mike calmly.

Relief flowed through her as Kelly lowered the gun to her side, her hands still trembling. 'You scared the living daylights out of me.'

Mike's voice came out rough, hard. 'Yeah, well, I just wanted to see how ready you actually were if any unwelcome visitors turn up. Why the hell didn't you lock the door before you went out?'

She frowned. 'I thought I did.' She glanced around carefully, noticing everything was just where she had left it. Nothing seemed to be missing or interfered with. Perhaps she had forgotten to lock the door after all.

'Where have you been?' he asked.

'At the homestead. Had dinner with your family.' She shrugged. 'Somehow it seemed like a good place to go.'

'Are you sure that was wise?'

Kelly put her gun on the bench, feeling dispirited. The last thing she wanted was to argue with him. 'I was very careful. No one could have possibly followed me at the speed I was travelling. And I checked in at the station to let them know where I was.' Seeing his doubtful look, she added quietly, 'I would never put them in danger. You know that.'

He nodded.

'I called around to your place as we'd arranged,' she continued, 'but then I saw the blonde journalist on your doorstep.'

'Julie? She'd heard the SCDEA officers had arrived and called in to talk about it. That was all,' he dismissed.

'Nice timing,' uttered Kelly. 'And my cover?'

'It's safe,' he reassured her, 'although I had to take her out to dinner to buy her silence.'

'Dinner?' exclaimed Kelly. 'Was that really necessary?' The thought of the blonde girl and Mike out for dinner in an intimate candlelit setting did wonders for her morale.

He arched a brow. 'Jealous?'

'No,' she said sharply.

She started to move past him, but he caught her wrist, saying softly, 'Liar. Blondes don't turn me on. But redheads do.'

'Is that supposed to make me feel better?'

He gave a short laugh, but she could tell it was strained. 'All right. I'll try again,' he said. 'I've been worried about you. That's why I'm here.'

She lifted her head to meet his gaze full on. 'Mike, I . . . ' But her words trailed off at the intensity of his gaze.

'Kelly, why didn't you tell me who you really were? Didn't you trust me enough?'

It was the question she had been dreading.

She fumbled for the right words. 'It was just impossible to tell you at the time,' she pleaded. 'It wasn't safe to tell anyone.'

'Yeah . . . but I'm not *anyone*, am I? Not one word,' he said, accusingly. 'That's all it would have taken.' She heard the pain in his voice but felt helpless to do anything about it. 'But Poulsen knew, didn't he?'

'Yes, he knew,' she admitted.

'And the Interpol file?'

'That was false,' she explained. 'It was designed to protect me in case there were any informers at the police station.'

'I see,' he replied carefully.

'I'm really sorry.' She hoped Mike believed her.

'Yeah . . . so am I.' His voice was flat, empty. It spoke volumes.

'Mike, listen to me. You're a good cop.'

'But not good enough, obviously,' he said drily. 'I can't even detect one of our own. I suspected something, but never in a million years did I think you were an undercover agent.'

She didn't know what to say except, 'You wouldn't be the first.' She took a breath. 'Listen to me. You only did what you thought was best. But if you think you've let the force down by lying to them over me, you're wrong.' She hated herself, talking to him like that, but she knew she was right. She had to make him see sense.

His mouth hardened; anger surfaced. 'A fool because I'm honest? Or at least I was, until I had to lie to Poulsen about knowing who you really were.' He snorted. 'Yeah, easy for you to say, especially since you make a living out of deceit.'

'That's unfair and you know it.' Hurt sliced through her.

'Is it? And what about us? Was that just a lie too?'

How much could she say without giving herself away? She hesitated a shade too long. 'Is that what you really think? That I was just using you? I suppose it was just a fling on your part.' She was testing him, hoping he'd deny it. But disappointingly, he didn't.

When he spoke, the coldness of his voice sliced through her. 'That's some insult, Kelly. Did you really think I would risk my job for a fling?'

She held his gaze, unable to answer. If he had any deep feelings for her, why didn't he come out and say it? There was no way she was going to act like some lovesick female and tell him she needed him — even if it was true, she thought desperately.

She could accept he was furious at being placed in an awkward position with Poulsen and having to lie about her but she had done it for him. Only she couldn't tell him that. Not yet anyway. But knowing Mike, if he found out the truth that the detective inspector had placed leverage on her in such an underhand manner, he was liable to march into the police station and punch Poulsen's lights out. It would lose him his job. Hadn't he realized yet she had asked for that new identity to stay in New Zealand for one reason only? So they could have a chance to be together.

Until then she couldn't allow him to become involved in the operation, even when he wasn't on duty. He didn't even carry a firearm.

'There's no point in our discussing things between us while I'm still undercover,' she said plainly, hoping that might defuse the situation between them.

Mike's voice came out cold. 'All right. If that's how you want things to be.'

No, she almost threw back at him, she didn't want it to be like this at all.

Mike continued. 'Rogers gave me a full account of your showdown with Carlos. So I'm supposed to be a bent cop now.'

'Just a ruse,' she explained, feeling awkward. 'You're in the clear. Only Carlos thinks otherwise.'

'As long as only Carlos thinks that.'

'What are you intimating?'

'Surely you can guess? The last thing I want is my colleagues thinking I'm bent.'

'You're in the clear. Absolutely,' she told him. 'Poulsen has even issued a written statement. Rogers endorsed it.'

He pursed his mouth. 'At least that's something.' He paused. 'You'll be relieved to know, Rogers has changed his mind about the surveillance. He's got men watching you.'

'I know. Poulsen rang earlier.'

'For Christ's sake, be careful. These men you're dealing with are ruthless. They won't hesitate to kill you.'

'You think I don't know that?'

'You're either very brave, or very foolish. I just can't make up my mind which.'

She stared at him. 'I wish it didn't have to be like this.'

He gave a worried smile. 'But it is. And right now there is nothing we can do about it.' His voice deepened. 'You'd best get some sleep. You look all in.' His knuckles touched her cheek briefly. Then he turned to go.

Suddenly, she realized, she was wrong. She couldn't possibly let him leave like this.

'Wait, Mike!' she cried out. 'There's something I need to tell you. Something important.'

He stood there, looking at her, his eyes enigmatic. Then he took a step forward. 'Go right ahead.'

Kelly took a deep breath, trying to form the words in her mind. This was cleansing her soul. She needed to do it. Had to do it. There was no way she could move on to any future if she didn't. It was time to tell him exactly what had happened all those years ago.

She took a deep breath. 'You know so little about me.'

He gave an almost bitter laugh. 'It's not from a lack of trying. But I'm trying to sort out the lies from the truth. That's going to take some time.'

'What I'm about to tell you isn't a lie.' She took another deep breath, hoping the pain would ease as she talked. 'I was married to a cop once.'

Surprise widened his eyes. 'A cop?'

She nodded. 'It seems just like yesterday somehow.' Her mind started to go back in time. 'We were working undercover, trying to bust some drug dealers in Glasgow. It was pretty rough. Hard drugs were hitting the large housing estates and getting out of hand. Jeff and I volunteered to go in to see if we could put a stop to it.'

Mike's forehead furrowed. 'Jeff?'

She swallowed hard. 'My husband.'

'Go on,' he urged.

She took another breath to steady herself. 'We were selected for an undercover operation as a couple. It was something we both wanted. We'd been plain clothes cops for several years and had some idea of what we were getting into. We figured if we could work together, then maybe . . . just maybe . . . we could contribute something of value. Looking back, perhaps we were a little naïve but we caught on pretty quick.' She paused briefly. 'Things were moving fast . . . really fast. Jeff had got word he was to rendezvous with one of the big players. They'd been showing interest in him and had even offered him a deal to work with them on a closer basis. It was the break we had been looking for.'

Kelly closed her eyes. She could feel her heart starting to pound.

As if Mike sensed her distress, he slipped his hand in hers. 'Kelly. You don't have to tell me this right now.'

Kelly shook her head, and pulled away. His touch distracted her. She looked up, uncertain, but his gaze steadied her. 'No. I want to. It's the only way.' She swallowed. 'We had always made a pact not to meet anyone by ourselves,' she explained, 'but Jeff broke it this time. He decided to go on his own or he could lose out on the deal. We were desperate to know who these players were. I pleaded with him to take me, but he wouldn't listen. We argued. Anyway, he left. I was out of my mind with worry, so I followed him. But by the time I got there — ' Her voice stopped suddenly. 'I was the first to find him, dying on the floor of an old warehouse. They'd pumped him full of heroin. Before he died, he said two words. Tino Chang.'

'Chang?' exclaimed Mike.

'Yes.'

Mike's arms slipped around her. She leaned into his embrace. 'Now I'm beginning to understand,' he said.

Her throat tightened. 'You see, I blamed myself. I should never have let him go alone. I've lost count of how many times I've asked Jeff to forgive me. But I never hear his answer. I'm still waiting.'

She felt the pressure of Mike's arms around her, reassuring her. Somehow it gave her strength to continue.

'It changed me,' she told him. 'Not immediately. I was too distressed at first. But eventually, as time passed, I decided that I owed it to Jeff to keep on going.' Her voice lowered. 'That's when I realized. That to stop the drugs, it had to be done at the source. So I offered to work with the Scottish Crime and Drug Enforcement Agency on a solo basis.'

Mike's brow furrowed. 'A personal crusade?'

She laughed bitterly. 'Maybe some would call it that. But to me it made sense. I had lost my focus and working undercover gave me a reason to go on.' She took another breath. 'After Jeff's funeral, I left Scotland and moved to London. Through the contacts I made, I managed to infiltrate one of the biggest drug cartels in south-east Asia and gain the trust of Tino Chang. It hasn't been easy. But every time I see another kid hooked on P or I remember the day I found Jeff, I think it's been worth it.'

'You can't win them all,' he said gently. 'And you don't have to spend your whole life trying.'

'I know that now.' She gave a smile. 'It's taken you to show me that. But I don't regret what I've done. I remember part of my training was not getting emotionally involved while undercover. I never thought that would happen to me. Up to now, it was so easy to remain detached. I always focused on the job because that's what mattered in the end. And I knew that someday I'd come face to face with Jeff's murderers.'

'And Chang is one of them?'

'Evidence points to his involvement with the Triads in Glasgow. There were actually two gangs, operating side by side. The other one was a Colombian outfit. The Fortuna cartel. Though at that time they weren't in partnership. It was Tino Chang who set up the deal to bring that particular shipment of heroin into the housing estate. Jeff's last words confirmed it.'

'You slept with Chang. Didn't you?'

Kelly gasped. Shame washed over her. She had hoped Mike would never find out. Somehow he had. Maybe it was for the best. 'It was Joe, wasn't it? He told you.'

Mike nodded, his eyes narrowing. 'So it's true then.'

'Yes.' Desperation entered her voice. 'Please . . . please don't judge me too harshly. My life was in danger.'

Mike stared at her intensely, the silence lengthening between them. She could face insults, even accusations, but not his silent disapproval.

Kelly lifted her chin. 'I know what you're thinking. What kind of woman would do that?'

His voice came out quiet. 'I'd be lying if I said it hadn't crossed my mind.'

'I did what I had to do,' she justified. If he

thought she was going to ask him for forgiveness, he was mistaken.

'I'm not sure I agree.'

She flinched at the accusing note in his voice, feeling that the distance between them was widening, in spite of what she had told him.

'You *are* judging me.' Disappointment shot through her.

'No. You're wrong. It's just that . . . ' His voice trailed off. 'Listen to me, Kelly. You don't have to finish this assignment for Rogers. You've done enough. Let it go.'

If only she could tell him that she was now doing this for him. 'I can't. I have to see this one through. But I promise it will be the last time.'

'And afterwards?' he asked questioningly.

'I . . . don't know.' Her voice faltered as her eyes met his. 'I guess that depends, doesn't it?'

There were still unanswered questions between them, and neither was willing to make that final move, she realized with a sinking heart. Perhaps realistically, it was impossible to until the undercover operation was finished. Once all the barriers were out of the way.

'I know I've misjudged you,' he said softly. 'In so many ways . . . but when you walked out on me, I had to go to Poulsen.' He shook his head. 'If only you had told me then — ' He hesitated, unsure. 'Damn you. Did you even realize how I felt?'

'I would have done the same,' she reasoned. 'I don't blame you for being angry with me, or for telling Poulsen about your involvement with me. It was the right thing to do.'

'Kelly — ' He pulled her into his arms. 'We have to try to make sense of this.'

'We're not playing ordinary rules here, Mike.'

'I know.'

'I'm scared.'

'Why?' he asked gently, pulling back and framing her face between his hands.

'Since Jeff died, I've put my personal life on hold. Somehow it just seemed easier that way. Then you came along and challenged all that.'

Mike spoke firmly. 'Everything is different now. Don't be afraid. Come with me. We can sort things out together. Tell Rogers you've changed your mind.'

She heard the caring note in his voice and fought against it. There was too much at stake. 'Not yet . . . I can't. I gave my word to Joe.'

'Rogers would understand. He seems a

286

reasonable sort of guy.'

But Poulsen wouldn't, she added silently. And therein lay the problem. 'No.' She shook her head adamantly.

Mike spoke slowly, his eyes puzzled. 'My gut feeling tells me something isn't right still. I can't explain it exactly.'

'There's nothing else,' lied Kelly.

'I don't want to leave you here, all alone like this.'

She smiled, making a determined effort. 'I'll be fine . . . honestly. Like you said, the surveillance team are nearby. So I'm safe.' Then she amended quickly, 'Well, as safe as I can be considering the circumstances.'

His arms encircled her, holding her tight, so tight, she thought he would never let her go. Something intense flared through her. Her arms slid around his neck as his mouth clamped down on hers. She sank into the kiss, enjoying the closeness between them.

When they pulled apart, Mike murmured softly in her ear. 'Kelly, tell me how you feel.'

'I'm trying, but right now I can't think straight. Let alone answer any more questions.'

Minutes passed. She gave a sigh, nestled in his arms. His warmth was so embracing, so male. Her body ached for his touch.

Mike broke the silence, his voice deepening. 'Let me stay the night.'

'Too risky,' she uttered. 'We're taking a chance doing this.'

'Then I'd better go. Make sure you lock your door this time.'

She gave another smile. 'I will. You can count on it.'

With reluctance, she stepped back out of his embrace. She watched him walk along the path and fade away into the darkness beyond a thick line of trees.

Maybe she should have just told Mike she was in love with him. It wasn't really so hard, was it?

Her gaze lifted, looked out into the inky darkness of the ocean. A large cloud covered the moon suddenly, shutting out the light. More clouds, dark silhouettes, from the north were rolling in fast like black swirling curtains. Maybe it was an omen, she thought philosophically. She'd never got rid of her Scottish superstitions. She'd just learned to live with them.

It had taken a lot out of her to speak of Jeff like that. He had been locked up inside of her for so long, even saying his name had been difficult. A sob escaped, which sounded like a strangled cry, but she pushed it down and took a deep breath to steady herself. She had to get a grip. It was simply a delayed reaction to all she had been through the last few hours.

Too wound up to sleep, she decided to make a hot drink. She picked up the kettle, intending to make a cup of coffee, but noticed it was empty. Pumping the plastic handle over the sink to fill it, no water came through. Then she remembered she had meant to fill the water container in the cupboard earlier on, but had completely forgotten about it. Kelly grumbled to herself. She'd have to walk to the shower block to fill it. She set off. When she reached it, she turned the tap on full.

A soft footstep behind had her looking over her shoulder. Too late. Someone grabbed her and pinned her arms to her side. 'Agh — ' She choked, dropping the kettle. It clattered to the ground and rolled away on the concrete. A hand clamped over her mouth.

Kelly struggled, lashing out with her heel against the attacker's shin. She heard a grunt of pain, confirming she'd found her mark. The attacker's hold loosened momentarily, but it wasn't enough. He slammed her up against the concrete wall, winding her. Before she had time to right herself, he pressed something into her belly that felt like a gun.

'Don't move.'

Kelly froze, then gasped. 'What is it you want?'

The masked face loomed into hers. 'You'll find out soon enough.'

The tap was still running, forming a pool of cold water at her feet. She shifted position slightly, hoping she'd get another chance to run. But any plans of escape crumbled as she saw another figure come out of the bushes. Her attacker looked up, to the left. Sensing his distraction, she tried to break free, sprinting forward, but he caught her and dragged her backwards by her jacket. She stumbled. Quickly righting herself, she lashed out with her foot and elbow. She sprang forward again, intending to run, but yet another man hiding in the shadows ran out of nowhere and tackled her. She collided with him and hit the ground hard.

She screamed. 'Help! Help!' The second man shoved a rag into her mouth, muffling her cries. Then a large sack was pulled tight over her head and shoulders. Kelly plucked at it frantically, the stench of rotten fish making her reel. She hit out hard, kicking and writhing. Someone grabbed her wrists, forcing them together. A rope was fastened around her hands and she was lifted over a man's shoulder. The mobile phone clipped to her belt ripped off and fell on to the ground, crunched beneath someone's foot.

Dumped into what felt like the boot of a

car, she lay there shocked and trembling. The boot lid slammed down over her, muffling any further sounds. Stunned at the speed of the attack, she tried to think what to do next. Desolation swept over her. There was nothing she could do.

Within the darkness, thoughts whirled in her mind. Who had abducted her? Was it Carlos? But why? And where were the surveillance team?

The car rocked around. Thrown from one side to another, she lay there listening to the sound of the car engine, trying to gauge in what direction they might be travelling. She heard gravel spray the side of the car, and guessed they had gone off the tarmac road.

After a while the car appeared to slow, and finally stopped. Kelly's heart sank. Was this going to be the end? Suddenly she thought of her whole life. All those things she had never got around to doing because she had been too busy working, following leads, making contacts, living a life that she knew was dangerous. She'd probably never see her family in Edinburgh again. What about Mike? She couldn't bear the thought of dying and that he would never know how she really felt about him. Tears sprang into her eyes and ran down her cheeks.

Angry voices surrounded her. She half

expected the car boot to be sprung open, and to be hauled out, but nothing happened. Someone got in the car, and the doors were slammed shut. The car sped off again, climbing uphill. She could hear the change of gears, and the frantic speed they were travelling. She rolled downwards, her head crashing against the side of the boot. Pain blinded her. Time passed; minutes or hours, she didn't know. She felt bruised, battered and disorientated. Finally the car slowed. Kelly held herself rigid, expecting the worst. The car stopped and the engine turned off.

This was it.

The boot sprang open. Hands gripped her, dragging her out roughly. She kicked and writhed. She tried to scream but only a muffled grunt came out her mouth. When a fist thudded into her stomach, she almost fainted with the pain.

With sinking realization, she knew it had to be only a matter of time before the abductors killed her.

★ ★ ★

Mike had gone straight home after his visit to Kelly. The house was quiet. Far too quiet. He missed her. It didn't feel right to leave her on her own at the camping park but since

292

Rogers's men were there, it made sense for him to back off for a while.

All the same he wished Kelly would change her mind about the assignment. He'd come across her stubbornness before and when she set her mind on something it was nigh on impossible to budge her. Maybe that's why she was such a success in her undercover work. She never gave up.

Undercover work was a dangerous game and he knew enough about it to know it took a special person to carry it off. An undercover operative was someone who could change easily like a chameleon, blending in to the environment or situation. Kelly had done that admirably. But who was she really? Had he got to know the real person when she stayed with him? Or had she fooled him in that respect too? He gave a bitter laugh. How could a woman fake making love like she did?

And yet he felt he could trust her now. He was still absorbing what she had told him about her husband being murdered. Kelly's confession hadn't surprised him. The trauma of how he had died explained a lot of things. Revenge — one of the most powerful emotions in human nature and who was he to say it was wrong? Some might say it was rough justice. He hadn't quite made up his mind about it. But one thing he was sure of, he'd never have made the grade working undercover. He just didn't have the temperament for it.

An hour later, lying in bed, he was still awake, his thoughts refusing to settle. He had a sudden urge to phone Kelly, to hear her voice — and to tell her he loved her. Why hadn't he done that? He knew it was because he was too damned scared she'd throw it back in his face.

He flicked on the lamp switch and glanced at his watch. It was nearly four in the morning. Maybe he just needed reassurance she was OK. He picked up the receiver and punched in her number. The disconnected tone reverberated in his ear. 'What the hell?'

He tried again. But still the tone came over as disconnected.

Unease crept over him. He punched in Rogers's number. It rang several times before he answered. The man sounded as if he had just woken up.

'It's Mike McKenna. I've just tried to ring Kelly. Her phone isn't working.'

He heard the man's sharp intake of breath. 'We'll check it out. But she's probably just switched it off to get some sleep.'

'I'm not so sure. It's got a disconnected tone.'

There was a slight pause. 'Right. I'll get on

to it. I'll send someone over there straight away.' He hung up.

Rogers's words circled in his mind. *I'll send someone over there straight away.* What did he mean by that? He dialled Rogers again. It was engaged. He waited a couple of minutes, then tried again. Finally he answered.

Mike spoke quickly. 'Poulsen said you'd put Kelly back on surveillance.'

'Eh? He did? There must be some mistake. Poulsen offered to send a police officer out in plain clothes at my request, just to take a walk around the camping park a couple of times during the night. But that's all. We'd already agreed there'd be no surveillance.'

Mike sat up, then swore. 'The double-crossing bastard. Poulsen told me the surveillance team was back on. I'm heading out there now.' He hung up. He reached out for his jeans and a shirt lying at the foot of his bed.

A growl of thunder echoed in the distance. Mike drew back the curtains, his eyes searching the sky. A storm was brewing; lightning flashed spasmodically in the night.

'Great. That's all I need,' he murmured.

Within seconds, the rain started. It came down slowly at first, then it began to beat heavily on the windows and on the corrugated iron roof. The temperature had dropped too, he realized. Hurriedly, he reached for his oilskin hanging behind the door and put it on. Then he grabbed his car keys lying on the kitchen bench.

It took quarter of an hour to reach the camping park. First, he drove past it, intending to park further down the highway, then backtrack on foot along the beach. That way no one could see him enter the grounds.

Within five minutes, he had reached Kelly's house truck. The door was open. It swung back and forward with the wind. Everything was in darkness. Mike approached cautiously, climbing the steps on his toes, ready to dive for cover if he needed to run.

Inside the house truck, the bed hadn't been slept in. Kelly's gun was still lying on the bench. He stood on the step surveying the area outside, his eyes sifting through the darkness, trying to make out her familiar shape. But he couldn't see her. His instinct told him something wasn't right. He walked towards the concrete shower block, keeping his senses on high alert for any movement. He could hear water gushing. Switching on his flashlight, he pinpointed the source as a tap on the wall of the concrete block. He reached down to turn it off. Turning around, he skimmed the area. Nothing seemed out of place. And yet . . .

He paused, listening again. A morepork hooted in the nearby trees. But there were no other unfamiliar sounds. It was as he was turning away he saw it lying on the ground. A kettle. And just beyond that was Kelly's cell phone. Even from a distance, he could see it was broken into several pieces.

Mike started to run.

★　★　★

Light filtered through the sack on Kelly's head but the material was woven so close together it was impossible to see through it, no matter how hard she tried. When the sack was finally removed she blinked painfully, even in the dim light. She surveyed her surroundings as best she could. She was in a large room that looked like a derelict workshop. Large jagged stones were piled together in one corner beside a huge rusty saw. Above her, giant muddy-coloured pipes ran across the ceiling with chimney-like vents hanging over the long wooden tables.

Her gaze skimmed across a bench top, seeing the tools laid out. For a moment, she thought they resembled a dentist's equipment. But this was no dental surgery. She detected an acrid smell in the air. Some sort of laboratory, Kelly realized, spotting the line of small glass containers stacked neatly together beside a pair of plastic funnels.

Her mind clicked over. She'd be willing to bet this was an illicit laboratory manufacturing drugs. The electronic scales were in full view and the latex gloves draped over the sink top confirmed it.

A door opened and closed. Shadows approached her. Kelly's eyes widened when she saw who it was. 'Tino, what are you doing here? I thought you were in Hong Kong?'

Chang's face was a mask of fury. 'As you can see I am not. So what have you been up to, Kelly? My informers tell me you spent some time at the police station yesterday.'

Kelly kept her voice steady, though inwardly she shook. 'That's right, I did. I arranged to meet Mike McKenna. He's a cop I know. He had some urgent information for me.'

She paused slightly, knowing that the story she was about to relate to Chang had to be believable.

She cleared her throat. 'There's been some new developments. The police know about the P shipment. There's also word out on the street that Carlos is selling it to the highest bidder.'

Carlos stepped forward, a smirk on his face. 'That rumour has been put about to confuse the police.'

Kelly shouted, 'No, he's lying, Tino. He's out to double-cross you. Don't trust him.'

Chang glanced at Carlos, then back at her as if he was trying to make up his mind who to believe. 'You have contacts in the police, Kelly. Tell me. How did you manage that?'

She kept her gaze level. 'Through some friends of mine. The friends I was staying with.'

'And what did you pay him with?' he asked. He squinted. 'Or was it blackmail?'

'Both,' she replied, shifting uneasily. 'He took a bribe from me. After that it was easy.'

Chang walked up close to her, lifted her hair, then curved his hand around her neck. She kept absolutely still, though she wanted to recoil at his touch.

He whispered in her ear. 'Something tells me you lie.' He shot her a twisted smile, and stroked her cheek. 'We had some good times together. You and I. A pity you chose to betray me.'

Kelly's breath stuck in her throat. The thought of what he might do to her while she was being kept prisoner almost made her want to cry out with fear. But begging for mercy would go against her. Tino would despise any weakness, and take advantage of it. She lifted her chin a notch. 'You're wrong, Tino. But you need to watch your back.

Carlos is for the cartel. He wants the Triads out. He has plans on taking over.'

Chang spoke in Chinese rapidly, then reverted to English. 'You must think I am a fool.'

No, that she would never do. Chang was ruthless, vindictive and had a brilliant mind. He was a lethal combination.

Two of his henchmen stood at his side and moved forward at his command.

Chang said, 'Put her in the back room. Carlos and I have things to discuss first.'

Knowing it was futile to resist, Kelly let them lead her out of the room. She passed through the hallway. One of Chang's men was busy stacking the bags of methamphetamine into plastic crates. Her eyes widened. The drug shipment was here, she realized, but it looked as if they were moving it.

As soon as she stepped into the back room, she saw a man sitting on the floor. Kelly gasped. 'Shaun!' But when she saw his hands bound with rope and the side of his face swollen as if he'd been beaten, she realized he was just as much a prisoner as she was.

The Chinaman pushed her down on to the floor roughly and tied her feet. The door slammed shut behind them and the key grated in the lock.

'What are you doing here?' asked Kelly, in disbelief.

Shaun gave an uncertain laugh. 'I could ask the same about you.' Then he added ruefully, 'I saw some lights on. The place has been derelict for years, so I thought it was a bit odd. Anyway, I came closer to investigate and someone got me from behind.'

'You must have put up a fight,' she remarked, noticing his left eye had almost closed with the swelling.

He gave a grin. 'I did. But as you can see, I came off worse.'

'So what exactly are you doing walking about at this time of night?' she asked suspiciously.

Shaun gave a rueful grin. 'I might as well confess. I've been prospecting for gold in secrecy. Dad's dead against any mining on farm land. You know what farmers are like.'

'You need the money?'

He nodded. 'I didn't want to ask the family for help, so figured I'd try to make something on the side. Something not too big. I had to be careful Dad wouldn't find out. The sluicing machine is further up the valley well out of visual range. Shona and Mike are sworn to secrecy.'

Kelly nodded. 'So that's why you kept disappearing in the truck. I thought something was a bit odd.'

'I guess things have backfired a bit,' Shaun

commented. 'The last thing I expected was being locked up like this.'

'Did you know this place is an illicit drugs lab?' she informed him. 'Methamphetamine.'

'A P lab,' exclaimed Shaun, looking shocked. He shook his head. 'No. I didn't. But everything makes sense now. I suppose it's an ideal location. An abandoned workshop in a rural area.' Shaun's eyes narrowed accusingly. 'But you're involved with them, aren't you? I heard what you said out there.'

Kelly inwardly debated on how much to tell him, then decided not to tell him anything. If they decided to interrogate him, he could possibly give her away.

'It's not that easy to explain. And we don't have time to talk about it right now.' She gave him a quick reassuring smile. 'You'll have to be satisfied with that.'

Still, Shaun stared at her. 'So whose side are you on?'

She gave a small laugh. 'Side? That's a tricky question.' She leaned forward. 'Put it this way, the sooner those drugs are destroyed, the better for everyone. And that's all I'm saying.'

He gave a grin. 'I shouldn't have doubted you.'

Kelly had a quick thought. 'Is anyone likely to be looking for you?'

'Not unless I don't turn up for lunch tomorrow. I said to Shona I'd be back by then.'

Kelly gave a sigh. 'By the time Mike realizes I'm not at the house truck, we could both be dead and buried.'

Silence fell between them. Taking the opportunity, she surveyed the room, noticing it was small, obviously used for storage at one time. Empty shelves and cupboards lined the walls. High up on the wall was one small window, but it was too small to crawl through. A bare bulb hung from the ceiling throwing a halo around them. At least they'd left the light on.

Kelly slumped back against the wall thinking over the events of the last few hours. She'd been in some tight situations before but had never been taken prisoner like this. Somehow, she had to find a way out, though she didn't fancy the odds of them escaping. She thought of Mike. If only she had told him she loved him. The truth was, she just hadn't summoned up the courage to tell him — and now it would probably be too late.

She mustn't think like that. She was still alive, wasn't she?

Kelly made a quick decision. 'We have to do something.'

Shaun raised his head, his face glum. 'Yeah

'. . . but what? The door is locked, the window is too narrow. And we can't even fight our way out tied up like this.'

'If we could only get our hands free,' she murmured.

Kelly's gaze swept the room. Everything had been cleared out, apart from several cardboard boxes lying squashed on the floor. 'What sort of workshop is this?'

'Greenstone. Better known as jade.'

Again, Kelly's gaze swept the room. A small jagged stone lay on the floor within arm's length. Kelly shuffled over to reach it. The stone was sharp, uneven, but it might just do the trick.

'What are you doing?' asked Shaun, interested. He edged towards her to get a closer look.

'Turn your back to me,' instructed Kelly. 'I'll hand you this stone. Try to cut my ropes.'

'Even if we get free, we're still locked in,' he reminded her. 'Still, I might be able to kick the door down if I had my legs free.'

'We can only try,' she replied, more positively than she actually felt.

Sitting back to back, Shaun sawed at the ropes. Twice his fingers slipped and caught her wrist. She winced but didn't cry out. 'Be careful, don't get my veins,' she muttered. 'I don't want to bleed to death.'

'Sorry,' he gasped. 'I'm doing my best.'

Cutting Kelly's ropes proved difficult. 'This is hopeless. It's going to take too long,' said Shaun.

Suddenly they were plunged into darkness. Kelly half expected the door to be thrown open wide, and to be marched outside, ready to be shot. But after a few minutes, no one appeared.

'What's happening?' asked Shaun.

'I don't know.' A few more minutes passed. 'Maybe they're just going to leave us here for the night.'

Shaun continued working away. A door slammed shut somewhere in the building. Shaun paused again, his body stiffening. 'Footsteps. They're coming this way.'

Kelly listened again, straining her ears. 'No, they're leaving. Can't you hear the car engine starting?'

'You could be right,' he admitted.

After about an hour of sawing, during which Shaun dropped the shard of greenstone several times, the ropes finally loosened.

'We're nearly there,' she said encouragingly. She pulled hard and was free. Bringing her arms around to the front, she rubbed her numb wrists. As she bent over to undo the ropes at her feet, dizziness swamped her. She half fell, but steadied herself just in time.

'What's wrong?' asked Shaun.

'I knocked my head earlier on. They trussed me up in the boot of the car. It was a bumpy ride.'

'Take a few deep breaths,' suggested Shaun. 'It might help.'

Sucking in air, all she could do was lean against the wall until the dizziness receded, though a wave of nausea swamped her. Swallowing hard, she took a step forward.

'Kelly,' urged Shaun. 'You have to hurry.'

'I know,' she mumbled, trying to focus her eyes on him. Tiredness was taking its toll but even worse, her head ached badly.

Forcing herself to get a grip, she reached out to undo Shaun's ropes.

As soon as Shaun was free he stood up. Kelly pointed to the window. 'We need to see what's going on.'

'OK, sit on my shoulders. I'll lift you up.'

Keeping her balance by sitting on his shoulders and holding on to the top of Shaun's head, Kelly peered out of the grubby window. 'There's one car parked outside. A Holden truck.'

'That's probably mine,' informed Shaun. 'What's the car registration?'

She could just make it out under the light of the moon. She reeled off the numbers and letters.

'That's mine, all right. I parked further down the road, but after they caught me, the gang drove the truck into the yard.'

'There's no sign of any other vehicles. So it looks like they've gone for now,' said Kelly. 'The trouble is, we don't know for how long.'

Kelly straightened her back as she climbed off Shaun's shoulders. 'Now what?'

Shaun tried the door handle, shaking it furiously. 'Let's see if we can break this down,' he muttered. 'If there is a guard, he's going to hear it. But there's nothing we can do. We'll just have to take the chance. Besides, it's better than doing nothing.'

He stood opposite and swung his leg straight out, kicking the door hard. It wouldn't budge. He tried again and again until finally the door started to splinter at the lock. Suddenly it swung open with a crash and rebounded against the wall. Shaun grabbed Kelly's hand, giving a quick look down the hallway. 'There's no one about. Come on. Let's go.'

Kelly sprinted forward and made for the first door they came to, but was disappointed to find it locked. Further down the hallway, another door, but it too had a large bolt drawn across with a padlock through it.

Backtracking down the hallway, Kelly entered the small kitchen. There were two windows in the room, she noticed. She heaved herself on to the top of a counter but her elbow caught a bottle of liquid. It toppled over and the liquid contents pooled across the bench.

'Oh — ' She gasped, her eyes smarting. She started to cough. 'Ammonia,' she choked.

'Quick. Move out of the way,' shouted Shaun. He picked up what looked to be a jug of water and threw the liquid across the bench. 'That should help. Now try.'

Kelly reached forward and tried to unlock the window. 'It's no good. It's stuck.'

Shaun leaned past her. 'Here. Let me try.' But it still wouldn't budge. He swore softly.

Kelly turned to look around the room. 'What about the window over there, by the table. It's smaller, but I reckon we can still get through it.'

Suddenly, they heard the sound of a car engine. She swapped glances with Shaun, her heart increasing pace.

Shaun picked up a hammer lying on the floor. 'Let's break the window. It's the only thing we can do.'

Kelly shook her head. 'No, wait. They'll hear it.' Frantically, her gaze swept the room. A knife lay on the table. She grabbed it. 'This might do.'

She started to lever the old-fashioned

window lock that had stiffened with disuse. She had, at the most, about three minutes.

'Hurry, Kelly,' urged Shaun.

A door banged somewhere in the building. The lights flooded on. Finally, just as they could heard the sound of voices, the lock released and the window swung open. Kelly breathed a sigh of relief.

Shaun stepped back. 'Ladies first.'

Kelly didn't argue, and slid out, landing heavily on some bricks beneath the window. Shaun followed closely behind her, catching his sweatshirt on a nail. It tore with a ripping sound. Breaking free, they both ran across the yard. 'Head towards my truck,' he gasped.

Shaun reached it first, and swung open the door. 'Damn. No keys.' But he had a spare clipped to the chassis underneath the vehicle. He grabbed his mobile phone lying in the glove box. 'Here. Take this.' He got down on his knees, ready to crawl underneath.

A shot rang out, ricocheting against the small tin shed behind them. Then several more. The windscreen splintered. Glass showered all around them. Shaun swore profusely.

Both huddled against the side of the truck. Kelly punched in the numbers of the emergency services and within seconds Shaun had given them the location.

'We can't stay here. They'll find us,' Shaun said. 'If we can reach the bush we'll be covered.' He slipped his hand into Kelly's. 'On the count of three, run like hell.' He took a breath. 'One . . . two . . . three — '

Kelly sprang forward, but in her haste, the cell phone slipped from her hand. 'Oh no!' She lurched down to pick it up, but Shaun wrenched her away, half dragging her. 'No time. Just leave it.'

They were halfway across the yard when a sudden pain struck her shoulder. She stumbled, then righted herself, but the burning sensation that followed made her cry out.

'I've been hit. You'd best go on without me.' Her hand started to slip from Shaun's grasp.

His arm slid around her waist. 'No. I'm not leaving you . . . come on.' He pulled her forward through the foliage. Every jolting movement sent pain flaring down her right side. She kept on moving, but could feel herself slowing with the pain.

'Hurry, Kelly . . . they're gaining on us.'

'I'm trying,' she grunted.

'We're going to end up lost in the bush. But it's a damned sight better than them getting their hands on us.'

'You can say that again,' she replied weakly, as suddenly she felt her knees sinking slowly beneath her.

12

'So where the hell were the surveillance team?' demanded Mike.

Rogers stood there in front of him, looking confused. 'I told you. We hadn't deviated from the original plan. There was no surveillance team.'

'Well?' said Mike, turning toward Poulsen. 'What the hell is going on?'

Poulsen swallowed hard. 'I sent a plain clothes officer out to monitor Kelly's movements. After we got your call, I sent out a patrol. We found our man tied up in the car and Kelly missing.'

Mike couldn't believe what he was hearing. 'You sent only one man out on surveillance. One man against a whole gang of criminals. What bloody good is that? You said surveillance had been reinstated.'

Poulsen hesitated. 'Perhaps an overstatement. But Kelly agreed to keep the surveillance low-key. If the gang had spotted any tail, they would never have made a move. Now, by abducting her, they've led us straight to their laboratory. In my estimation, it was a chance worth taking. And it's paid off.'

Mike's face flushed red as he grabbed Poulsen by the collar and shoved him up against the wall, half choking him. 'That's not good enough. Do you know what they could do to her?'

Poulsen retorted angrily, 'You're way out of line. Seems to me you're getting too emotionally involved, McKenna. You're suspended.'

'Like hell I am.'

Mike felt a hand on his arm, dragging him back. It was Rogers. 'For Christ's sake, Mike. Let him go. There'll be time to sort this out later.'

'You're damn right,' Mike replied, still furious. He gave Poulsen another filthy look before letting his hands drop to his side.

Rogers tried to remonstrate with the detective inspector. 'We need every man tonight. I suggest you change your mind about suspending Mike.'

Poulsen glared. Then, as if he too had come to the same conclusion, replied, 'Until after this is over, McKenna. Then we've got scores to settle.'

Mike forced the words out through gritted teeth. 'Agreed.' He turned to the side table where several automatics lay ready to be issued. He picked up a Glock 17 and checked it. He had to keep calm, forget about Poulsen for now, and focus on finding Kelly. The phone call received from Kelly and Shaun confirmed their whereabouts, but that didn't mean they were out of danger.

Mike watched the Armed Offenders' Squad snipers quickly select their assortment of high-powered, long-range weapons. The men moved with efficiency. All trained. All armed. And all ready.

'Let's go!' someone yelled and the black uniforms and berets blended into the night-time darkness. Officers loaded up the rear of the squad van with an assortment of firearms and ammunition and followed them in. The door slammed shut and they were ready to move out.

'At least we know Kelly and Shaun's location,' Rogers said as he slid into the seat. 'So at least that's something.'

Mike nodded. 'We can only hope they made a run for it.'

'Kelly's resourceful,' pointed out the SCDEA man. 'She's one of the best undercover operatives we've ever had. I trained her myself.'

'She never told me,' replied Mike. His eyes shadowed. There were so many things he still didn't know about her.

Twenty minutes later, as they drove along the main highway, Mike said, 'The road leading to the old workshop should be just ahead of us. Keep a look out.' Mike could see an old rusty sign on a long wooden pole looming up at the side of the road. 'There it is.'

The driver slowed and squinted, his vision through the windscreen made difficult by the torrential rain. He pulled up, on to the grass verge, while the other vehicles behind him followed suit.

Rogers suggested Mike go first to check things out. 'You know the area.'

'Right.' Wired up with a radio, Mike jumped out of the van. He carefully approached the clearing where the workshop sat, skirting along the shadows of the native bush until he was only a few metres away from the building. After a few minutes of observation, he reported back. 'Four suspects in a Falcon. Looks like they're getting ready to leave. No sign of Kelly and Shaun.'

'Roger that,' came the reply. Within seconds, the Armed Offenders' van turned on to the track to intercept the gang. Seeing the police, the Falcon put on speed, but a patrol car swept in beside the van, blocking the gateway. The gang's car slid to a halt and the four men jumped out and into the bushes. Torchlight followed their movements while the police officers chased after them.

Mike's only concern was finding Kelly and Shaun. 'For all I know they could still be in the workshop,' he told Rogers. 'I'm going in.'

Mike skimmed around the side of the building. With his gun held across his chest, he approached a slightly ajar door and lashed out with his foot, kicking it open. It bounced against the wall. A shot rang out, just missing him by millimetres. He swore softly as he threw himself flat on to the floor, thankful he was wearing a bulletproof vest.

'One suspect inside,' he reported via his radio.

'Use tear gas,' instructed Rogers.

Keeping perfectly still, Mike searched the darkness. He listened carefully. Everything was quiet except for the sound of an abnormally loud dripping tap. Wriggling along the concrete floor, he came to the legs of a wooden bench and peered round the corner. The gunman was nowhere to be seen but Mike had a feeling he was probably hiding near the back of the workshop. He waited a few more seconds to get his bearings, then crawled forward. It was now or never, Mike thought. He slipped his gas mask on and threw the canister of tear gas.

Within minutes, he heard the sound of swearing in Spanish, then a bolt being drawn back noisily and footsteps running along the concrete floor. The gunman was leaving by another entrance. Mike knew there'd be someone waiting for him as he emerged. The sound of him resisting arrest outside confirmed it. That was the easy part, Mike grimaced. He still had to find Kelly and Shaun.

His eyes now accustomed to the darkness, he scoured the workshop. It seemed clear. Mike eased himself up slowly, keeping close to the wall. The tear-gas fumes would still be thick. He had to leave his gas mask on for the moment. He paused and listened again, looking out for anyone else lurking in the shadows.

Once along the hallway, he briefly checked two doors, but on opening them, found they were only small cupboards stacked with cardboard boxes. Curious, he flicked on his small flashlight. The name of the local hospital was printed in large black writing across the side of the boxes. So this was the missing equipment and chemicals which had been sent from the pharmaceutical company and had never turned up at their destination.

When he reached a third door, he noticed it was splintered. He approached cautiously, preparing himself for the worst. He pulled his mask off, leaving it slung over his free arm, then flashed the torchlight around the room until it fell on a pile of ropes in the middle of the floor. Kneeling, he examined them but didn't touch the jagged pieces of greenstone. The ropes were stained dark red. His chest tightened at the implication. Was Kelly hurt? What about Shaun? Grim-faced, Mike got up quickly and went back outside to see if he could find them.

★ ★ ★

Kelly and Shaun were moving deeper into the bush.

'Let's stop for a while,' suggested Shaun. 'At least, until I can get my bearings.'

'I need to rest,' said Kelly, her breathing ragged. She leaned against a tree, exhausted, her wet jeans sticking to her body like a second skin. Although they were sheltered under a canopy of beech trees, water dripped noisily around them.

Shaun eased her towards a rotten tree stump where she could sit. Lightning flashed in the sky directly above them, illuminating the trees and bush and making the scenery seem unreal in the stark blue light. Kelly blinked.

'Damn this rain. We couldn't be in a worse place during a storm,' Shaun muttered. The rain was heavy now, pelting from the heavens in an unceasing downpour. His hair was plastered to his face and rivulets of water ran down the back of his neck. He dabbed the rain from his forehead with his sleeve.

'I've heard of people being lost in the bush and never found again,' she said. She just hoped it wouldn't happen to them.

Shaun gave a short laugh. 'I've hunted around here for years. Come daylight, no problem. I'm more concerned with those buggers with the guns. Can you walk a little further? If we keep going we should hit the main road soon, otherwise we stay put.'

Kelly stood, and winced with pain. 'I don't know. But I'll try.'

Shaun put his arm round her waist as they staggered forward together. 'The search and rescue team will be out looking for us at first light,' he told her. 'That means Mike will be with them.'

Five minutes later Kelly stumbled, almost falling forward. Shaun took the full brunt of her weight.

'It's no good,' she gasped. 'I can't go any further. It's best you go on ahead. Get help.'

'No,' he said sharply. 'We'll stay together. If we split up, we may never find each other again.'

Pain flared down her side and shoulder. 'It's getting harder to breath.' A fusillade of shots rang out, making her jump. A dog barked somewhere in the distance. Voices, loud and angry, were drifting through the darkness towards them and they could only imagine what was happening. There was the sound of people running through the undergrowth and then a deathly quiet.

Shaun finally answered. 'That was probably the Armed Offenders' Squad turning up.'

'Will Mike be with them?'

Shaun flashed a brief smile. 'You bet he will.'

The thought of Mike nearby gave her a warm feeling. Yet worry niggled at her. The night wasn't finished yet and anything could happen.

'Hang in there, Kelly. Help won't be far away,' said Shaun quietly. Now he was really concerned. He hadn't realized her wound was as serious as it obviously was. If they waited for dawn it could be too late for her. He gripped her tightly, holding her steady. Too weak to move anymore, her head rested on his shoulder. A few more minutes passed. Neither of them talked, just waited, hoping someone would find them soon.

'It's getting cold,' murmured Kelly. She started to shiver. Shaun was just about to take his jacket off and put it around her shoulders, when a twig snapped behind them.

Kelly stiffened. 'Shaun,' she murmured. 'There's someone following us.'

'I hear them,' he whispered. 'Keep very still. Let me handle it.' Sliding his arms away from her, he bent down and picked up a small log lying on the ground. Backing up against the thick bushes, he raised it and braced himself for impact. A tall, black figure emerged from behind a tree, carrying a handgun. Kelly couldn't make out who it was.

Suddenly, her name was called. There was no mistaking that voice. Tino Chang. He loomed into view, pointing the gun at her. Oh my God . . . he was going to kill her.

A shot rang out. At first she thought Chang had fired the gun, but when she saw Chang stagger she knew he hadn't.

Mike stepped out from behind a tree. Another flash of light. Chang fell, a startled look on his face.

'Kelly!' Mike called out, sprinting towards her.

She desperately wanted to move, to answer, but when she opened her mouth, no sound came out. Suddenly things became hazy; a multitude of black dots blocked out her vision no matter how hard she tried to focus her eyes. A buzzing sound droned in her ears, growing louder and louder, as Kelly felt herself slowly sliding to the ground.

When Mike reached her, she was out cold.

★ ★ ★

The morning dawned with wisps of cloud high in the sky as if an artist had dipped his paintbrush in white paint and twirled it across carelessly in one stroke. Kelly opened her eyes. The vast blueness stared down at her, echoing the blankness of her mind.

Her gaze travelled slowly at first, settling on the flowery curtains, absorbing their bright colours, the reds and yellows vivid against white walls. A sea breeze blew the curtains upwards, disturbing the stillness of the room, the cold air skimming across her face and catching the tendrils of her hair. And, as if to counterbalance one element, the sun decided to make its appearance, peeping round the corner of the window and sending warm streams of sunlight flooding across her bed. One glance at the room told her she was in hospital. But where? Her mind felt confused as if she had emerged from a long deep sleep and yet instead of waking refreshed, she was still so very tired.

When she moved her hand to brush her hair back from her face, she realized her wrists were firmly bandaged. She tried to sit up, but couldn't. Her head fell back on to the pillow.

'I wondered when you were going to wake up,' a deep voice said.

'Have you been waiting long?' she murmured.

Mike laughed, leaned over towards her and brushed her forehead with his lips. 'Yeah, you could say that.' He touched the bruise on her cheek tenderly with his fingertips. 'How are you feeling?'

'Awful,' she admitted. She tried to remember what had happened. Everything was coming back to her now, though slowly, in flashes.

'Is Shaun all right?'

'A bit shaken up. But he'll be fine. It's you we're worried about.'

The nurse bustled in carrying a chart and threw Mike a disapproving look. 'Don't tire her out, please. She needs her rest.'

Mike promised he wouldn't. 'Just a few more minutes. Please . . . '

The nurse nodded her approval, quickly taking Kelly's temperature and making a note of it. With deft fingers she adjusted the drip and long plastic tube leading to Kelly's arm.

After the nurse left, Kelly said, 'What about the methamphetamine? Has it been found?'

Mike nodded. 'It was in the boot of the car

when the gang tried to leave.'

Kelly felt relief flow through her. 'Thank God. I thought we'd lost it for good.'

'If we'd been a few minutes later in arriving, we probably would have. It was Williamson's sister and one of the Black Snakes gang who stole the missing medical equipment.'

'And Carlos?'

'He's been arrested. He's now trying to cut a deal with the SCDEA.'

Kelly frowned. 'What sort of deal?'

'He's offered to give us names of the Triads in return for dropping some of the charges.' Mike shrugged. 'I don't think Rogers is too keen. Not after what he did to you.' Mike paused slightly. 'Tino Chang is dead. But your cover is blown.'

Kelly sucked in a breath. 'How did that happen?'

'Rogers had to tell the Hong Kong police.' Mike gave a sigh. 'Kelly . . . the SCDEA have taken your resignation seriously. I had a long talk with Rogers. He's putting out a notice that you were killed on your motorbike. He thinks it would be safer. Tino Chang has associates who could come after you.'

She smiled at the irony of it. 'Perhaps it's better that way. The old Kelly Anderson killed off for good.'

Mike smiled. 'That's a pity. I'm going to miss her.' He took her hand in his. 'Seems to me you and I have to sort a few things out. So there are no misunderstandings this time.' Lines of worry were etched deeply around his eyes. 'God, I'm stupid,' he said. He started laughing. 'I didn't see it.'

'See what?' Kelly wanted to know.

'When you first arrived,' he said, shaking his head. 'The speeding, the attempted bribe, all that aggro. That was all intentional, wasn't it? All a bloody act. If I hadn't picked you up as you came into town, you would have made sure someone else did at the first opportunity. Right?'

'Right,' said Kelly with a tired smile. 'I needed to get the bad girl image out there and to meet Poulsen without putting the syndicates on high alert. What better way than by getting nicked for speeding and attempted bribery.'

'And I was the lucky copper, huh?'

'Didn't I do well?' Kelly replied softly.

His hand slipped into hers, and tightened. 'Rogers told me about the deal you made with Poulsen. I also saw the letter Poulsen wrote. It's obvious you were trying to protect me from disciplinary action.'

'I just didn't want you to get into trouble. It wasn't your fault you got caught in the middle.'

'Don't underestimate me on that score. I'm putting a complaint in about Poulsen. Some of the things he's done . . . he put your life in danger by misleading me about the surveillance.'

She tried to explain. 'Maybe he did, but I didn't let Poulsen have it all his way. Don't forget I made a few conditions of my own. Besides, he was just doing what he thought was best in the only way he knew how. He didn't want organized crime getting hold in New Zealand. And I can't say I blame him.' She shook her head. 'You know, the last thing I want is a police inquiry dragging on for weeks on end, splashed across the newspapers. I couldn't bear that.'

'It won't happen that way. Trust me.'

She nodded. If he wanted her trust, he had it. 'OK. If you want to make a complaint about Poulsen I'll back you up.'

'Good,' he said, satisfied. 'The last thing I need is Poulsen breathing down my neck, especially since my position with CIB has been made permanent.'

Kelly gasped. 'Permanent? That's wonderful.'

Mike gave a grin. 'Rogers put a good word in for me. A special unit is being set up to combat drug crime.'

'When?' asked Kelly.

His gaze deepened. 'Not until after we're married. I want you to myself for a while.'

Stunned, Kelly could only stare at him. 'Is that a proposal?'

'You could say that. I don't want to settle for anything less.'

'Oh, Mike . . . ' she murmured, feeling at a loss for words. Mike loved her. How could she ever have thought otherwise?

'But that's not all.' From his jacket pocket he pulled out a small white box. 'Got a surprise for you.'

Kelly looked closely. 'What's this?'

'A gift,' he said softly.

She opened it. A single earring of polished greenstone, shaped like a teardrop, lay snuggled against the soft material.

She looked up at him, holding his gaze. 'It's really beautiful, Mike. I don't know what to say. Except that . . . I love you.'

'I guess that will do for a start.'

He lifted out the earring and fastened it on to her ear lobe. The stone lay against her skin, as smooth as a lover's kiss. 'Just you and me, Kelly.'

'Yes.' Her heart soared. 'You know what? I think I got more than I bargained for.'

Mike smiled. He couldn't argue with that.

EMERALD GREEN

Heather Graves

Laura Flanagan leaves Ireland to go to Australia and begin a new life there. During the flight to Australia she meets young horseman Declan Martin, taking the Irish champion Lancelot's Pride to race for the Melbourne Cup. But when Laura tells him she must find an Australian husband in order to live there, Declan doesn't handle it well and in Singapore they part bad friends. However when he walks into the Irish pub where she's working in Melbourne, the attraction is still there. Can Laura recognize true love before it's too late? Will Lancelot's Pride win the Melbourne Cup?